REBEL, BULLY, GEEK, PARIAH

ALSO BY ERIN JADE LANGE
Butter
Dead Ends

REBEL, BULLY, GEEK, PARIAH

Erin Jade Lange

BLOOMSBURY

NEW YORK LONDON OXFORD NEW DELHI SYDNEY

First published in the United States of America in February 2016
by Bloomsbury Children's Books
www.bloomsbury.com

Bloomsbury is a registered trademark of Bloomsbury Publishing Plc

For information about permission to reproduce selections from this book, write to
Permissions, Bloomsbury Children's Books, 1385 Broadway, New York, New York 10018
Bloomsbury books may be purchased for business or promotional use. For information on bulk purchases
please contact Macmillan Corporate and Premium Sales Department at specialmarkets@macmillan.com

Library of Congress Cataloging-in-Publication Data
Lange, Erin Jade, author.
Rebel, bully, geek, pariah / by Erin Jade Lange.
pages   cm
Summary: After a party gets raided by the police, four teenagers who barely know each other find
themselves on the run in a car with a trunk full of stolen drugs—and in the next few hours they will make
decisions that will determine the course of the rest of their lives.
ISBN 978-1-61963-498-5 (hardcover) • ISBN 978-1-61963-499-2 (e-book)
1. Teenagers—Juvenile fiction. 2. Fugitives from justice—Juvenile fiction. 3. Juvenile
delinquency—Juvenile fiction. 4. Interpersonal relations—Juvenile fiction. 5. Trust—Juvenile fiction.
[1. Fugitives from justice—Fiction. 2. Juvenile delinquency—Fiction. 3. Interpersonal relations—Fiction.
4. Trust—Fiction.] I. Title.
PZ7.L26113Re 2016   [Fic]—dc23   2015014043

Book design by Nicole Gastonguay
Typeset by Newgen Knowledge Works (P) Ltd., Chennai, India
Printed and bound in the USA by Berryville Graphics Inc., Berryville, Virginia
2 4 6 8 10 9 7 5 3 1

For Derik.
This is a book about friends, and
you were one of the best I ever had.

REBEL,
BULLY,
GEEK,
PARIAH

AFTER

EVERYTHING IS GRAY.

The concrete floor is littered with ashy dirt and dust. Grime is packed down at the edges of the floor like a gray glue holding the walls and this whole awful place together. My eyes wander upward. Even the fluorescent lights seem to glow gray here. I never knew there were so many shades of such an awful color.

A hollow beep sounds, followed by a loud clang, and the iron bars in front of me slide to the left, shrieking as metal scrapes metal. A guard holds out a stiff hand, and I follow her past the first set of bars to a second, identical set. The holding area is so small, it would make me claustrophobic if I couldn't see past the bars. I stare through them across a room full of tables bolted to the ground. The tables are a cold, hard gray, like everything else, but they're shaped like picnic tables—funny, since it seems to me that picnic tables are usually happy meeting places.

Beyond the tables, another iron gate stands exactly opposite the one I'm behind, and the face waiting on the other side makes me feel like I'm staring into a mirror. I lean into that reflection, wrapping my hands around the cold metal bars as if I could press right through them to get to her.

"Step back!" The guard's voice is booming, and it's too warm and round for this quiet, cold place with all its sharp gray edges. Only beeps and clangs and other metallic sounds belong here. Everything else should be a whisper.

I flinch and let go of the bars. "Sorry, Kate," I mumble.

I've been on a first-name basis with this guard for years. After enough visits, you get to know some of the jail staff, and I've visited more than most.

Her voice is quieter now. "Just don't want you to lose a finger." Then the second wall of iron slides left like the first, and I step into the room of picnic tables, taking a deep breath as if the air will somehow taste different on this side.

Across the room, my mirror image repeats the process—sliding bars, stepping through—like a reflection on delay. The guards hovering around each of us usher us to a table at the center of the room, and we sit on opposite benches, our movements identical. But now that we're close, the mirage is fading, and the woman across from me is definitely not my mirror image. Our eyes are the same, maybe—that startling shade of green that makes strangers stop us on the street—but hers are creased at the corners, and her skin is pulled tight over sharp cheekbones. Her mouth is pinched, and I see deep lines there, too.

"Hi, Sammy," she says.

"Hi, Mama."

A spell is broken, and suddenly we can both be soft in this hard place. We lean in simultaneously, elbows pressing into the table and hands reaching for each other. Those hands clasp and become a single knot of intertwined fingers, so I can't tell where hers end and mine begin. The knot falls to the table, and the clunk of a metal chain linking two cuffs interrupts our moment to remind us where we are.

I frown down at the cuffs. *As if these are necessary. As if there's any danger here.*

"I can't believe they still use these things," Mama says. "When I was over at Richter, it was all zip ties."

Her tone is light, and I know she's trying to make conversation. I open my mouth to say something, but I've never had her knack for pretending everything is fine, so all that comes out is a whimper.

"Oh, Sam, don't cry." Mama's hands squeeze mine, then squeeze them again, over and over, so our knot now feels like a beating heart.

I sniff. "I never do," I remind her.

She watches me not cry for a moment, then says, "I broke a promise to you."

I don't respond, because she's broken so many promises I can't imagine which one she means.

"I swore to you we'd never be here again."

"No more bars," I whisper, echoing something she's said to me many times—every time, in fact. I untangle my fingers from hers and pull away, examining my hands so I don't have to meet her eyes.

"It's not your fault," I say.

The words would have sounded hollow even if we weren't in a place where sound bounced off the walls and came back to you changed and muted and as dull and gray as everything else. I've had so much practice telling Mama "It's not your fault," the phrase is empty now, its meaning all worn out from overuse.

"It's always my fault," she says.

"Not this time."

"Especially this time."

Her fingers stretch across the table for mine, but I lean back and hold up a hand to stop the "I'm sorry" about to pour from her mouth. I've been listening to Mama's apologies for sixteen years, and I can't listen to one more. It's my turn to talk. For once, we're going to sit at one of these metal picnic tables and it's not going to be all about her.

"Mama, I need to tell you a story."

1

MAMA HAD BEEN to jail more times than I could count and to prison exactly twice. It took me a long time to figure out the difference. Grandma always said jail was for people who did a little bad and prison was for people who did a lot of bad.

Beep. Ninety-nine cents.

Mama said jail was the place you went first and prayed really hard that you didn't get sent to prison. Aunt Ellen used to grumble that the only difference was the prisons were farther outside of town, which meant she had to spend more time and gas to drag me there for visits.

Beep. Thank you for your coupon.

The truth is that jail is a place where you can still hold on to hope—hope you'll be bailed out, hope you'll be found innocent, hope you'll get a second chance. Prison is the place where hope has left the building.

Beep. Ninety-nine cents.

"Excuse me? Miss? Excuse me!"

I pasted on a smile. "Yes, sir?"

"This machine is broken."

I eyed the self-checkout machine—the worst idea River City Market had ever come up with. People in this town were too stupid to do something as simple as checking out their own groceries. It *was* rocket science, after all. That's why they hired me—to man the little computer at the end of the self-checkout aisle, a job that pretty much consisted of pressing a Clear button when customers messed up and calling a manager when they got rowdy. This guy looked like he might be about to get a little rowdy.

"What's the problem?" I asked.

"It's broken," he repeated. He slapped the side of the machine a few times and then pounded it once with a fist.

Rowdy.

"Sir, please don't bang on the checkout terminal." I gritted my teeth, hoping whatever expression I was making still looked like a smile. I wasn't that great with customers . . . or with people in general; lack of practice, I guess. But Mr. Dugan kept telling me all I had to do was be polite and use words like "sir" and "please."

I stepped over to the man and eyed the terminal screen. "You're trying to use a coupon?"

"I'm not trying. I *am* using a coupon. And this thing can't count. It keeps saying ninety-nine cents, but my coupon should make it fifty-nine cents."

Yes, obviously you can count better than this computer.

"Can I see the coupon?"

The man passed me the little paper he'd been scanning: forty cents off tomato soup. I glanced down at the can in his hand. Clam chowder. A real genius, this guy.

"This is for tomato," I said.

"Then why did it thank me for my coupon?"

"It says thank you for every coup—"

He punched the terminal again.

"Stop that!"

So much for being polite. But it was a computer, after all, not a vending machine, and I was pretty sure that rule about the customer always being right stopped short of letting him destroy store property.

The man's jaw dropped slightly. "But this stupid machine . . ."

"Yeah," I muttered, keying an override code on the terminal screen. "It's the machine that's stupid."

At least I thought I muttered it, until a woman at the next kiosk gasped.

"What did you say to me?" The man seethed.

I pretended not to hear, my cheeks burning as I quickly worked out how many free cans of soup I would have to give him or how polite I'd have to be to make up for what I'd just said.

Please, stupid sir, don't tell my boss!

"Sam." A voice wheezed behind me, and I slumped.

Too late.

I turned to Mr. Dugan, a frail, wispy-haired old man who'd probably been working at River City Market ever since people carted away their groceries with horses and buggies. I stared at his shoes to avoid meeting his eyes. I liked

Mr. Dugan. He was patient, and he let us blast music over the intercom after closing. He was the kind of guy you didn't want to disappoint.

"What seems to be the problem here?" Mr. Dugan rasped.

The man spoke before I could.

"This girl just called me stupid!"

On a slow night, with no witnesses, I could have denied it, but the self-checkout kiosks were full of Friday-night folks stocking up on booze and TV dinners to get them through their lonely weekends, and now they were all staring, waiting to testify to what they'd heard.

"Sam, is that true?" Mr. Dugan asked.

"He punched the machine. . . ."

"Did you call this customer a name?"

I closed my eyes and let my silence tell him all he needed to know.

He sighed, a thin, tired sound. "Please turn in your name tag and clear out your locker."

Apparently all hope had left this building, too.

It took all of thirty seconds to "clear out my locker." One summer of watching people bag their own groceries hadn't exactly given me time to settle in at River City Market. All I ever kept in my locker was my purse, a postcard, and a hat—always a hat. Today it was a vintage newsboy cap that I shoved down over my curls. When I was little, my hair was straight and wheat colored, but after the accident it grew back all curly and kind of orange. Mama called it strawberry blond. I called it Little Orphan Annie.

I peeled the postcard off the inside of the locker door—a night scene of Paris that I'd snagged from one of the over-stock bins in the back room. I didn't have the faintest idea why the market would sell postcards from foreign cities, but I liked the tiny lights and the Eiffel Tower in the background all the same.

Someday, I thought.

I shoved the postcard into my purse and tossed my name tag into the empty locker, too chicken to carry it up to the front office, where my former coworkers would all be watching. I'd had enough of people looking at me for one night. Then I slipped out the loading-dock doors and headed straight for downtown.

The city got decidedly seedier the closer you got to the river, and I shifted my purse strap into a more secure position across my chest as the evening shadows stretched into the street. I kept my eyes peeled for HELP WANTED signs. It wouldn't be hard to top River City Market, but at least there I'd been able to zone out and pretend I was somewhere else. I flew over Egyptian pyra-mids, climbed the Great Wall of China, and explored markets in Marrakesh—all from the end of the self-checkout lane.

Aunt Ellen always said I spent too much time daydreaming, and Grandma used to pat my head and say, "Only children are lonely children." But Mama understood. She said I had inherited her wandering spirit, and she even bought me the corkboard in my bedroom, where I pinned up pictures of all the places I planned to go. I know she secretly hoped the pictures would be enough—that I wasn't actually plotting an escape from River City. But she should have known better. She escaped once, too.

I wondered what Mama would say about me getting fired from my first job. I decided I wouldn't tell her until Sunday. Tomorrow night was going to be special, and I didn't want to spoil it.

I put a hand in my purse to feel the wad of bills at the bottom: everything I'd managed to save over the last two months—which wasn't much, thanks to a few too many new hats and a summer-long spending spree on travel magazines, but it was just enough for what I needed.

What I needed was at Pete's Pawn, and I had to weave my way through a cast of characters to get there: the tattoo-covered guy with the shaved head who always parked his butt on a folding chair outside the liquor store, drinking forties and acting like he owned the street; the guy in the suit who tried to make himself look small as he slipped in and out of the dirty-video store and stared too long at teenage girls. The usual crew on River City's main drag, who all belonged in prison.

I should know. I'd seen enough people in prison while visiting Mama.

I looked past the suit and the tattoo man, at the lights flickering on inside an old Italian bistro, the crosswalk signs blinking permission for crowds to rush through traffic, and I listened to the sounds of impatient car horns and the lady shouting down from her second-floor window to the owner of the Chinese market on the sidewalk below.

"It smells like oysters up here! What did I tell you about that?"

"Sorry, ma'am. New delivery today."

I had to smile. I loved the hustle of downtown, even if I didn't like the hustlers.

I saw all of them, but they didn't see me. Invisibility was a talent I had perfected over the years. Don't make eye contact; keep the hat pulled low; step light. It's funny how many people say they would choose invisibility as a superpower, when really all it takes is practice.

I started practicing after the accident, back when I just wanted people to stop staring. Kids who didn't stare teased, and if they didn't do either, it was only because they felt sorry for me. And the pity was the worst of it. I made it all disappear by making myself disappear. But it's possible to get *too* good at a thing, and one day you wake up screaming inside, *Look at me! Look at me!* And that's when you realize you've forgotten how to be seen.

The clerk at Pete's Pawn saw me, at least. As soon as I pushed open the door, he looked me up and down with suspicious eyes. I didn't blame him. Most people who wandered into Pete's were either looking to steal or looking to sell something they'd already stolen. I made a beeline for the back wall, where all of the musical instruments were hung. Some of them were chained to the wall to keep them from being lifted by sticky fingers. But the one I was looking for wasn't all that valuable—at least not to this shop.

My eyes scanned past the stacks of guitars and piles of drums until I found the row of small stringed instruments and, in the center of that row, the curve of blond wood I was after. I let out a small sigh of relief that it was still here.

Mama's violin.

I lifted the violin gently from the rack and blew a layer of dust off the top. The price tag, tied to the neck with a piece of thread, fluttered with my breath and landed faceup, balanced on top of the strings. The number on the tag caused me to gasp.

Four hundred dollars?!

Still gripping the violin in one hand, I reached into my purse with the other. My stack of twenties looked meager now—only two hundred dollars, which had been the price of the violin for the last three years. You'd think, after all that time collecting dust, the violin would have gone down in value, not doubled.

I carried the violin to the clerk to show him the offending price tag.

"I think this is marked wrong. It used to be half this much."

He shrugged. "I don't set the prices." He flipped through a magazine with sports cars splashed across the pages and deliberately ignored me.

So, Pete's Pawn is all about eyeballing anyone suspicious but can't be bothered with an honest customer. Nice to know.

I stared at him until he finally looked up.

"The owner sets the prices. Maybe he looked it up on eBay or something, and it's worth more than he thought."

It *was* worth more. A *lot* more. But at four hundred dollars, I doubted "Pete" or whoever owned the place had actually done any research. If he had, he might have noticed the autograph carved crudely into the neck—might have looked up the name and discovered that this violin had been played on the stage of the Grand Ole Opry, in the hands of a woman people once upon a time thought could be a huge country-music star.

But that's the thing about stars—they all fizzle out, one way or another, and Mama's star had never burned bright enough to earn her a name outside Nashville. So here in Illinois, her almost-famous fiddle was worth only four hundred bucks. Four hundred bucks I didn't have.

The clerk went back to his magazine, and I retreated to the instrument wall. My eyes burned, but I didn't cry. I tried sometimes to bring on the tears, but all I ever got was a sore throat from straining. Apparently, crying wasn't something you could practice, like being invisible or polite.

But if I could cry, this would be the moment. Mama and I had big plans for tomorrow, and I was going to be empty-handed. I didn't have time to research another gift, and a card just wasn't enough.

Although, they probably did make a card for this. They made a card for everything else.

Dearest Mother,
Cheers to another year.
Thanks for staying sober.
Love, Sam

2

I STARED DOWN at the violin in my hands and cursed quietly, pissed at myself for wasting money on hats and magazines. Now I didn't have enough to buy back something that belonged to us in the first place. I counted my cash again, as if there would suddenly be an extra two hundred dollars in the pile, then shoved the whole wad into my back pocket. I wiggled my hand up under my cap to finger the rope-like scars beneath my hair—a nervous habit the hats were supposed to help prevent.

"You got lice or something?" a voice asked, startling me so much I almost dropped the violin.

I spun and stumbled back a step, knocking into the row of stringed instruments so that they banged together with the hollow echo of thin wood and the shriek of scraped wire.

"You break it, you buy it!" the clerk called from the front of the store.

I opened my mouth to answer the stranger who had sneaked up on me but was struck dumb when I saw she wasn't a stranger. Not completely.

She pointed a pale finger at my hand shoved up under my hat. "Lice? Bugs? You look like you're about to dig a hole in your head."

I yanked my hand down. "I don't have lice."

The girl tilted her head, a row of long dreadlocks cascading to one side. "Wait, I know you. Samantha, right?"

"Sam," I corrected, surprised she'd even come close. Despite the fact that we were in the same class—both about to be juniors at Jefferson—the nearest we'd ever come to conversation was me coughing as I passed through her cloud of cigarette smoke every day on the way into school.

"Yeah, Sam." She snapped her long white fingers, which were tipped with black nail polish. "Sam . . ."

"Cherie."

"Cherry, yes."

I scowled back at her. "No, not *cherry*. Cherie, with a '*sh*.'"

I noticed with some irritation that she didn't bother to tell me her name, but I guess when you're Andi Dixon you don't worry about people forgetting it.

"So why are you drooling over a piece of old wood, Sam Cherie?" Andi reached for the violin, and I reflexively smacked her hand away.

She lowered her voice to a hiss. "Watch it, little girl. I'm trying to be nice to you."

I doubted "nice" was a word anyone ever used to describe Andi. Not back when she was the girl in designer jeans with the whole school wrapped around her perfectly polished pink fingernails, and definitely not now that she'd swapped all that pink

for her signature green army jacket and earned a reputation for
flipping off teachers and cutting class.

"Sorry." I squeezed the neck of the violin, feeling stupid.
"It's just—it's special. It's sort of a family heirloom."

"Ah." Andi relaxed. "You're buying back something that
shouldn't have been sold."

"Well, I was."

"Was? Change your mind?" Andi's eyes flitted around the
shop, piled to the ceiling with other people's abandoned belong-
ings. "See something you want more?"

What I wanted couldn't fit inside Pete's Pawn. It was a train
through Europe; it was the ruins of Machu Picchu; it was a life
unshackled by addiction.

My fingers traced the worn edge of the blond violin. Every
year when we celebrated Mama's sobriety, I also secretly celebrated one year closer to the day when I could leave her alone
without worrying about a relapse.

The longest stretch I'd ever lived with Mama was the first six
years of my life, the six years when I'd learned to call her "Mama"
and everyone else "y'all"—two words Mama had brought home
with her from Nashville, along with an unplanned baby and a
drug habit.

Mama's jail-parole-jail rotation started when I was six, and
I spent the next few years in the custody of my grandmother
and, when she died, my aunt Ellen. I still saw Mama all the time,
though. Whenever she was on parole or in between rehabs, my
world was full of supervised Saturdays at halfway houses and not-
so-supervised Sundays giving each other mani-pedis on Aunt

Ellen's couch. Those memories were a checkerboard of light and dark, of here and gone, of one day Mama pulling me out of school for a shopping spree and the next day trying to block out the sound of her standing on the front lawn crying and shouting that Aunt Ellen was trying to steal her baby. It's confusing when your mom is both the scariest and most exciting person you know.

When I moved back in with Mama permanently at age thirteen, the seesaw finally stopped, and somewhere between the manic highs and the scary lows I met my real mom. This mom didn't let me cut school or buy me lavish gifts, but she still painted my toenails every Sunday.

She'd been sober a year by then, and we'd celebrated her one-year chip from Narcotics Anonymous with takeout pizza in our brand-new apartment. I'd given her a locket that had belonged to Grandma—one Mama had pawned for drug money years before. She didn't know that Grandma had bought it back, and then passed it down to me.

It became our ritual. Every year, on the same day in August: the NA chip, the pizza, and a gift of something precious that Mama had pawned. It was lucky for me that she'd pawned almost everything at the same two shops downtown.

"I never see anyone else my age in here," Andi said, her eyes still combing the shelves. "Especially not on a Friday night."

"You come here a lot?" I asked.

"I stop in from time to time."

"To do what?"

"Whatever I want," Andi answered, with a casual flip of her long dreadlocks. Then, as if to punctuate the point, her hand slipped over to a shelf of knickknacks and palmed a cheap-looking snow globe. She tossed it in the air once, caught it, and with only the slightest glance over her shoulder at the clerk at the front counter, slipped it into the pocket of her oversize army jacket.

"Most of this stuff is junk," she whispered. "But sometimes you find a gem."

I felt my mouth drop open and then close again. Or more like clench than close. I was no fan of stealing. Stealing had landed Mama in jail more than once, and it seemed like such a stupid crime to risk your freedom for, especially when the goal was usually to turn the loot into something powdery and white that was gone the second you sniffed it up your nose. At least, that was always Mama's endgame, back when she was using.

I looked down at the violin one last time. *Next year, then.* It would make a better five-year anniversary gift anyway. I returned the violin to the rack, but no sooner had I set it down than Andi snatched it up. She spun it carelessly between her hands, keeping it just out of my reach.

"Put it back," I said.

Instead, she dangled it between two fingers from the end of the neck, letting it swing dangerously back and forth above the tile floor. "You said it belongs to your family?"

"No." I held my breath as the violin slipped from her fingers, and she caught it silently with her other hand. "I said it *used to* belong to my family."

"It still does," Andi said. She gripped the neck firmly now and held it out to me. "This place was just borrowing it. Take it home now."

"I don't have enough money."

Andi didn't answer; instead she held the violin steady in the air between us, daring me to do what she'd done with the snow globe. But even if I'd wanted to, I didn't have a giant green jacket like she had, and if I did, the jacket still wouldn't have pockets big enough to hide a violin.

As if reading my mind, Andi tugged with her free hand at a black strap running diagonally across her chest, and an oversize messenger bag attached to the strap swung out from behind her. The next thing I knew, Mama's violin was disappearing into the messenger bag, the neck poking awkwardly out one side.

"You could have had it for free," she said. "Now you'll have to buy it off me."

Then she spun on her heel and ran for the door before I could even breathe.

3

FULL DARK HAD now fallen on the street outside Pete's Pawn, which was steaming with summer humidity and glowing with the light from neon signs. The green glare of a beer advertisement and the flickering pink neon of a dancing lady lit my path as I pounded down the sidewalk after Andi.

I could see her just ahead, skirting a group of guys headed into a bar, her dreadlocks sailing behind her and the messenger bag with its violin handle bouncing dangerously against her back. Behind me, the pawnshop clerk shouted "Hey! Hey!" over and over again, but I could tell by the way his shouts got thinner and quieter as I ran that he wasn't coming after us. I wished he would. He probably had a better chance of catching Andi than I did. My short legs were pumping double-time compared with her long, easy strides, and already my chest was starting to ache. I was wheezing by the time Andi reached the end of the street and took a hard left toward the river. I skidded to a stop at the corner and bent over, my hands on my knees.

The road Andi had turned down was empty and quiet, all the shops shuttered for the night, in contrast to the party just picking up on the street behind me, and next to every other storefront, alley after alley opened up dozens of paths she could have taken.

I stood to stretch out a cramp in my side and was about to turn back when movement under one of the shop awnings caught my eye. I darted into a doorway and peeked around the edge, holding my breath.

Andi crept slowly out from the shadow of the awning, twisting her head in my direction. I ducked back into the doorway, and when I dared to peek again, she was walking away down the street, clearly in no hurry now. I moved on my tiptoes and used the cover of the yawning alleys and deep doorways to creep behind her.

I followed her all the way across the wide road that ran along the river into the vast expanse of River City Park—a tangle of trees, sloping hills, and dirt paths so sprawling you couldn't even see the river from the road that followed its banks. The park was the perfect place to disappear.

River City liked to pretend this place was its emerald jewel, a shiny stretch of green along the famous Mississippi. But the only part of the park that really fit that bill was the bit I was pounding across right now. The city kept the lawn between the road and the woods perfectly groomed, and it was always installing fancy new water fountains and the latest playground equipment. But beyond the tree line, River City Park became wild, and I don't just mean the landscape. Dirt roads cut narrow paths through the woods, where you were as likely to run into a fallen tree as you

were a group of homeless people making camp for the night.
The shadows of the park hid all kinds of things, from hookers
with their clients to druggies looking for a quiet place to shoot
up. Grandma had found Mama passed out in the woods more
than once.

I knew all the ugly that lay beyond those pretty trees, and I
wanted nothing to do with it. But across the green space, Andi
was disappearing into the woods with Mama's violin, so I hesitated only a second before diving in after her. Flickers of light
flashed through the dense forest, and I could hear the distant
thumping bass line of a familiar song.

Well, at least I knew where she was headed. I raced through
the trees and exploded into a clearing full of bonfires and a sea
of people.

People I recognized.

All around me, kids from Jefferson were clutching red cups
with liquid sloshing over the sides as they grinded against each
other in time with the music. To my right, four guys held a fifth
one upside down over a keg as he sucked beer straight out of the
tap, while a crowd around them cheered him on.

I leaned against a tree to catch my breath and peered through
the haze of bonfire smoke. So this was what a high school party
looked like. I usually tried not to think about the stupid small-
town parties I wasn't invited to and focused instead on the great
big cities where I would someday live. But now that the scene
was laid out in front of me, it wasn't as lame as I'd hoped. In
fact, once you got used to the stink of sweat and beer, it almost
seemed kind of cool.

Not that I spent a lot of time *woe-is-me*ing over my lack of invitations. I'd been to a slumber party or two, even made a few friends over the years—mostly other kids from family support groups, where it was pretty much impossible to be invisible. But those friendships were fleeting. Sometimes kids moved away to get a "fresh start" or went into their own downward spirals, but mostly we eventually discovered we just didn't have anything in common outside of our screwed-up parents.

Besides, Mama seemed more friend than family most days. Sure, we weren't doing any keg stands together, but we shopped in each other's closets and laughed at each other's dumb jokes, and she was the only other person on earth who understood that ramen noodles and ketchup was a gourmet meal. As long as she was sober, she was all the friend I needed. Or at least that's what I told myself whenever I saw kids my age clustered together.

The thought of Mama reminded me of exactly what I was doing lurking at the edge of this end-of-summer bash, and I peeled myself away from the tree, determined to find Andi. I squinted at the crowd, searching for a head full of dreadlocks.

Before the dreads, Andi's hair had been a mass of lush brown waves, the kind of thick and shiny you usually only see in magazines. It had made her stand out, even among the rest of the Barbies who were always bobbing along in her wake. The Barbies all still had their perfect hair, but sometime freshman year, they started following someone else around. I wondered whether Andi had violated some pretty-girl code when she twisted her hair and started sporting that green army jacket. In

any case, I hadn't seen her with her former clique since freshman year.

And I couldn't see her at all now. Either she had a chameleon's
knack for blending in, or she had skipped past the party and run
deeper into the woods. Which meant the violin was gone, too.

"Attention, upperclassmen!" someone over by the keg bellowed. He was answered with a few cheers and whistles. "Junior
year is going to ROCK!"

I sighed. *If you say so, dude.*

A hand touched my shoulder then, and the stink of beer
breath blew across my face.

For one irrational moment, I was five years old again, and
Mama was drunk and trying to kiss me good night, but all I
wanted to do was pull the comforter over my face so I wouldn't
have to smell whatever she'd been drinking.

"Why susha waffle?" the beer breather said in my ear.

I leaned away from the voice, from the smell, and felt the
hand slip off my shoulder.

The girl attached to the hand wobbled for a second on long,
thin legs, but managed to stay standing. She smiled down at me,
waiting for my answer to whatever question she thought she had
asked.

"I don't—I didn't hear you right," I said.

She leaned close to me again, her breath now hitting me
smack in the face. "Why. Such. A. Wall. Flower?"

The smell. The *smell*.

I reached up to grab her forearms and push her away. Once I
got her upright and out of my personal space, I could see she was

one of Andi's former followers—the Barbies who controlled what was cool and what wasn't at Jefferson. I was pretty sure you weren't supposed to touch the Barbies. I braced myself for her wrath.

But she only smiled as though I'd done her a favor. "Thanks," she said. "I'm tipsy."

If by "tipsy" she meant about to tip *over*, then yeah, I had to agree.

"I'm not a wallflower," I said.

"No?"

"Can't be a wallflower without walls. I'm a . . . a . . ." My eyes landed on the tree I'd been leaning against. "I'm a tree flower."

Oh my God, please let the earth open up now and suck me and the tree both down a big black hole.

"I mean—"

"A treeflur," she slurred. "That's pretty. You're pretty."

"Oh. Um . . . thanks."

This Barbie wasn't so bad.

"Tess, if you think that's pretty, I'm cutting you off."

The Barbie—Tess—and I spun at the sound of the voice, but the spin was too much for Tess, and she sidestepped into the tree behind me.

"Whoa," she said. "Tree."

"Yes, Tess, tree. See tree stand. See Tess stumble." The voice belonged to a blond ponytail and comically high cheekbones. Georgia Jones—the new Andi, after Andi became . . . something else. Maybe there was always a new Barbie waiting in the wings to step up if the chief B went AWOL.

"Do I know you?"

It took me a second to realize Georgia was talking to me. How do you answer a question like that? How should I know whether she knew me? We were in some of the same classes, and I certainly knew *of* her, so maybe she knew of me, too—but did that mean she *knew* me?

"You look familiar," she said.

"She's a tree flower." Tess reached an unsteady hand out to pet the curls spilling out from under my hat and fixed an unfocused gaze on me. "Look at her eyes. Pretty green. Pretty flower. Can we keep her?"

"Tess! Go puke," Georgia ordered.

Someone snickered, and I realized that Georgia had backup—two more unfairly pretty girls at her flanks.

"Okay." Tess obediently stumbled away, already half-bent into hurling position. Her clumsy fingers had tangled in my hair, skewing my hat. I hurried to jam it back down, but Georgia's eyes had already snagged on the few jagged edges of scars that crept past my hairline onto my forehead.

"What's your name?" she asked.

One of the backup Barbies answered for me. "They call her Worms."

I choked. Did people still call me that? No one had said it to my face in years, but then, since I'd started high school, nobody had really talked to me much at all. That was the upshot of being invisible. It was lonely, but at least it was safe.

"Gross." Georgia flinched. "Worms? Why?"

The backup Barbie shrugged as if it didn't matter why, and I pulled my hat down tighter on my head. Kids didn't need a reason to call you names. You could cover up your secrets with hats until a boy teased that you only wore them to hide your greasy hair. You could pull the hat off to prove he was wrong, exposing your orange curls, until another boy laughed and covered his eyes, shouting, "Ugh! Put it back on!"

I'd learned all that back in seventh grade. Junior high meant a new wave of students who didn't know about Mama or my scars or that my hair used to be as straight and blond as Georgia's. So I had opened myself up just an inch, making eye contact in hopes of making friends. Once I realized that I would be a target with or without my scars, I crawled back under my hats and embraced invisibility for good.

Georgia lifted her chin. "Well, no offense, *Worms*, but if you weren't invited, you really shouldn't—"

"I invited her." A body filled the space where Tess had been, and it was much more imposing, with all those crazy dreadlocks and that hard stare.

Georgia's voice turned to acid. "Well, I *know* nobody invited *you*, Andi."

"I'm pretty sure I have a standing invitation to these shindigs," Andi said.

"Not this one. This 'shindig' was my idea, and—"

"Your idea?" Andi interrupted. "Is that why it's so lame?"

One of the Barbies next to Georgia made a choking noise, and I couldn't tell whether it was a gasp or a stifled laugh.

Georgia's cheeks flushed, and her hands flailed for a moment before landing on her hips, as if she was trying to make herself look bigger. "The only lame thing I see here is you and your . . ." Her eyes slid to me. "Friend?"

There was something in the way she said the word "friend"—some echo of pain, or even jealousy. Whatever it was, Andi caught it, too.

And she laughed at it.

"That's right," Andi said. She linked an arm through mine. "And my friend and I wish you would go away."

"I'm not going anywhere. This is *my*—"

"Yeah, yeah. It's your lame party. Oh, Georgia," Andi sighed. "I liked you so much better when you just did what I told you to."

Georgia huffed. "I never did anything just because you told—"

"I'm bored," Andi said abruptly. She turned to me and waved a hand at the other girls as if flicking away a cloud of gnats. "Let's go find some more interesting people. There must be one or two here."

Then, her arm still linked with mine, she dragged me away.

BEFORE

"I LOVE THE black strapless one, but Mark likes me in blue. He says it matches my eyes."

"Please. Mark prefers you in *nude*."

The two girls started snickering, and one let loose an unattractive snort. It was the only unattractive thing about either of them. I shifted in my seat behind them, trying not to listen in. In every classroom, every bathroom, every stairwell at Jefferson, all anyone could talk about was homecoming. It was like they'd all come down with the same sickness—diarrhea of the mouth—and all they could spew was football-game this and formal-dance that.

I forced myself to look away from the long, dark waves and the blond ponytail in front of me and flipped through my world history textbook, letting the words blur by until something caught my eye—a full-page color photo of the Roman Colosseum taken with a fish-eye lens, so its curves seemed even more dramatic and impossible. I folded the page as close to the binding as possible, then tugged until it tore at the crease. The ripping noise echoed through the mostly empty classroom, and I was glad I'd beaten Mr. Spencer to first period.

The girls turned at the sound, surprised to find they weren't alone, and I wiggled my fingers up under my sun hat self-consciously. The one with the ponytail barely glanced at me, but Andi Dixon's eyes zeroed in on my textbook and the damage I'd done. Before she twisted forward again, I thought I saw one corner of her mouth twitch. It wasn't exactly a smile, but it was something like approval.

"Okay," Ponytail said. "So you've got the limo covered, right?"

Andi tilted her head to one side, her hair moving like a waterfall. "I guess."

"I mean, we can all pitch in, but I figured your dad would pay."

"It's not that," Andi said. "It's just—limos are so boring. Everyone will have one."

"Exactly. That's why we—"

"What about a school bus?"

"Uh . . ."

"Or a monster truck!"

I smirked. Seeing these girls in their satin and tulle trying to climb out of a monster truck would almost make the homecoming dance worth attending.

Ponytail was quiet for a moment, then seemed to recover. "Well, we can work on transportation after we've worked out your date. Mark says Harry Sims is going to ask—"

"No," Andi said abruptly. "Tell Harry to invite Alexia. He's a perv, and she puts out. They'll be perfect together."

Ponytail turned her head, and I could see shock in the profile of her face. "But Harry's hot for *you*. And he's just hot, *period*."

"So?"

A bell rang, and students spilled into the classroom, shuffling their feet and scraping the legs of their chairs against the floor. I found myself leaning forward, no longer trying to ignore the conversation in front of me. I didn't know Harry Sims from Harry Potter, but there was something electrifying about overhearing other people's secrets.

"So it's freshman homecoming," Ponytail insisted. "It's our first dance. Who we go with is *everything*."

Was it? This seemed like an important piece of information—something they should have included in our freshman orientation booklet, in between how many electives we could take and what kind of offensive T-shirts would get us sent home.

"But I don't like Harry," Andi said.

"Okay, well, who *do* you like?"

There was a long pause before Andi answered in a low voice. "You know who."

Unfortunately, *I* never got to know who, because Mr. Spencer charged in just then, clapping his hands and launching right into a lecture about ancient Egypt. I quickly folded my pilfered photo of the Colosseum and tucked it into my backpack. When I got home, it would go up on my bulletin board next to all the other pictures and postcards of places I'd rather be.

I have no idea whether Andi went to homecoming with Harry Whoever, but I know a week after the dance she and Ponytail started sitting on opposite sides of the classroom, and by the end of the year, the name on everyone's lips was no longer Andi Dixon but Georgia Jones.

4

I HEARD THE Barbies whispering behind us for a second before their voices were swallowed by the music. As soon as we were out of sight, Andi dropped my arm and reached into her jacket pocket for a pack of cigarettes. She pulled one out and then tipped the pack upside down.

"Shit. Empty." She tossed it into the nearest bonfire and lit her last smoke. She took a deep drag and squinted at me as she exhaled. "You're kind of a trip, huh?"

Was I?

I crossed my arms to keep my hands from crawling up into my hair.

"Are you going to give me the violin or not?"

"Depends," she said, inhaling again. "What are you going to do with it?"

"Keep it." I knew the words were true as I said them. The right thing to do would be to return the violin and hope for some kind of reward, but I doubted Pete's Pawn was in the business of giving things away. And after all the trouble of chasing this thing down, it felt like I'd kind of earned it, even if I hadn't paid for it.

Andi laughed. "No you won't. You'll take it back, and I'll get in trouble. Can't do it."

"The clerk already saw you," I pointed out. "You're in trouble anyway."

Andi dropped her cigarette butt and ground it into the dirt with her boot heel. "Tell you what, Worms—"

"Don't call me that."

She looked up, surprised at the venom in my voice. "Okay, *Sam*. I'll sell you this here fiddle for whatever price you were planning to pay."

I smirked. "I was planning to pay five dollars."

She shook her head in mock disappointment. "Sorry. I don't play with liars."

"And I don't play with thieves."

A noise in the trees to my left cut off our argument. We were on the fringes of the party, next to the thicker part of the forest that led down to the river, and my heart galloped for a second as I worried what—or who—might be hiding in the darkness beyond the bonfires.

But Andi didn't share my fear; she bravely tiptoed into the woods toward the sound. I wouldn't have followed, but as she turned away from me to the trees, I saw the neck of the violin sticking out of her messenger bag. An invitation.

Take it now, while she's distracted.

It wasn't really stealing if it didn't belong to Andi in the first place, right? As the thought flitted across my mind, I realized it was pretty much the same argument Andi had made back in the pawnshop. I inched up behind her, my hand stretching silently toward the violin. My fingers were only a whisper away from closing around the neck when Andi suddenly spun back to me.

"Shh!" she hushed me, even though I hadn't made a sound. She held a finger to her smiling lips, then pointed it straight ahead.

I had to squint to follow her finger. We were under the canopy of trees now, and my eyes were still flashing with the echo of firelight, so it took a moment for them to adjust to the dark. I heard what she was pointing at before I saw it. Someone was grunting up ahead. No—two someones. I could hear each of them breathing to a different beat—one labored and slow, the other quick and gasping. I heard fallen branches crunching beneath them, and as we crept closer, I could see them rolling over the ground, locked in an embrace.

Oh! I looked away. I didn't want to see that.

Or did I? I peeked again, first with one eye, then the other.

The pair half tumbled, half skidded away from us down a slope, and now their embrace looked more like a choke hold. A huge boy—probably a senior—had his hands wrapped tight around the neck of a skinny kid who looked too small for high school. The forest shadowed their faces.

Unable to look away from the train wreck in front of us, Andi and I followed their rolling fight down the hill, slipping as the slope grew steep and treacherous, until finally they spilled out of the woods and into a patch of moonlight along the riverbank. Now that I could see them both clearly, I recognized the older boy as York Flint—one of those obscenely good-looking guys who made himself ugly by always cutting people down. His friends thought he was hilarious, but personally I thought he was kind of an asshole. The smaller boy was familiar, too. I could never remember his name, just his face and his distinct mass of freckles.

It was hard to make out those freckles now, in the dark, but I could see enough to tell his expression was more pissed than panicked. He clawed at the hands around his throat, but they never moved, and I knew I should help, but I didn't know how. I looked at Andi, expecting her to shout, to step in, to do *something*—but she only cocked her head toward me and said, loud enough for the boys to hear, "Fifty bucks on the big guy."

"What?" the big guy and I said at the same time.

"The big one," she repeated, pointing him out in case it wasn't obvious. "York."

He gaped at Andi and loosened his hold until Freckles's wheezing breaths sounded almost normal. Their rumble had come to a halt, the fight scene frozen in place.

Andi snapped at York, "Hey, keep a grip there! I've got fifty bucks on you."

"She's kidding," I said.

I had no idea if she was kidding, but Andi seemed like the kind of person you apologized for. Like Mama.

She looked at me with a gleam in her eye. "Or, better yet, I'll bet one violin against your fifty bucks."

Tempting, but the smaller kid didn't stand a chance.

"Nice try," I said.

"Hey, shut up!" York sat up and shook out his hands. Apparently, choking someone could make your hands tired. In that moment, the skinnier kid, his legs still pinned, sat straight up and smacked York's face. And not just once—he thrashed around with both hands, slapping York's cheeks over and over again, like he was tapping out a drumbeat.

Andi found this so hysterical she actually doubled over in laughter, holding her stomach, while I looked away, embarrassed for him.

York grabbed both of the flailing wrists in one hand and yanked them to the side. "Knock it off. Give me the keys."

He wasn't slurring quite as badly as Tess had been, but I could still hear the alcohol in his voice.

The pinned boy responded by spitting directly into York's eye.

"Wow, nice shot," Andi said, startled out of her laughing fit.

York rolled away, wiping his face. "Sick, man!"

Freckles scrambled to his feet and dug something out of the front pocket of his jeans. A second later, he was dangling a set of keys in front of York.

"These keys?" he taunted.

York bent forward and hunched his back, but before he could pounce, the other boy reared back and threw the keys with all the force his skinny arm could muster. We all held our breath for a moment—just long enough to watch the keys fly, arcing into the sky, glittering as the moonlight reflected off the metal, until they landed with a soft splash and disappeared under the water.

York opened and closed his mouth twice before he could finally make words. "You—you—" He grabbed his own hair with two fists. "I'm gonna—I'm gonna—"

"You're going to what?" Freckles taunted. "What are you going to do?"

York let go of his hair and waved his fists at the sky instead.

"I'm going to tell *Mom*!"

5

THE SKINNY KID with the freckles laughed, but it came out more like a groan as he rubbed his throat, which was red with marks from York's fingers.

"Yeah, you go ahead and tell Mom. Tell her I wouldn't let you drive drunk. I'm sure I'll get in a lot of trouble."

"Shut up," York growled.

Andi elbowed me. "You should have taken the bet. It kind of looks like the little guy won."

The smaller kid dropped his hand from his throat and glared at Andi. "Could you not call me 'the little guy,' please? My name is Boston."

"I'm Sam," I piped up.

Boston and Andi both cocked their heads at me like I'd said something strange.

"I thought we were doing introductions," I mumbled.

"You're the girl with all the hats." York flashed a grin that would have looked good on him if he wasn't all scratched up and sweaty from the fight. "Hat Girl."

I tugged my newsboy low over my face, partly so he wouldn't see my surprise that he recognized me and partly to fight the urge to smile back.

Andi turned her attention to York. "I didn't know you had a brother."

"I didn't know it was any of your business," York spat back, his smile gone now.

I looked back and forth between the two of them, trying to remember if I'd ever seen them together in school. Maybe everyone just knew everyone but me.

York yanked his shirt up to wipe the sweat and dirt from his face, and my gaze caught on everything rippled and lean that had been hiding under that shirt. He wasn't exactly a Calvin Klein model, but I imagined boys didn't get built much better than this in River City. Maybe people forgive you for being an ass if you have abs like that.

I forced myself to look away from his stomach and spotted a tattoo on his chest. I barely had time to register a thin scrawl of black before he dropped his shirt again. Probably the name of some girl he was trying to impress. River City boys made smart choices like that.

York lumbered over to Boston and grabbed him roughly by the shoulder, dragging him toward the river. "Go get 'em."

Boston pulled out of York's grasp and smirked. "You go get 'em. Oh, wait, that's right. You can't."

York's fists clenched and I tensed, expecting another beating, but he only popped a finger out of one of those fists and pointed it in Boston's face like a warning.

"Hey, *little guy*," Andi said very deliberately. "You shouldn't poke the yeti. Yeti big. Yeti get angry."

She laughed at her own joke, and I took a step away from her. It seemed to me that she was the one poking the yeti, and he didn't appear to be above taking a swing in our direction.

"Who are you calling a yeti, slut?"

Whoa.

He may as well have thrown a punch.

Andi pinched her lips and took a step toward the boys, as if meeting a challenge. The moonlight hit her dreadlocks, making them look like thick icicles. "Call me a slut again," she dared him. There was ice in her voice, too. It cast a decided chill over the otherwise sweaty August night, and for a moment we were all frozen, watching the stare-down between York and Andi.

York caved first—whether because Andi had intimidated him or because he'd had too many beers to win a staring contest, I couldn't be sure. He looked away with a shrug and turned back to Boston. "Keys. Now."

Boston crossed his arms. "Like I said—you want them, be my guest." He nodded at the water.

York stayed rooted to the spot, his eyes darting between the river and us girls, and even in the dark, I could see his cheeks turning red.

Boston grinned in our direction. "He can't get them, because he can't—"

Whatever he was going to say next was lost in a muffled thump as both boys hit the ground. It was hard to say whether York had tackled Boston or just drunkenly stumbled into him, but I took an involuntary step forward in case they started brawling again. It seemed like someone should help, even if Andi was right—the little guy *was* poking the yeti.

I managed only that one step before I bumped into something long and hard—Mama's violin. Andi was holding it out like an extended arm, a barricade to keep me back.

"Stay out of it," she warned.

I reached for the violin but she swung it away, and my fingertips only brushed the strings, releasing a soft chord of music into the night. Andi moved a good distance away from me and tucked the violin back into her messenger bag.

"If you're going to be shadowing me all night, it looks like I'll need a ride." She snapped her fingers at the two boys, still sprawled on the ground. "I've got fifty bucks for whichever one of you fishes those keys out of the water and drives me home." She pulled something out of her pocket and waved it around—a wad of bills.

My wad of bills.

My chest clenched as I scrabbled around in my purse and came up with only crumpled pages torn from magazines—a beach in Thailand, an iceberg in Alaska— *No, wait*, I'd put the cash in my pocket at the pawnshop. I shoved a hand into the back pocket of my jeans, but all I found in there was lint.

"That's my money!" I shouted.

The boys startled at my explosion, and I realized it was the first thing I'd said since stupidly blurting out my name.

Quiet, but prone to outbursts. That's what the family therapist at Mama's old halfway house once said—as if I was the one who needed psychoanalysis. Also *antisocial* and *unpredictable under duress*.

I was pretty sure I was under duress right now. Standing in these woods that I hated, out of a job, robbed of all my money, and just steps away from the only thing I wanted but couldn't get my hands on—even I couldn't predict what I was going to do next.

And I never found out, because just then the wail of police sirens sliced through the woods, and the dull hum of music and laughter from the party somewhere above us turned into a roar of shouts and stampeding feet.

"Cops!" York shouted.

Andi shushed him and cursed in the same breath.

He ignored her and shoved Boston toward the water, still yelling. "Keys! Now! I'm not screwing around!"

Those keys were already buried under the Mississippi mud, but Boston obediently kicked off his flip-flops and waded into the river up to his knees, the water soaking the edge of his cargo shorts.

"There's no way," he said. "I threw them too far out."

"You are dead!" York punched at the air. "Dead!"

"Shut your face!" Andi barked, and it came out with such force that the boys did, indeed, shut their faces. "You're going to get us busted," she said.

Busted for what?

I hadn't had so much as a sip of alcohol, and while I'd never been to a party like this—or any party, really—I doubted the kids up the hill would get anything more than sent home for the night. I knew from personal experience that cops had bigger fish to fry than underage drinkers.

But Andi had something to fear. She was carrying stolen goods. I had half a mind to shout out that there was a shoplifter and pickpocket down here. I would relish watching the deputies handcuff her. But something held me back—something deep and distrustful of police for all the times they'd been unfair to Mama. Plus, I reasoned, they'd probably take the violin as evidence, and then it would be gone for good.

Andi opened her mouth to say something, but it was drowned out by the distorted sounds of police barking into megaphones, ordering people to line up. Elsewhere, deeper in the trees, some geniuses were still trying to make a break for it. Shouts echoed through the woods like a round-robin song. "Ben! Katie! This way! This way!"

I wondered which way they could possibly think would keep them out of trouble.

"York!" Boston whisper-shouted, still knee-deep in muddy water. "They're making people get in line!"

"Citations," York agreed.

Boston splashed out of the river and squished his wet feet back into his sandals. "I'm not signing one of those stupid pieces of paper saying I was drinking. That goes on your record."

"I'm not signing it, either," York whispered back. "One more and Mom and Dad—" He didn't finish his thought, running a hand through his hair instead. "We're getting out of here," he said, sounding shockingly sober now. "Car or no car."

He started moving down the riverbank, away from the hill. "This way," he commanded, and Boston scurried behind him.

"No!" Andi said, forgetting her own order to be quiet.

The boys ignored her and kept moving. I watched Andi, waiting to see which way she would go. Neither direction scared me, since I hadn't done anything other than have a conversation with the wrong girl in the wrong place at the wrong time. I planned to follow the violin and my money, whichever way they went.

"Shit," Andi whispered. "Shit, shit, shit."

She pulled at one of her dreadlocks and flicked her eyes back and forth between the sounds of police above us and the retreating backs of the boys. Finally she seemed to make a decision, and uttered one last "shit" before running after Boston and York.

"What are you doing?" Andi asked when I caught up. "Go back!"

"Give me my money," I demanded.

"Your money? I thought you wanted the violin. Make up your mind, girl."

I wanted to push her into the river.

Just ahead of us, Boston and York were arguing and not bothering to be quiet about it.

"I told you I didn't want to come here," Boston said. "Now we're screwed."

"We're only screwed because you tossed the keys, you little worm."

I bristled at the word "worm" for a split second until I realized it wasn't directed at me.

"I have a spare set at home," Boston shot back.

"But how are we *getting* home, asshole? We can't outrun the cops."

"There's a dirt road up ahead. It goes down to the old boat dock."

"Wait," Andi said. "Not the boat dock."

York glanced back at us. "He's right. There's a road—"

"I know." Andi grabbed at the back of York's shirt, trying to slow him down. "That road meets up with the one to the party. We'll get stopped. Let's just wait here until everyone's gone, and—"

"We *want* to get back up to that road." York walked faster, his shirt pulling out of Andi's grasp. "We can catch a ride with someone on their way out."

It was strange how much they all seemed to know about the forest back roads. Maybe their parents were all druggies, too. *Or maybe some people actually use the woods for regular old recreation. Imagine that.* It's possible the woods were nice during the day. I wouldn't know.

"Do whatever you want," York said, not breaking his stride. "Say hi to the cops for us."

Andi looked pained, almost panicked, but she continued stomping after the boys.

"What's the big deal?" I said to her. "Forget them. Go wherever you want. Just give me my stuff first."

"Fine." Andi surprised me by lifting the bag from her shoulder. "If I give you your shit, will you go back to—"

A megaphone crackled through the woods behind us.

"Attention in the trees!" There was almost an edge of laughter in the officer's voice.

What fun, breaking up a party and terrifying teenagers!

"We have your license-plate numbers. We *will* be following up on any cars left behind. Come on out."

He sounded close—much closer than the hum of teenage voices and the music from the party, which had inexplicably been turned down but not off. Someone really liked their hip-hop.

Boston stumbled on a tree root. "He means our car! *Our* license plate."

"Relax." York grabbed Boston's elbow to keep him from falling. "We'll say we got a ride home with someone else after you lost the keys. You won't even have to lie."

"But Mom and Dad will know we were at this party! And the police will probably automatically cite us for drinking just for being here."

"How would you know?" York said. "You've never been busted for anything."

"Yeah, well, I've got this big brother who gets busted all the time, so I know—"

"All right! I'm sorry, okay? Sorry I tried to show you a good time."

It didn't sound like much of an apology to me, but it seemed to settle the argument, and they kept walking.

The megaphone blared again. Another warning. Or was it a threat?

My body thrummed with something like fear, or maybe a thrill. I had no reason to worry about the man behind the megaphone, but instinct told me to keep moving.

Or maybe it was just in my DNA to run away from cops.

6

"HE SOUNDS CLOSER," I said to no one in particular.

"Then move faster," York answered.

At that moment, someone finally cut the music back at the party, and the woods went suddenly silent. The twigs snapping under our feet were as loud as cannons now, and we all stopped in unison, as though we were part of some choreographed marching band.

"Shh," Boston said unnecessarily.

"It's over," Andi whispered. "We should just go back. I know a path—"

"No, we're here," he said, tiptoeing around a large tree in our path. "The dock is just on the other side of— Crap!"

Boston ducked back behind the tree, and York leaned around him to get a look.

"Awesome! A car! I wonder who parked down here. Maybe we can hitch a—"

Boston pulled York back with a force his skinny arms didn't look capable of. "Not the car. The cops!"

This time we all peeked around the tree, leaning against one another so our heads stacked up like a totem pole next to the tall oak. A silver SUV glimmered under the summer moon, its front doors wide open, and next to it, two police officers stood talking quietly.

"They're searching cars," York said, his voice a breath below a whisper. "Probably stealing all our beer. Pigs."

The officers appeared to be standing guard over the SUV, waiting to bust whichever partygoer thought they were clever for parking at the bottom of the hill. After a moment, one of the officers turned away and disappeared into the trees in the direction of the river, probably heading to the boat dock, though I couldn't see it from here. The other cop rested a hand on the holstered gun at his side and turned in our direction.

We scrambled back behind the tree, tripping over one another's feet in the process.

Boston looked at all of us and swung an arm in a circle over his head.

We're surrounded, he mouthed.

Andi replied by pointing a finger at herself and each of us in turn, then jerked her head violently back up the hill. Her message was clear. *Let's go.*

York held up his hands as if to silence the both of them, even though they weren't making a sound. Then he pointed one finger, telling us to hang on, and scratched his head, apparently trying to think.

This game of charades was so ridiculous, I had to suppress a giggle.

At least, I *tried* to suppress it. I really did. I held my lips together as tightly as possible to seal them closed, but when I looked at the trio around me, it was too much. The charades had exploded. Andi was waving her hands back and forth, warning me not to make a noise; York was reaching toward me as if to put a hand over my mouth; and Boston was shaking his head so fast it looked like it might wobble right off his neck.

I lost the fight.

It wasn't a laugh that escaped so much as a gasping snort, like a giant face fart that echoed through the trees all around us.

The response was instantaneous.

"Who's down there?" The megaphone blared behind us.

It was followed by the much quieter but more chilling sound of a gun being cocked.

Now *that* killed the laughter.

The three faces around me were murderous. Yes, obviously, this whole scenario was my fault. Never mind that at least one of us had been drinking and another was a thief—my laughter was the real crime. I scowled back at them, then squared my shoulders, making a decision.

I marched out of our cluster of trees with my hands up, because "hands up" seemed like the proper response to an officer drawing his gun.

That gun was aimed and ready to fire.

I swallowed hard. I hoped the moonlight was bright enough for him to see that I was just some unarmed kid and not the usual trash that prowled these woods at night. To my left, still sheltered by the huge oak and its surrounding trees, three sets of eyes bulged. In front of me, the officer's gun pointed steadily at my chest. *If only there were a way to make myself invisible now.*

I forced myself to lift my gaze from the gun to his face. *Make eye contact. Look innocent!*

But I probably just looked confused, because the face above the gun was familiar. I couldn't place the guy, but for some reason, his mug made me think of Mama. Confusion hardened into anger. No doubt this must be an officer who had busted Mama once upon a time. How many times had I seen cops put her in handcuffs over the years?

Twice, when Grandma called the cops on her. Once when Mama was in the hospital. *My fault, sort of.* Once when I was in the hospital. *Her fault, definitely.*

I wondered whether the officer recognized me, too, or whether he'd seen so many traumatized children that our tear-streaked faces all started to look the same. Maybe he wouldn't remember me without those tears. I hardly recalled what I looked like with tears myself; it had been so long.

Behind me, but definitely closer now, the megaphone cop spoke again.

"If you're down there, best come on up now."

The boom of the disembodied voice shattered my silent standoff with the trigger-happy officer. His head swiveled in the direction of the megaphone, and his gun arm finally, mercifully, lowered to his side. I waited for him to answer back, to let the other officer know he had everything covered down here, but instead he did something inexplicable: he whipped around and raced off into the trees after his partner, toward the river.

My breath came out in a whoosh—*How long have I been hold-ing that in?*—and I lowered my arms, which ached from hanging in the air.

"He left," I whispered. I turned to the trio hiding in the shadows to my left and repeated, louder, "He left!"

York tentatively stuck his head out from behind the tree to confirm what I was saying, and then he spun around in place as if looking for someone. "Whose car is that?" he asked, his voice low. "We need a ride."

"They're probably up there getting a ticket," Boston said, equally quietly. He pointed back in the direction of the party.

"I think it's Carrie's," York said to himself. "It looks like hers."

There was a faint but distinct noise then, from the direction of the river—the sound of feet on wooden slats. The cops were coming back up the dock.

York grabbed Boston by the arm and started dragging him toward the wide-open SUV, then turned and called back to us. "Let's go!"

I stared stupidly after them, not sure what they were doing, until the megaphone opened up one more time.

"Stay where you are!"

The party police had heard us. I looked back up the hill into the thicker part of the woods and saw a bright light flashing as it bobbed around trees, slicing through the dark in our direction.

Andi shoved me hard toward the SUV. "Move. *Now.*"

I stumbled, letting her push me into the clearing. Ahead of us, the boys were climbing into the front seats of the SUV, York behind the wheel.

"No way!" York cried. "The keys are in the ignition!"

Andi dragged me to one of the back doors, and I pulled out of her grasp.

"We can't ride with him. He's been drinking!"

It would occur to me later that it was also a bad idea to steal a car and run from the police, but in the moment, I only had the wits to focus on one drama at a time.

Andi jumped into the backseat and dropped the messenger bag with the violin at her feet. To my right, labored voices were floating up a path cut through the trees—the path to the boat dock. The SUV would be gone before they got here, and so would Mama's violin, along with all of my money. I was already thinking about how I would track Andi down later to claim my stuff when she yanked the violin out of the bag and held it high.

"Get in, and it's yours," she said.

I couldn't understand the intensity in her voice, but it was that sense of urgency, even more than the lure of the violin, that pulled me into the SUV.

"Drive!" she screamed, and the engine roared in response.

Within seconds, the SUV was flying backward as York did the three-point-turn maneuver I'd learned in drivers' ed last year. The SUV rocked back and forth until it faced up the road and away from the river.

I opened my mouth to—I don't know, protest, maybe? Or suggest another plan, or maybe just ask to be let out of the damn car. But whatever I was going to say got knocked right out of my brain as York hit the gas and slammed us back in our seats.

We sped all of ten feet down the road before a bright flash of light glared off the windshield, followed by something large flying out of the woods to our left. It was a blur of black, and it made an awful *thump* as it hit the front fender and rolled up the hood of the SUV.

York slammed on the brakes, and the body—*Oh God, it's a body!*—rolled back down the hood, the megaphone attached to its hand *clunk-clunk*ing against the car all the way down.

7

THIS IS WHAT people mean when they say silence is deafening.

The quiet shock that filled the car was a tangible thing, and it swelled until it felt like the small confines of the SUV would burst with it. A car door opened, and the *ding-ding* warning bell cut through our hush.

"Stay here," York ordered.

So, naturally, every one of us opened our own doors and followed him to the front of the SUV. The officer had fallen to the side of the dirt road, half-concealed in the weeds and grass. He was not moving.

"He's dead," Boston said in a strangled whisper. He said it again, and this time it was a scream that reached all the way to my bones. "HE'S DEAD!"

Jail is for drunks and accidental car thieves. Prison is for cop killers.

I backed away from the officer's body and fumbled in my purse for my phone. It had been so long since I'd had to dial

9-1-1. *My mama is missing. My mama won't wake up.* It made me sick to my stomach.

But before I could punch the numbers, York let out a 9-1-1 call of his own.

"Help!"

It took me a second to realize he was shouting his SOS directly out toward the river.

"HELP!"

He was calling for the other police.

And they answered.

The first shot whizzed by us far to the left, lost somewhere in the woods.

The second bullet burrowed deep into a tree just over the fallen officer's body.

By the time the third bullet screamed into the rear bumper, we were all back inside the SUV.

Andi yelled for York to "Go! Go! Go!" but he really didn't need her prodding. His foot was on the gas before our doors were even closed.

Two more shots rang out, and I couldn't help but turn around and look out the rear window. Through the cloud of dust we were kicking up, the cops finally emerged from the trees, still firing their guns, until they became so small I couldn't distinguish them from the trees. I wondered if the familiar cop knew he was shooting at the child of a woman he had arrested.

Small world, I thought as I collapsed back into my seat, because in this chaos, it was the only thought I could spare.

The SUV roared out of the woods, and our heavy breathing paused for only a moment as we passed the fork in the dirt road that led toward the party and held a collective breath. But there were no signs of any cop cars, and the only thing that followed us out of River City Park and onto the road was our own fear.

As soon as the tires hit pavement, the silence in the SUV broke.

"Pull over," Andi ordered just as Boston said, "Slow down."

York told them both to shut up, but a moment later, he side-swiped a curb and seemed to change his mind.

"Maybe I shouldn't be driving," he mumbled as he slowed down *and* pulled over.

"You think?" I muttered.

The SUV rolled to a stop in a dark parking lot behind a boarded-up fast-food restaurant. A giant plaster taco dangled from a rusted chain over the old drive-through window. I was suddenly hungry, and not just because I'd skipped dinner but because hunger was an easier feeling right now than horror.

"Is everyone okay?" York asked.

"We're fine," Andi snapped. "You just hit a curb."

"No, I mean—what happened . . . we—are we okay?"

In the passenger seat, Boston's head dropped into his hands, and his shoulders shook.

Oh shit, a crier.

"Oh my God, are you crying?" Andi said. "We don't have time for your meltdown."

It was harsh, but I had to agree.

"Hey!" York whipped around and pointed at Andi with a finger backed by a fist. "You don't talk to my brother. He's scared, all right?" He turned and ducked his head toward Boston's. "But dude, you really can't cry right now. We're gonna be okay, trust me."

Boston wiped his nose on the back of his hand and sat up straight again. "We just killed a cop. There's nothing *okay* about that."

"We didn't kill a cop," York said. He turned to look each of us in the face. "Right?"

"If he's dead, we killed him," I said, emotionless. My brain wasn't really connecting with the truth of those words yet.

"But maybe he's not dead." York latched onto the bone I'd thrown. "Maybe he's fine, and—"

"He didn't look fine," Andi said. "And either way, the little one is right. We are *not* okay."

Boston pounded the dashboard suddenly. "I'm not the little one!"

His punch sent something clattering off the dash and into his lap. He picked it up and turned it around. It was a flat black box with an old-fashioned-looking digital display running along one side.

"What is this?" Boston fingered the display, which was blank. Whatever it was, it was off. "What is *all* of this?" He gestured around the dash and the center console, and Andi and I leaned into the gap between the front seats, finally taking in our surroundings.

The SUV was full of custom equipment. The stereo was the biggest one I'd ever seen in a car, with more buttons and knobs than you could possibly need to tune a radio. It, too, had a display window, which was constantly scrolling a series of nonsense numbers and letters that didn't match any radio station I'd heard of.

Boston spun one of the knobs until a soft crackle sounded from the speakers. He turned it farther, and a voice cut through the static, loud enough to startle us all back into our seats.

"All units River City Park, Forest Road 6."

My heart raced, and I imagined it beating in time with the three pounding hearts around me.

Another voice answered through the radio. "Dispatch, this is Twelve, en route to Forest Road 5, juvenile disturbance backup."

"Negative. Forest Road 6. Nine-one-eight, officer down. Possibly related to disturbance."

Boston's hand flew off the knob like it was on fire. "What the hell?!"

My thoughts exactly.

8

BOSTON SPOKE AGAIN, and his voice was choked down to a whisper. "Whose car is this?"

York shook his head. Actually, his whole body seemed to be shaking, and I wondered if he was crying now, too. "I thought it was Carrie's, or someone from the party. I figured we'd give it back later."

"York." Boston seemed to be struggling to keep his voice even. "Is this a *cop car?*"

"It's just some SUV. I didn't—how could we—"

"It's a cop car!" Boston shouted.

I felt a pang of guilt. If it *was* a cop car, it seemed like I should have known somehow. I'd certainly seen enough of them. But this one wasn't marked, and I was ever-so-slightly distracted by the gunfire and the running away before.

Boston slammed around in the SUV, flipping down the visors and opening the center console compartments. Then he yanked on the glove compartment door and pulled out a small walkie-talkie. "Undercover!" He shook the walkie-talkie as if it was proof. "I am so screwed!"

"*You?!*" York exploded in return. "Of course *you*. It's always about you! We are all in this. We all hit that cop!"

"Actually," Andi spoke up, sounding almost bored, "you're the only one who hit a police officer."

"And drove drunk," Boston added.

"And stole a cop car," I said, because it felt like my turn.

York caught my eye in the rearview mirror. "We all left."

"No," Andi said. "The rest of us were kidnapped. We're innocent."

"You're a thief," I reminded her.

She rolled her eyes. "Hardly ranks now, does it?"

"Look," York said. "Whatever happened back there, for all intensive purposes, every one of us was a part of it."

Boston shook his head. "You mean 'intents and purposes.'"

"That's what I said."

"You're an idiot." Boston tossed the walkie-talkie back into the bowels of the glove compartment and kicked the door shut with his foot.

The radio in the center console spoke again, the dispatcher directing cars and calling for more units.

The shock started to wear off then, and in its place the gnarled claw of reality crept in, twisting my guts. This whole night had felt sort of like a dream—the kind where you follow yourself around, observing but not actually controlling any of your actions. But those were real police responding to a real emergency—a real officer possibly real *dead* in the woods—and the dream was quickly becoming a nightmare.

I opened the door and tumbled out of the car. *Air. I need air.* It was a good thing I hadn't eaten dinner, or it would have all come back up in that moment. Instead, I bent over and faced the pavement, convulsing with dry heaves. Not much of a replacement for tears, but I felt a release all the same.

I am on a beach. I am on a beach in the Caribbean, all sunshine and white sand, with steel drums and the crash of ocean waves mixing to make a new kind of music.

I heard the sound of car doors opening behind me, accompanied by the constant static of that awful reality radio.

I turned up the steel drums in my mind. *My feet are sinking in the soft sand. There's a tropical drink in my hand, and a cool breeze blowing my hair, for once not held down by a hat.*

"Is she puking?"

"Gross."

I straightened up and looked around. *I am in a dark parking lot in shitty River City, streaming with sweat. Damn it.*

I pulled my phone out of my purse to check the time. Only 10:00 p.m. I should have been getting off work now. I couldn't believe just hours ago I'd been wondering how to tell Mama I got fired. I guess telling her about all of this would really soften the blow of my lost job. It would have been funny if it wasn't so damn tragic.

"Grab her phone!" The voice was Andi's, but the rough hand that snatched my cell away was York's.

"Hey!" I lunged after him, but he held the phone out of reach.

"You were trying to call nine-one-one," Andi accused me.

I should have.

"No," I swore. "I was checking the time. I thought my ma—my mom might be worried."

"She's lying," Andi said.

"You don't trust your own friend?" York tucked my cell phone into his back pocket.

"We're not friends," Andi and I said in unison.

York squinted at me. "What did you say your name was again?"

"Sam."

Boston tipped his head to the side. "Yeah, but they call you Worms, right?"

Who is this "they"?

"No," I said sharply. "They don't."

"Well, Sam," York said, "you need to get back in the car and—"

"We need to ditch the car," Andi interrupted.

Boston scoffed. "Yeah, with my brother's fingerprints all over it."

"Not my problem."

"Then what do we do?" I asked. But the answer was obvious. We had to call the police, of course. We had to explain what happened and throw ourselves on their mercy. I just didn't want to be the one to say it out loud.

Boston said it for me.

"We'll tell them it was an accident," he said.

Yes, perfectly reasonable.

"A drunk-driving accident," York said quietly.

Well, okay, that sucks for him, but like Andi said, not our problem.

"We need to start walking," Andi said. "Now. They're going to come after us."

As if in response, from inside the SUV, a radio voice—it sounded like a different dispatcher this time—called for a perimeter around the park.

"Fine," York said. "We get out of here. But we take the car until we figure out what to do."

"No, we *leave* the car," Andi protested. "If it's a cop car, they'll be looking for it."

York came at her so fast, I thought he was going to shove her to the ground. Instead, he leaned in close and seethed. "We're taking the car. In case you hadn't noticed, nobody follows you around anymore."

Andi looked like she'd been slapped.

"I'm driving," Boston told York.

"My ass."

"I can do it."

"You're only fifteen."

I hardly thought that mattered. When I was eleven, I drove Mama's station wagon all the way to the River City Hospital emergency room. She was on parole, and Aunt Ellen had let me stay the night with Mama. We'd fallen asleep on the couch while watching a marathon session of the *Scream* movies—our favorites—but when I woke up, I was alone. I'd finally found Mama in the parking lot, passed out behind the wheel with the car still running. I smacked her a few times, hard, but she didn't wake up.

Aunt Ellen had given me a cell phone to call her in exactly this kind of emergency, but I was more afraid of getting Mama in trouble with Aunt Ellen than with the police, so I left the phone off and shoved her into the passenger seat. It wasn't hard. She was so skinny back then—she weighed barely more than I did—and her frail body tipped easily onto the car's front bench. I remember her head hitting the inside of the passenger-door window with a little *thunk*, and the thin line of white foam that dribbled out of the corner of her mouth.

My small eleven-year-old hands shook as I stretched the seat belt across my lap and adjusted my mirrors, like Mama had taught me just weeks before. The emergency room was only a few blocks from the apartment. I cried the whole way.

I hadn't cried since.

"I'd rather ride with the fifteen-year-old than the drunk," Andi said.

"So you're coming?" York asked.

"Yeah, we're coming."

It took me a second to realize she meant both of us.

"Not me," I said.

"Come on." She stuck an arm out like an impatient mother ordering a child to take her hand.

Something about that motherly gesture caused anger to boil up inside my chest. It bubbled and bubbled until I thought I might explode, so when I opened my mouth, I made an effort to keep my tone even.

"No. Thank you."

There. That was even polite. Good for me.

York tossed my cell phone at me before climbing into the passenger seat.

"Don't give her that! She'll call the cops." Andi looked like she was about to boil over herself.

"We can't leave her downtown with no phone," York said. He leaned out the window and called to me. "You okay out here, Hat Girl?"

I nodded.

Then he looked me over in a way that made me feel naked. "She doesn't look like a narc to me."

I'm not! I'm not a narc!

I don't know why I cared what the hell they all thought. I'd learned a long time ago not to care what *anyone* thought, and I'd been called a lot worse than a narc.

"You can't leave," Andi said, pleading now. "We're all in this together."

"I'm not *in this* at all," I said. "I don't even know how I got here. All I wanted was what you stole!"

"This?" Andi whipped the violin out of her oversize messenger bag and swung it back over her head like she was winding up a pitch. But she didn't throw it. She seemed to think for just a moment, anger flashing in her eyes, and then she shoved the violin into my chest.

"If this is really all you care about after a man's been run over and probably killed and we've been shot at, then you have some serious problems."

My cheeks burned. Of course it wasn't all I cared about. But the violin was part of Mama, and I normally didn't have room to worry about much more than that.

"There you go," she said, releasing the violin into my clutching hands. "You've got it. Now go." She pointed out toward the road.

Inside the SUV, the boys had turned down that awful radio and were listening closely. Boston looked anxious to get on the road. I felt like a coward for abandoning them.

"And my money," I said.

"Consider it payment for your stupid violin. Now, please. Get. Out. Of. Here."

Why did it sound like she was begging me?

"GO!"

But I didn't want to go.

The feeling hit me like a wrecking ball.

I had Mama's violin. I had my phone and permission to leave. Maybe I didn't have my cash, but who cared? I was going to spend it on the violin anyway. This was my moment to escape this whole crazy night.

And yet my feet didn't move.

Move, feet!

But I was sure if I took a step, it would be in the wrong direction. My brain's compass told me to hit the road, but my gut was pulling me back toward the SUV.

For a few crazy hours tonight, I had been part of something—something silly and then stupid and then downright awful—but something other than Mama and endless daydreams. And now here I was, standing apart again, watching others from the outside, and it gutted me. It wasn't that I wanted to get in the car so much as I didn't want to be left out.

"We have to go!" York called.

A siren wailed off in the distance, somewhere inside the woods, punctuating his words.

I probably stood there weighing my options for only a few seconds, but it felt like a lifetime. Andi must have seen something in my face—some change—because her angry shout dropped to a conspiratorial whisper.

"Come on, Sam. You're with us."

I yanked off my hat and let my fingers wander over the scars on my scalp, tracing the wide raised lines, smooth in spots where the hair had never grown back. I ruffled up my curls to make sure those spots were covered, which was pointless, because I just hid them back under the hat a second later anyway.

The siren grew louder, more urgent, and Boston punched the car horn in frustration. But it wasn't the horn that propelled me back into the SUV with three strangers and a world of trouble. It wasn't the ominous wail of the police sirens, either. I climbed into the backseat and slammed the door shut behind me because, for once, I was invited.

BEFORE

LOOK AT ME.

I stretched the thought across the wide hallway to the lockers on the other side. Or, more specifically, to the boy standing in front of those lockers. He was cursing as he spun a lock dial back and forth, every so often tugging on the latch and then throwing his head back when it refused to budge. I liked the way his muscles moved under his shirt when he tensed up to try again.

"Thirty-two, thirteen . . . no, thirteen, thirty-two . . . Shit!"

He banged his head on the locker in frustration, then turned to lean against it, blowing a thick lock of hair out of his eye.

Look at me. Look at me.

Not that I had any idea what I would do if he *did* look at me, but I wasn't exactly practicing my invisibility. I had pushed my gray ski cap back off my face—not far enough to tease out any curls, but far enough that if he looked my way, he might see my eyes. Some people seemed to like my eyes, when I let them look.

But he didn't. Look, that is.

His gaze was focused on one end of the hall instead, his eyes narrowed in a laser-like search. I wondered who he was watching for and hoped, beyond reason, that it wasn't a girl. He looked too old to have a locker in the freshman wing, and it occurred to me he might be trying to break into someone else's. Maybe he was on the lookout for teachers so he wouldn't get busted.

It was unlikely. Most teachers retreated to their lounge during lunch hours, to get a little peace or hoover up some coffee or take a Xanax—who knows?—but I doubted they'd come marching down the halls of F-wing. The only action this hallway ever saw at this time of day was a few kids running back and forth between the cafeteria and the good bathrooms . . . and me, eating my lunch on the floor in front of my locker.

"York!"

The shriek came from the cafeteria end of the hallway, and a whirlwind of skinny arms and legs propelled itself forward— too fast; the kid was going to fall! As though my thought had triggered it, just then the boy pitched forward, tripping from his own momentum. His bony arms, all elbows and freckled skin, stuck straight out in front of him, Superman-style, and for half a second it looked like he might actually fly right past the boy with the lean muscles and floppy hair.

But instead, the boy called York threw out an arm and hooked it under not-so-Superman's chest, catching him before he face-planted on the floor. A smile touched my lips. Now who should be wearing the hero's cape?

The scrawny kid—I searched my brain for his name but came up blank—straightened himself up and glanced in my direction. I ducked my face into my tuna sandwich so fast I nearly inhaled mayonnaise up my nose. I didn't want the poor guy to think I'd watched his almost-fall. When I dared to look up again, his back was to me.

"I got your text," he said breathlessly to York.

York. Three months into the school year, I hadn't learned many names outside of the freshman class, but this one sounded familiar for some reason. By the looks of him, there was every chance his name was written on bathroom walls and whispered between giggles around school.

I felt a pleasant little rush of relief that York had apparently been waiting for this awkward kid and not one of the Barbies. That's what everyone called Andi and Georgia and their clique—the Freshman Barbies. Although, come to think of it, I hadn't seen Andi with the other Barbies for a few weeks.

"The combination's not working," York grunted, pounding the locker once with his fist.

The skinny one huffed and held up his phone. "That's your nine-one-one? I thought something was wrong."

"Something *is* wrong. You gave me a bunk combo."

"No, you just have to be smarter than the lock."

The smaller boy twisted the dial as York grew impatient. "See, that's why I was confused. There are only three numbers, but you spin it four times."

"I have to."

"You don't have to. You're just a freak."

"And you're a moron."

York shoved him roughly to the side in response.

Boys.

"What is all this garbage?" York dug in the bottom of the locker like a dog, sending out a spray of loose papers and gum wrappers.

"It's called homework. You should try it sometime."

"You should try being human sometime."

I stifled a laugh.

"Why can't you just use your own locker?" the freckled kid complained.

York finally stood up, a textbook clutched in his hand. "I don't want to see . . . anyone."

"Just because you're not on the team anymore doesn't mean—"

The textbook hit the floor with a bang that echoed down the hall.

"Shut up about it!" York's hands pulled at the sides of his hair. "You're lucky I'm using your locker—that I'm even willing to be seen with you."

"What's that supposed to—"

"You're embarrassing!"

I tugged my ski cap back down low over my forehead and crumpled up the remains of my lunch, my appetite gone.

"Got it," the small boy said in an even smaller voice.

York softened almost immediately, stammering out, "Look, I didn't mean— It's not you I'm—"

But the other boy was already slamming his locker shut and rushing away down the hall. I thought I saw him brush something from his cheek as he ran, but I couldn't be sure. Across from me, York looked like he might run after the younger boy—one arm was stretched out, and his mouth was open as if to shout—but after a second he only turned back to the locker and leaned his head against its smooth surface.

He stood that way for a full three seconds before straightening up and punching the locker hard with his fist, leaving a slight dent. Then he scooped up his textbook and jogged off toward the cafeteria.

I watched him go, feeling a squeeze of disappointment in my chest. Of course he couldn't be hot and nice at the same time. That was just too much to ask of River City boys.

I pushed my squashed lunch bag to the side and tugged my algebra binder out of my backpack. Beneath the binder's plastic cover was a patchwork of old photos Mama had dug out of a box in Grandma's attic after she died: Mama in front of the St. Louis arch, Mama playing her violin on an outdoor stage surrounded by red rocks, Mama posing with roadies on top of a skyscraper in New York, Mama splashing through the waves on a beach who-knows-where.

Inside the locker behind me I'd created a similar collage, but with much more exotic locations. I was going to travel as much as Mama had, and then some. I was going to get as far away from River City as I could, and when I got there, I was going to tear off my invisibility cloak and let people see me. Until then, I just had to keep my head down and try to survive high school.

Alone in the hallway, I squared my shoulders and lifted my chin.

I'm glad he didn't look at me.

But the problem with having only yourself to talk to is you always know when you're lying.

9

AS SOON AS the SUV started moving, uncertainty set in.

"Where are we going?" I asked.

"Our house?" Boston suggested as he pulled onto the road.

"Hell no," York answered. He turned to us in the backseat. "What about you guys? Are your parents home?"

"Yes," I said.

Andi looked away from us, out the window. "My dad's always home."

"Are they cool?" York pressed. "Can they help us?"

Andi let out a low, sarcastic laugh. "Yeah, right."

"My mom's cool," I said. "But not this cool."

For all Mama's run-ins with the law, when it came to me getting in trouble, she was decidedly *un*cool. The way she lectured me about drugs and sex and anything criminal, you'd think *I* was the one with the bad habits. I guess she just worried that she'd passed on more to me than her green eyes.

"We could go to the cabin," Boston offered, but he didn't sound too sure.

York faced forward again and seemed to consider the idea for a moment. "It's far," he finally said.

Boston shrugged. "Not *that* far."

"Maybe just far enough," York mused.

"You think?"

"I think."

"Hey, Tweedledee and Tweedledum," Andi said. "You want to fill us in?"

"There's a . . ." Boston hesitated and cast a sidelong glance at York. "We have a cabin." He stopped at a red light and drummed his fingers on the steering wheel, craning his neck around as if expecting police to surround us at any moment.

"Yeah, we got that," I said wearily. "Where?"

"North," York answered. "About an hour. Right before you get to Wisconsin. We'll just go there long enough to figure out what to do."

Andi looked at me. "What do you think?"

I think driving out to the middle of nowhere to some deserted cabin with two boys I don't really know is the kind of genius idea that gets girls raped and murdered in the movies. But the blond bimbo always gets killed first, and since neither of us is a blond bimbo, maybe this won't turn into a slasher flick.

"I don't have a better idea," I said.

"We can't be driving around town in a stolen cop car," York pressed.

"We shouldn't be driving *anywhere* in a stolen cop car," I argued.

What a colossally bad idea it had been to get back into this SUV.

"We should drive it right to a police station," Boston said.

Agreed.

"I told you . . . ," York said.

"I know, I know." Boston waved off York with one hand. "You don't want to get a DUI."

"I don't want to get arrested for killing a cop!"

"Don't say that again," Boston said. The light turned green, and he pressed the gas, careful to stay under the speed limit.

A fifth voice spoke up then, quieter than ours and muffled.

"Attention."

The sound sucked the air out of the SUV.

"Attention," the distant voice repeated.

"I thought you turned the radio off," York said, running his fingers over the knobs and dials.

"I did, I did. It's off!" Boston insisted.

The voice spoke once more, and this time it sent a chill down my spine.

"Attention, all you little bitches in the stolen car."

The others looked around, searching high and low for the source of the voice, but I had already found it. I raised a shaky hand and pointed to the glove compartment in front of York.

"Get off the main road," York ordered Boston, who obediently turned down a dark side street. York opened the compartment and gingerly lifted out the walkie-talkie Boston had found. It was crackling with life now.

He turned it over in his hands, then pressed a button on the side and spoke tentatively.

"Hello?"

My hat was off my head and whipping him on the shoulder before he'd even released the button. Andi came at him from the other side with a hard slap to the head.

"Don't talk to it!" I said.

Maybe he was still drunk.

York hunched his shoulders, looking ashamed, but the damage was done. The voice knew we'd heard it.

"Do you know what happens to cop killers in this town?" It was a man's voice, low and threatening.

"Yeah," I muttered to myself. "They go to prison."

"They don't get arrested," the voice said, almost as though he had heard me. "They get dead."

I swallowed hard and heard Andi whisper "Fuck" beside me.

"It's the police," Boston said. "The ones who—"

"Who shot at us," York finished.

"Cop killers don't make it to jail," the voice said. It was cold, emotionless.

"That's not true," I said aloud. "He's trying to scare us."

"It's working," Boston breathed.

Well, that much I couldn't argue with.

"But there's no need for that," the voice said. "It was an accident."

Here it comes. The part where they try to reason with us—to lure us out.

I wouldn't take much convincing. I figured we were going to end up in a police station one way or another. At least this way we could talk to the cops before they cuffed us.

The voice spoke again. "You'll be safe if you just tell us where you are."

"He's offering to help us," Boston piped up hopefully.

"Sounds more like a threat to me," I countered.

Boston pouted and steered the SUV down a narrow alley. "Police don't threaten you."

I rolled my eyes. "Except they just did."

It must have been nice for him, to live in his little bubble where all police were good guys and everyone behind bars was a bad guy. How conveniently black and white.

"You have two options." The voice paused as if waiting for a reply, but we all just stared at the walkie-talkie until it spoke again. "Door number one: you tell us where you are. Door number two: you run like rabbits."

Yes, definitely a threat.

One by one, I studied the faces around me. None of us made a sound.

When the walkie-talkie crackled again, the voice had dropped to a sinister hiss. "All right then, little rabbits . . . *run.*"

We sat in silence for a full thirty seconds before it became clear the voice was done. Then Andi leaned toward the front seat, her voice slow and casual.

"Sooo . . . you mentioned a cabin?"

10

YORK DIRECTED BOSTON to keep to back roads, and the SUV wound slowly through neighborhoods and then industrial areas as we made our way toward the interstate. Boston whined a little about trusting police and *not* trusting York, but his arguments were thinner now.

"Boston, that was the scariest cop I've ever met," York said.

"Met a lot of cops, have you?" Andi scoffed.

I answered before York could. "I've met a few. And they're not like that. That was . . . personal," I finished.

Boston finally exhausted his protests as the sign for the freeway rose overhead. "Can they use that two-way to trace us?" He took a tense hand off the wheel long enough to point around at all the equipment in the SUV. "Can they use any of this?"

"You watch too much TV," York retorted, but he looked over the equipment anyway. "It all looks like radios to me."

"Not every cop car has a GPS," I said.

I didn't add that I knew this from too much time spent sitting in police stations, waiting for Grandma to bail Mama out and listening to officers bitch about their lack of funding and everything they didn't have enough of, from GPS tracking devices to SWAT team gear.

"There's nothing else here," York said.

Boston sighed as he turned onto the interstate entrance ramp. "You know, the longer we wait to deal with this, the worse it could get."

"Just go to the cabin."

"You owe me so big."

Then we were on the freeway and flying north.

The first ten minutes on the road were made of utter silence. Andi twisted her dreads absentmindedly and watched the night fly by the window. In the front seat, Boston kept a laser focus on the road ahead, while York actually dozed off. I briefly wished I'd had some drinks myself, if it would help me sleep through this.

I clasped my hands together to keep myself from calling Mama. I didn't want to risk getting my phone confiscated again, but I knew she would start to worry soon. And a worried Mama worried *me*. She was four years clean, but Mama's sobriety still seemed like it was balancing constantly on the fine point of a knife, ready to tip off in any direction if the wind blew the wrong way. If she thought I was missing, it wouldn't be a breeze. It would be a hurricane.

Mama always said I was her reason for living—or, worse, her reason for staying sober. I guess a kid is a pretty damn good reason to get clean, and I should have been glad for that, but it weighed heavy on me whenever she said it. With Grandma gone and Aunt Ellen all but done with the drama, I was the only one left to look out for Mama. And, selfishly, I knew a setback for her would be a setback for me. I was happy back when we first built our little cocoon for two and didn't invite anyone else in. We were making up for lost time. But now time stretched out before me, full of places and possibility, and I was ready to fly away. But with one wrong move, Mama could pin my wings.

The quiet in the car was giving me too much time to think—about Mama, about the cop tumbling off the hood of the SUV, about my extremely poor decision to go along on this ride. The silence was making my mind scream, and when I thought I couldn't take it for one more second, I poked Andi.

"Ow. What?" She glared at me, and I made an emphatic gesture that I hoped would convey that she should say something. But judging by the arch of her eyebrow and the sneer on her lip, apparently the only thing my gesturing conveyed was that I might be mentally ill.

"Did you have too much to drink?" she asked.

"I don't drink."

"And you don't talk so good, either. What are you pantomiming at me?"

"Well," Boston said.

Andi turned her sneer on him. "What?"

"It's 'You don't talk so well,' not 'good.'"

"I know, moron. I was just kid—never mind." She looked back over at me. "What are you trying to say? Spit it out."

I shook my head. "Forget it."

But Andi was engaged now. She shifted in her seat to rest her back against the car door and propped her feet up on the bench next to me.

"So you don't talk much. You don't drink. What else don't you do?"

I don't answer questions that are nobody's business.

"I don't cry."

"Ha!" Andi crowed. "We'll see about that. You've got cry-baby written all over you."

"I think you have me confused with Boston," I deflected.

I felt like an asshole the second the words left my lips. The kid had every reason to cry. Crying was probably downright normal in this situation. I was about to open my mouth to apologize when York whipped around in his seat, not so asleep after all.

"Don't you talk about my brother, you little nobody!"

"Whoa!" Andi pressed her palm hard against York's forehead and pushed him back into his seat. "Somebody's awake."

A nobody. I guess I shouldn't have been surprised that being invisible pretty much made me nobody at all, but the word stung just the same.

After a moment, York turned again. "I didn't mean— It's just . . . I can't let people shit on my brother, y'know?"

I said nothing, instead staring at my hands as though I could actually see them disappearing.

"Come on, Hat Girl. I'm sorry."

"Her name is Sam," Andi said.

York watched me for another second, but when I refused to meet his eye, he flopped back in his seat, huffing. "That's a boy's name."

Andi laughed. "You should talk, *York* and *Boston*. What the hell is that about?"

"They're cities," Boston said. "Obviously."

"York is a city?" Andi raised an eyebrow.

"As in *New* York," York said.

"Were your parents hippies or something?"

Boston eyed Andi in the rearview mirror. "If our parents were hippies, we'd be named Sunshine and Willow."

Andi shook her head. "Nope. I don't think anyone would call either of you Sunshine."

"Our parents are venture capitalists." Boston puffed out his chest, but York deflated it with a backhanded smack.

"Don't try to make them sound cooler than they are."

"What's a venture capitalist?" I asked, glad the focus was off me.

Boston answered, "They invest in start-up companies. They give money to entrepreneurs to get something going, and when it takes off, they make a profit."

"They help people open restaurants and shit," York said. "It's not like they funded Google or something."

"Our parents are really important people!" Boston was getting loud now.

Andi shrugged. "Sound like hippies to me, Sunshine."

"If they're important," I said, "maybe they can help us."

What would that be like? I wondered. To have a parent in a position to help instead of one who was perpetually on parole.

"They won't help us," York said. He and Boston shared a look, and then he added, "Okay, they won't help *me*." He flipped the visor over his seat up and down a few times, then said quietly, "Our parents are assholes."

The silence that followed lasted only a second before Andi laughed. "Hey, whose aren't?"

11

"WE'RE ALMOST OUT of gas," Boston said a few minutes down the road.

"Perfect," I muttered.

York pointed into the darkness ahead. "I think the next exit has a gas station."

"You can't stop!" Andi sat up straight in her seat.

"We can't?" York turned around, eyes wide with mock surprise. "Gee, thanks for letting us know. We'll be sure to keep driving until the car dies, then. Good call."

Andi returned his sarcasm with a withering stare. "Well, we can't just roll into a gas station in this car."

"We could dump this car and get a new one." The words were out of my mouth before I could think them over. "What?" I said when York and Andi gaped at me. "That's what they do in the movies."

And this must be a movie, since it can't possibly be my life.

"Brilliant idea," York said, using the same tone with me that he had with Andi. "Except, wait . . ." He made a show of patting his pockets. "Yeah, damn. Left my carjacking kit at home. Bummer."

I put a hand over my mouth to stifle a laugh. He was right. The idea was so stupid it was almost funny, but I wouldn't give him the satisfaction of a smile, not after what he'd called me.

"I'm not stealing any more cars," Boston said decisively as he breezed past the exit.

Our headlights fell on a sign looming up alongside the freeway, making it glow against the night sky. A cheery cartoon cornstalk with googly eyes and stick legs waved from one side of the sign.

NOW LEAVING RIVER CITY.

All I'd ever wanted to do. But not like this.

The words burned bright in my vision even after we'd passed the sign, and I sat up with a jolt as the message really hit me.

"Guys," I said, breathless. "We're not in River City anymore."

"That's right, Dorothy," Andi chirped. "We're in hell. Toto, too."

I ignored her and plowed ahead. "I mean, we're not in the River City police jurisdiction."

"So?" York said. "They'll be looking for us everywhere."

Boston checked his mirrors as though a highway patrol car might pull up at York's very suggestion.

"But they won't be as pissed," Andi said, my meaning settling in. "We didn't kill *their* cop."

"We didn't kill anyone," Boston said.

York sighed. "Keep telling yourself that."

"Those other police—I don't think they want to arrest us at all," I said. "They threatened us. They shot at us. But the county cops . . . they might actually *listen* to us."

York twisted in his seat, and this time he didn't mock my suggestion. "So, tell us what to do."

We huddled at the center of the SUV as I laid out a plan. At the next populated exit we saw, we'd pull off for gas and look for a county cop car. There was usually a deputy or two cruising around the tiny towns that didn't have their own law enforcement. If we didn't spot one, then we'd call 9-1-1 as a last resort, but it would be better to tell our story in person, before word went out over all the law-enforcement frequencies that the River City cop killers wanted to confess. We'd still be in deep shit, but we'd be safe from cops bent on revenge.

York nodded emphatically as I talked, and though Andi twitched and sighed a few times, she didn't argue. Even Boston, with his eyes on the road, offered the occasional "Yeah" and "Good idea." I smiled inwardly. Maybe all of this wasn't really my problem, but it still felt good to be part of the solution.

Finally, Boston pulled off the freeway onto a strip of road with two fast-food joints and a single filthy gas station. My mouth watered at the sight of the pair of golden arches over one of the drive-throughs, and I imagined I could smell burgers and fries.

I cleared my throat. "Could we maybe stop for—"

"Oh my God, food!" Andi said.

"Exactly," I laughed. I actually *laughed*.

Boston parked at a gas pump. "We're only here long enough to fill up. You can grab something inside. And hurry," he urged. "We want to find a deputy before they find us, remember?"

Andi pouted and opened her door.

"Wait," Boston commanded. He ducked low in his seat, peering up and out the windows like a turtle sticking out its neck.

"Uh, what are you doing?" I asked.

"Checking for cameras." He sat up straight again. "It's clear. If anyone in there asks, we're camping nearby and getting supplies, okay?"

Andi and I agreed, but York only growled as he got out of the car. "Whatever. Stop acting like you know what you're doing."

I rounded the back of the SUV and started to pass by York as he fumbled with the gas pump, but his arm shot out, blocking my path.

"Hey," he said.

"Hey, what?"

"I really am sorry about before. I didn't—"

"Whatever; forget it."

"Um, here." He dug around in his pocket and came up with a wadded bill. "For the gas. I don't think we should use our credit—"

"Fine." I snatched it out of his hand and stomped away without looking back.

The inside of the gas station was sweltering.

"Sorry. Air conditioner's broke," the clerk greeted us.

I dropped York's twenty on the counter, and Andi peeled off her army jacket, revealing a black tank top and bare arms. Well, not entirely bare—her inner forearms were covered elbow to wrist in tattoos. She caught me staring and held them out to give me a better look. Two identical tree trunks stretched the length of each arm, their roots wrapping around Andi's slender wrists and their branches fading away at the top as if the leaves didn't matter.

"They're teak trees," she said. "The strongest on the planet. Like me."

The detail of the bark was mesmerizing, almost three-dimensional, and I reached out a hand to feel it, but Andi snatched her arms back. "Yo! No touching. I don't know you that well."

"Really?" I stared her right in the eye. "You don't have a problem touching *my* things."

She gave me an appraising look. "Touché."

"York has one, too," I said. "A tattoo. On his chest. I think it's a name. . . ."

I trailed off when I saw Andi smirking.

"So, just the trees?" I asked.

She shook her head. "I have seven total. The trees, a snake, cherubs—"

"Cherubs?" I raised an eyebrow. "Like angels?"

Andi grinned. "They're ironic."

"Which one's your favorite?" I asked.

She turned and lifted the bottom of her tank top to reveal a leprechaun dancing on the small of her back. "This guy. I designed him myself. Cool, huh?"

I wondered if she would still think it was cool when she was eighty-five with sagging skin, and that leprechaun fell into her butthole.

"You know, there's an island in Tahiti where they still do tattoos in the traditional way, with needles made out of sharks' teeth," I said. "I'm going there someday."

The last bit came out in a rush, and I held my breath, waiting for Andi to laugh, but she only nodded.

"Sounds awesome."

I smiled as we started combing the shelves for snacks. "So your parents don't care? About all the ink?"

"My dad. And not only does he not care, he doesn't even notice."

"Kind of hard to miss," I said.

Andi picked up a box of powdered doughnuts, then put it back down again. "You'd think."

"No mom?"

"Dead."

"Sorry."

She shrugged. "I don't remember her, so it's no big deal."

I understood that. My dad wasn't dead, but he'd left so long ago, I couldn't remember him, either.

Andi pulled a few bags of beef jerky off a hook and quickly tucked them under her jacket, which she draped over her arm.

"Oh, come on!" I complained in a low voice. "We're in enough trouble."

"Don't remind me." Andi tucked a package of pink Snowballs into her messenger bag.

"I'm just saying, we're already—"

"No, *seriously*. Don't remind me. I'm trying to pretend for a minute that this whole night isn't happening."

I turned away, and the moment my back was to her, Andi shoved something into my rear jeans pocket.

"What the—"

"Shh." She pushed my back. "Just keep walking."

I planned to pull whatever it was out of my pocket as soon as Andi stepped away, but she stayed right on my heels, herding me toward the front door. We were just feet from the exit when the clerk's voice stopped us.

"Hold it," he said.

Damn it. Damn kleptomaniac!

We were so screwed. It was just a hop, skip, and a jump from shoplifting to stolen cop car spotted to teenage killers caught. Andi's stupid habit was going to get us busted before we had a chance to tell our side of the story.

We turned slowly toward the clerk, and I started to put my hands up, but Andi grasped my wrist and forced it down to my side. She winked at the clerk, who was leaning deep over the counter. "Yes?"

"What are you ladies up to tonight?" His eyes raked Andi's body from head to toe, and I mentally thanked her for taking her jacket off.

"We're going camping," she said.

"Oh, yeah?" He leered at her for another second, then his gaze shifted to me, and his jaw went a little slack. "Your eyes," he said. "They're . . ."

Unnatural? Bizarre? I'd heard it all, including, occasionally, *beautiful*, but usually people looked more frightened than
impressed by my eye color. Mama's eyes were an identical shade,
and she liked to call it "palest green, like the inside of a lime."
Or, as a boy in third grade once told me, "a freaky alien green."
I had thought that was rude, but Mama said it was just a third-
grade boy's way of telling me I was pretty and he noticed.

Most of the time I liked that Mama and I had this in common, this thing that made us inextricably mother and daughter.
But other times, I knew people—teachers, counselors, even Aunt
Ellen—looked into my eyes and saw only Mama, and it just gave
me one more reason not to be seen.

"They're contacts," I lied. Much easier than getting into
some drawn-out conversation with a guy we shouldn't be talking to in the first place.

"You girls need help putting up your tent?" The clerk
grinned, and I noticed one of his teeth was capped in silver. "I
know how to light a fire."

We were saved from declining that sick offer by the boys
bursting through the door behind us.

"We have a problem," Boston said in a low whisper.

"Boyfriends?" All the flirt had gone out of the clerk's voice.

Andi shrugged apologetically and threw an arm around Boston's waist, steering him back out the door. I followed her lead,
grabbing York's hand and winding my fingers through his as we
retreated. He looked at me like I had grown another head, and I
dropped his hand the second we were outside.

"Impressive," Andi said to me. "We make a good team."

I reached into my back pocket to pull out whatever Andi had stashed there and saw it was a bag of cashews.

"I'm not really a team player," I said, tossing them to her. "And I don't even like nuts."

She caught the bag and tore it open with her teeth. "Good. More for me."

Boston was pink cheeked, his shirt pressed against the sweaty skin where Andi had wrapped her arm around him. "Guys, I said we have a problem."

"We have several," I agreed.

"Well, now we have one more," York said seriously. He led us to the back of the SUV and opened the hatch. Inside, a long black bag ran the width of the trunk, zippered closed.

"Oh God," I said. "Is it guns or something?"

Of course we accidentally stole an arsenal when we accidentally stole a cop car. Of course we did. Naturally.

York shook his head. "It's worse."

Then he leaned in to grab the zipper tab, took a deep breath, and pulled.

He was right.

It was worse.

12

THE SUV AND parking lot disappeared around me, replaced by stained yellow walls and an unmade double bed. Foil crinkled in Mama's hands as she balanced it over the hissing flame of a Bic lighter. An aroma like too many Easter eggs being colored at once soaked the tiny motel room. Chasing the dragon, Mama called it, but I thought chasing dragons sounded like a lot more fun than whatever she was doing.

By age five, I was tall enough to turn on the fan in the bathroom. Then I would crawl into the rusted tub and pull the stained plastic curtain closed. It was as far away from Mama and her smell as I could get. It wasn't far enough.

Beside me, Andi leaned deep into the SUV to inspect the contents of the bag. Not that they needed close inspection. Small rectangular packages wrapped in clear plastic were laid out in tight, neat rows. The boys had already torn one open, and its dusty brown contents spilled like sand.

"It's drugs, right?" York said, looking over his shoulder to confirm we were alone in the lot.

"This is bad," Andi said.

York brushed a finger over the powder he'd set free and held it close to Boston's face. "It's too dark to be coke. Cocaine is white, isn't it?"

"How should I know?" Boston pushed his brother's hand away and then rubbed his own hands on his shirt as if they were contaminated. He began to pace back and forth behind us.

"Very bad," Andi repeated to herself.

York lifted his tainted finger to his nose, and I shot out my hand instinctively to stop him, my fingers closing around his wrist.

"I wouldn't," I said.

"I just want to smell it."

"It's heroin." I let go of his wrist, but his hand still hung frozen in midair, and three faces turned to stare at me. "And if you want to know what it smells like, go stick your face in a bottle of vinegar."

I could think of only one scent I hated more—so distinct in my olfactory memory that I couldn't pin down just one thing to compare it to. It was like urine mixed with cleaning supplies and poured over burning plastic. I'd smelled it only once, cooking on our stove in the little apartment Grandma had rented for us to get us out of the motels. When I was six years old, other kids' moms were cooking SpaghettiOs. Mine was making meth.

I closed my eyes, wishing the thought away. It happened like that sometimes: one bad memory bleeding into the next, as if my past were a patchwork quilt of ugly moments and I was chasing the seams, trying to find an exit but only bumping into new patches, new memories.

I forced myself to focus on the drugs in front of me instead of the drugs Mama had left behind.

Drugs. We are standing in a gas station parking lot with a wide-open bag of who-knows-how-many pounds of heroin.

I couldn't wrap my brain around what it meant to be part of a hit-and-run involving a police officer and a stolen cop car, but I knew exactly what could happen to us if we were caught with drugs. I reached up to pull down the hatch, barely giving Andi and York time to duck out of the way.

"Watch it," York said, but he glanced nervously around the lot, understanding my urgency. "Get in the car."

Andi was talking before I'd even settled in my seat.

"We can't turn ourselves in like this, with a car full of heroin."

"But it's not ours," I said, clinging to my initial plan. "We'll just explain that we found it like this."

"We found it," Andi repeated, staring at me. "In the back of a cop car. Would *you* believe that?"

"But it's true," Boston said.

"It doesn't matter if it's true," York countered, sounding defeated. "It matters if it *sounds* true."

"And it sounds like bullshit," Andi added.

The truth of Andi's words hit me hard, and I felt my plan unraveling.

"What it sounds like," I said, hating to admit it, "is a really good reason to run over a cop."

"Motive," Boston whispered.

I nodded, and a quiet fell over the car.

"Well, we can't just sit here," Andi finally said.

Her words seemed to snap Boston out of his trance, and he turned the ignition. He checked all his mirrors twice—left, center, right—and then he reversed the order and checked them again. He'd gone through the same ritual back before we'd left River City. I didn't know what it was, but I was losing patience with it.

"Can we go already?"

He shot me a dirty look in the last mirror he adjusted and finally put the car in gear.

No one protested when he got back on the interstate heading north. Something felt wrong, and I was fine with driving away from that wrong until we figured out how to right it.

"What the hell are police doing with a bag of drugs?" York asked, turning to me. "And how do you know it's heroin?"

"How do you know it's not?" I pivoted.

"This is bad," Andi muttered. She kept repeating this same phrase, and it was starting to freak me out.

"Maybe it was a bust," Boston said. "Maybe it's from a drug deal they were breaking up."

"Doubt it," I said. "If there was a bust that big going on, the police wouldn't have been wasting time at a stupid high school party."

York pulled the walkie-talkie out of the glove compartment; it was so still now, as though it had never been turned on. He held it up, a question on his face. "They didn't tell us. They didn't say a word."

"And they didn't exactly demand we turn ourselves in, either," I said, my mind clicking and whirring now. "All they wanted to know was where we were."

York nodded. "And you said that cop standing by the car ran *away* when he heard the cop with the megaphone?"

"Yep." Something wrenched inside my gut. Andi was right. This was bad.

"And then they tried to shoot us," York finished.

"Maybe we didn't see what we think we saw," Boston offered.

"Yeah," York scoffed. "We all simultaneously hallucinated flying bullets."

"No, I mean, maybe it just wasn't what it looked like. Like this car—undercover."

"That's another thing," York said, getting loud. "What kind of undercover cops wear uniforms? This whole thing reeks."

I wished they would both shut up so I could think.

"We just don't have all the pieces of the equation—" Boston started.

"No." York shook his head. "This is not some algebra problem you can just solve—"

"Uh, I take calculus, not algebra. At least I will, if Mrs. Doyle—"

"Boston, they *shot at us*! They tried to kill us!"

Andi pounded the back of York's seat with a fist. "Settle down up there!"

"I'm sure they didn't know they were shooting at kids," I said. "There are a lot worse things going on in those woods than high school parties, trust me."

"How would you know?" Andi asked.

I slumped back in my seat, suddenly tired. "I just know."

Boston latched onto my suggestion. "Maybe they were aiming for the tires."

"And you're supposed to be the smart one," York huffed.

"You got any better ideas?"

York thought a moment. "One."

"What's that?" I asked.

"They weren't busting up a drug deal. They were the ones *making* the deal."

York let his words settle over the car.

Arresting druggies by day, feeding them by night. The idea sickened yet somehow didn't surprise me.

"Oh, come on." Boston rolled his eyes at his brother.

"They obviously had some sort of alternate motive for being at the docks," York insisted.

"'Ulterior,' not 'alternate,'" Boston corrected. "And I don't think police really need a 'motive' to be anywhere at all."

"They're crooked," York whispered, ignoring Boston. He ran his hands through his hair and leaned forward in his seat. "Holy shit. Crooked cops."

Andi narrowed her eyes at the back of York's head, and Boston opened his mouth but found no words. None of us could disagree.

I didn't know exactly what had happened back there in the woods, but whatever it was, it was definitely crooked.

13

WE PASSED A bag of beef jerky around the car and went over our options. Boston still wanted to go to the police, drugs and all, but York convinced him it would be our word against the crooked cops'. I didn't add that my mom's history might make our claim a little less convincing. Andi suggested twice that we dump the SUV and everything in it and just pretend none of this had happened, although she had no solution for how the hell we would get back home.

In the end, the only thing we could agree on was that we needed to get out of sight until we figured out what to do, so Boston kept the SUV's wheels pointed toward the cabin. Mostly we practiced proclaiming our innocence to one another. *Not our drugs! Not our bullet in the bumper!* Of course, there was still the issue of running over an officer. That one was definitely on us.

"But if we ran over a *crooked* cop," Boston argued, "maybe we won't be in as much trouble."

"*That* cop wasn't crooked," York said. "He was one of the police busting up the party."

"But!" Boston stuck his finger in the air as though inspiration had just struck. "What if the only reason they were breaking up the party was to get everyone away from the drug deal? What if they were in cahoots with the crooked cops at the dock?"

"Um." York stared sideways at his brother. "Did you just say 'cahoots'?"

This dissolved into several seconds of mocking, and I curled up in my seat, thinking of the officer we'd left in the woods. Did he have a family? Did the crooked cops help him after we left? The poor guy thought he was just busting up a party. He probably never imagined he'd end up dead. I pulled off my cap and put both hands in my hair, fingers massaging my disfigured scalp as I tried to make sense of the senseless. I didn't understand why the police were in uniform if they were up to no good, but it was the only hole I could drill into York's theory.

I tried again to muster up even a little bit of surprise. Cops who used their uniforms as beards for their real moneymaking job? It didn't sound so different from the pervert downtown who wore a suit to hide his disgusting habits, or the not-so-tough guy who held court outside the liquor store to cover up his insecurities. Walking lies, all of them.

"Look, this could be a good thing," York was saying as I tuned back in. "We're not the bad guys now. Or we're not the *only* bad guys, anyway. It's almost like we stopped a crime. We're kind of vegemites."

"You mean vigilantes?" Andi said, disdain in her voice.

"That's what I said."

"Not even close," Andi retorted. "And if you think you're going to turn in those drugs and get rewarded instead of hand-cuffed, you're an even bigger moron than I thought."

"Call me a moron again, and we'll leave you on the side of the road to—"

"Stop!" The word flew out of my mouth unbidden. "Everyone, just stop talking."

They fell silent and watched me, waiting. It was a second before I realized they expected me to speak.

"Oh; I didn't—I wasn't—" I stuttered. "I don't have anything to add."

York rolled back in his seat, and Andi shook her head at me. "God, you're so weird."

Yeah, and you're so normal, you violin-toting klepto.

Boston caught my eye in the rearview mirror. "You're sure that stuff's heroin?"

"I'm sure."

I heard the second, silent question he didn't ask, and answered that one, too.

"I don't do drugs."

He dropped his eyes back to the road and, thankfully, dropped the subject as well.

"York's right," Boston said. "This is good. We have—we have . . . *leverage.*"

He and York shared a tight smile and a nod, apparently soothed by the idea that the drugs were somehow our ticket out of trouble. But until we cashed that ticket, we were still just a bunch of teenagers driving around with an insane amount of heroin.

We might as well be sitting on a bomb.

"I think the best thing to do is type up our story, like a statement," Boston said. "We can do that from the cabin and then find a way to get it to the police—the *good* police."

"As long as we get it to them before they get to us," York said.

We fell into a tense silence that York broke by turning on the radio. He avoided the police scanner and played with a few knobs until he found what sounded like an actual station.

A couple of guys were talking politics, and I imagined Mama talking back to them like she always did. Sometimes she ended up shouting at the TV or radio, and I'd tell her to turn it off, but I think she secretly liked her one-way conversations. My hand went involuntarily to the cell phone in my purse. Why hadn't she called to check on me? It was after eleven now.

The guys on the radio told us to stand by and introduced a woman at the "news desk."

"We have a breaking news update on that hit-and-run involving a River City police officer," she began.

The SUV made a violent lurch as Boston swerved in shock.

"Access roads to River City Park remain closed at this hour, and police are searching for suspects. Several officers were in the park earlier this evening, issuing citations to underage drinkers, when one officer was apparently hit by a vehicle that left the scene."

Every muscle in my body clenched. The air seemed to have been sucked out of the SUV.

"That officer remains hospitalized tonight, but we're told he is in stable condition with no serious injuries."

And just like that, my taut muscles unwound, and the sigh of relief that went around the car was like oxygen rushing back in.

We didn't kill him. We didn't kill *anyone*.

"He's alive!" Boston cheered.

York shushed him, and we all crowded in close to the radio to hear the rest of the report.

"Police say the hit-and-run happened in a different area of the park than the underage drinking, and at this time, they do not believe the two incidents are related."

"This just keeps getting better," York breathed.

"Shh!"

The reporter continued, "Investigators are looking for a silver SUV with oversize tires. A witness reported seeing an SUV matching that description leave the park. We were able to talk to that witness, and here's what he told us."

The next voice we heard sounded like an old man's.

"They come tearing out of the trees like a bat out of hell; only slowed down for a second when they hit that curb over there. I told my wife, nothing good never happens in River City Park."

You got that right, buddy.

The woman's voice took over again. "That same witness told us there were three or four people inside the SUV, including two males in the front seats and someone in back who may have long dreadlocks."

Andi clutched her dreads, looking guilty.

The reporter finished by saying the man had given the same description to police and a search was under way.

"Hey!" York shouted at the radio. "You forgot to mention that they tried to shoot us!"

When the DJs went back to their political chatter, Boston glanced away from the road to give a wide-eyed look to the rest of us. "It's . . . good. Right?"

"It's weird," I said. "Why didn't they give a license-plate number? They should know it; it's their car."

"But it's not all bad," Boston insisted. "At least that cop is fine."

"He's not fine. He's in the hospital," York said.

"But he's alive," Andi pointed out. "You dodged a bullet, dude."

"We all dodged a bullet," he countered. "Three of 'em. Why didn't they say anything about that?"

"Maybe those cops didn't stick around," I said. "The, um . . . *other* ones." Calling them crooked was starting to sound childish to my ears. "Maybe that's why the police don't know we're in an undercover car—the other cops didn't report it."

"I wouldn't," York said. "Not with that load of shit in the back."

"So then, we've got evidence," Boston said. "The cops who drove this car weren't supposed to be there. Just having the car is proof they were doing something wrong." He was excited now. "When the police see that, they'll believe us about the drugs, too!"

York shook his head. "Sure they will."

"Okay, maybe the police won't believe us," Boston said, shimmying in his seat to pull his cell phone out of his pocket. "But Mom and Dad will."

"What are you doing?" York grabbed for the phone, but Boston elbowed him out of the way and started to dial.

"Watch the road!" Andi shouted as Boston veered across the center line.

York lunged again, and this time Boston pushed back, taking both hands off the wheel. The SUV squealed to the right as the wheel spun free, and I felt a skid as our tires hit gravel.

Well, at least if we die right now, we won't go to prison.

Boston corrected in time, but he still had only one hand on the wheel. The other was wrapped around the cell phone, which York also had a fist around. He was trying to pry Boston's fingers away.

"Just once," York said, breathing heavily, "just once, can you not go running to them? Just once, can you take my side?"

Boston didn't answer, but I saw some of the struggle go out of his arm.

York released his grip. "Thank you."

Boston's hand hung in the air, still clutching the phone, even after York sat back, satisfied.

"Promise you won't call them," York said. "Promise."

But Boston hesitated for just a moment too long, and the next thing I knew, Andi was reaching into the front seat. With one hand, she snatched the phone out of Boston's now-limp grip while the other hand lowered her window. Wind rushed into the car, and Boston's phone rushed in the other direction, sailing out the window and into the dark.

14

"AND THAT SETTLES that," Andi said, calmly raising her window with the push of a button.

I gaped at her and held my purse a little tighter, in case she reached for my phone next.

"You bitch!" Boston said. "You psychotic bitch!"

"I'm just helping you focus on the road," she said. "You almost killed us fighting over that phone. You obviously *are* too young to drive."

"I have my learner's permit," Boston shot back.

"So you'll be a sophomore this year?" she asked him, totally conversationally, like she hadn't just thrown his five-hundred-dollar phone out onto the highway.

Boston just shook silently in the front seat. I imagined I could see steam coming off his head.

"He's a junior," York said. "He started kindergarten early."

"I've never seen you in school," Andi said, still talking to Boston. There was doubt in her voice that set my teeth on edge.

"Well!" I spit it out like something hot, surprising myself as much as everyone else. "If you haven't seen him, then he must not be a junior. He probably doesn't go to Jefferson at all. Maybe, if you haven't seen him, he doesn't even exist!"

In the silence that followed, I wanted to gather up all the words I'd spilled and shove them back into my mouth. Five-second rule! But I only sat there seething. It was one thing to keep your head down and try to go unnoticed; it was another to have someone basically call you a ghost in your own school—as if being invisible wasn't a choice.

Andi rolled her shoulders like she was physically shrugging something off, then tilted her chin toward Boston. "I just meant you're not in any of my classes . . . right?"

I enjoyed the tiny tinge of guilt she layered onto the last word.

Boston glared at her in the rearview mirror, and she pointed a finger, directing his eyes back to the road.

"I'm in your grade, not your classes," he said through clenched teeth. "I've never had class with any of you except her." He jerked a thumb back at me.

I quickly scanned my memory for Boston in biology, composition, or any other subject, but if he was there, I couldn't see him. I'd only ever noticed him in the hallways. I wondered if that made me as guilty as Andi.

"And not since third grade," Boston finished. "That's when we switched to a private elementary school."

Well, that explained how he knew about Worms. I guess some things were just written on the world in permanent marker, no matter how much you tried to erase them.

"Now I'm splitting my schedule between AP and college courses so I can graduate early."

"Cool," I said.

York let out a bitter laugh. "Yeah, cool. My brother, who is two years younger than I am, will graduate the same day as me."

"*If* you graduate," Boston retorted.

York shot a hand out as fast as lightning and shoved the side of Boston's head. To his credit, Boston kept the car straight.

"God," I complained. "Are you guys always like this?"

"Like what?" York and Boston said in unison. Then they both cracked up, their shared laughter instantly outweighing any sibling spat.

Andi poked me. "What was that?"

"What was what?"

"You're mostly quiet, and then . . ." She made a sound in the back of her throat and pantomimed an explosion.

"Sorry," I said. And I was, a little. "It just came out."

"Well, lighten up," Andi said. "Things are looking better. At least we didn't kill a cop. No one's going down for murder."

"If not murder charges, then what?" York asked. "Hit-and-run? Is that a charge?"

"Leaving the scene of an accident." Andi ticked crimes off on her fingers. "Assaulting a police officer. Assault with a deadly weapon."

"What weapon?" York scoffed.

"The car," she answered.

"How do you know that?"

"Everybody knows that."

"She's right," Boston said. "And add attempted vehicular homicide to that list."

These charges were starting to sound made-up.

"We didn't *attempt* anything," York said. He looked back at us girls. "Boston thinks he's going to be a lawyer or something."

"I'm going to be a judge," Boston corrected. "And then a Supreme Court justice." He lowered his voice. "At least I *was*. Before this."

"Oh stop," York said. "This isn't going to ruin your perfect plan. Shit doesn't stick to you. It just rolls right off."

"This isn't getting busted drinking at some stupid party," Boston protested. "This is, like, multiple felonies. The longer we wait to tell our side of the story, the more guilty we look. And if they don't believe us, then . . . God, our whole lives— *poof*. Gone. I can't get into an Ivy League school with a criminal record."

"Right," York said. "It's all about your precious college applications. As long as you get a perfect SAT score, I'm sure schools won't care if you got caught up in some crime spree."

A crime spree? Is that what this was? One crime could be chalked up to accident, but a *spree*? I shivered despite the heat.

Outside the car, pinpoints of light stabbed through the darkness, every one of them a searchlight seeking us out.

"What is that?" I asked. "A town?"

"Not really," York said. "Just a few houses, a couple of gas stations, and a Walmart. We stop here for supplies when we go to the cabin."

A few minutes later, we flew past the exit for the town, and in the distance I could see a sign lit up with spotlights.

Welcome to Prison.

I blinked and looked again.

Welcome to Pitson.

AFTER

"TWENTY MINUTES, LADIES."

I don't bother to protest that I'm in the middle of a story. I know the drill. When visiting time is over, it's over. Once, when I was little, I threw a temper tantrum and refused to let go of Mama's leg for, like, fifteen minutes past visiting hours. The prison told Grandma if it happened again, I wouldn't be allowed to come back. Jails were usually a little more lenient, but it's best not to push it. I'll have to be quick.

"Maybe I should just skip to the—"

"No," Mama interrupts. "Tell me everything."

Her fingers are splayed and stiff on the cold metal table. It's obvious my story is freaking her out—giving her some kind of guilt complex. A million questions are on her face, but she knows there's no time to ask them.

Instead, she whispers, "I wish you had called me right away."

"Would it have made a difference?" I ask.

Mama smiles weakly.

"Thank you for the violin, Sammy. That was very thoughtful."

"Not like I can give it to you in here, though, huh?" I say.

Mama shakes her head, and a single tear slips down her cheek.

"Anyway," I say, leaning back. "Don't thank me yet."

15

"I HAVE TO pee," Andi said a few miles down the road.

"Why didn't you say that back at Pit Stop?" York said.

"What's Pit Stop?"

"That town. Pitson. We call it Pit Stop, because that's really all there is to it."

"Fascinating," Andi drawled. "Pull over."

"Can you wait?" Boston asked. "We're only, like, ten minutes from the cabin."

"Ten minutes in a car that smells like pee is going to feel like a looong time," she said.

Boston checked his mirror to make sure there were no cars behind him and reluctantly pulled to the side of the road. "Hurry up."

"You have to go?" Andi asked me.

I shook my head. I did kind of have to go, but I wasn't excited about doing it in a strange field in the middle of nowhere.

Andi wandered off until the darkness swallowed her up, then York opened his own door.

"You, too?" Boston asked.

York slid out of the passenger seat and shook his head. "No, man. I think I have to puke."

The events of the night had sobered him up a long time ago, but it looked like he wasn't going to escape the hangover.

Boston stretched in the driver's seat. "Okay, but don't take too long."

"It takes as long as it takes." York slammed the door and loped off in a different direction from Andi.

Boston rubbed his face with his hands. He looked totally spent.

"Your brother's kind of a mean drunk, huh?" I said.

He dropped his hands and stared out the window after York. "He's kind of mean in general."

I recognized the beaten-down look on Boston's face; I knew what it was like to be someone's emotional punching bag.

"My mama's an addict," I blurted.

"Your what?"

"My . . . mom. She's an addict."

"Okay." Boston didn't look at me.

"I'm just saying . . ."

What *was* I saying? I had no idea. I guess I just wanted to let him know—from one target to another—he wasn't alone.

"York's not an alcoholic," Boston said.

"I know, I just meant—"

"Hey, no offense," Boston said, twisting in his seat to finally look at me. "But I don't really want to have a moment right now. I've kind of got enough to deal with."

Uh, me, too, ass.

"Sorry," I snapped. "I guess we should focus on what's important—like your college applications, right?"

I felt bad, but like Grandma always said, *Wounded dogs will bite.*

"Did you know Harvard accepts less than six percent of all students who apply?"

The way he said it, I wasn't sure whether he was talking to me or to the sky.

I answered anyway.

"No, I didn't."

"Yale and Stanford take less than seven."

"Uh-huh."

"If we somehow get out of this, I'll get accepted to all three."

Okay, so we don't have time for me to share something personal, but bragging is totally okay. All the time in the world for that.

Boston pointed after York. "He'll be lucky if he gets into community college. He's not a drunk. He's just pissed."

"At you?"

Boston shrugged. "A little. More at my parents."

"The assholes," I said, remembering what York called them earlier.

"They're not assholes. They're just . . . overachievers."

"Like you."

"Yeah."

"And York's not? An overachiever?"

Boston frowned at the dark outside the car. "He used to be. It was easier then, when it wasn't all on me, y'know?"

I didn't know; I waited for Boston to elaborate, but he fell quiet, and a moment later Andi and York were climbing back into the SUV.

"What'd we miss?" Andi said. "Did you guys make out in here?"

"Gross," Boston said.

I flinched, and angry blood pumped at my temples, especially when Andi laughed at Boston's reply, like she knew he would be sickened by the idea. York was less amused, and he growled at Boston to get moving.

"This again?" Andi complained as Boston started his mirror checks.

"I'm detail oriented," he said.

York rolled his eyes. "That's one way of putting it."

"More like OCD," Andi said, and in the stiff silence that followed it was obvious that she'd hit a little too close to the mark.

Boston rushed through the end of his routine, and as wheels met road once more, York gave Andi the finger on his brother's behalf.

Ten minutes later, as promised, we were turning off the highway onto a narrow, unmarked road. It was little more than a cleared dirt trail, and trees crowded in around the SUV, branches scraping the roof and windows. We might as well have been back in the woods of River City Park.

The forest opened up into a massive clearing, and the SUV's headlights illuminated a large cabin backed by a wide expanse of water glowing white in the moonlight. The cabin—if you could call it that—was two stories high, with a front wall made entirely of glass, from foundation to roof. It was closer to a crystal palace than a woodsy retreat.

We spilled out of the car and let our eyes adjust to the shift from headlights to moonlight. Pine needles crackled under our feet, and a cool breeze rushed in off the lake, whisking away some of our summer sweat. I felt a million miles away from River City . . . and a million miles away from River City is where I'd always wanted to be. I took a mental snapshot of the cabin—a postcard to hang on the walls of my imagination.

York stepped up next to me, his shoulder brushing mine. "So, this place is—"

"Amazing," I breathed.

He grinned. "I was going to say better than our place."

"I thought this *was* your place."

"Uh, yeah, I mean our regular house." He spread his hands in the air, framing them around the building. "Both the east and west facades are glass, so you can watch the sun rise over the lake and set in the woods."

"Not exactly a log cabin, is it?" I said.

"It's made from the same stuff—Douglas fir, cedar, spruce. And wait until you see the stonework inside. . . ."

His face lit up as he rambled on about trusses and struts and other things I didn't understand, and I found myself standing next to a very different boy than the one I'd seen tormenting kids at school.

"You know a lot about it," I said, impressed.

York shrugged. "I'm into buildings. I might become an architect."

"Yeah, right," Boston scoffed. "You need to go to college to become an architect."

York whirled on his brother. "I'll be whatever I say I'm gonna be."

"You could be a construction worker." The tone in Boston's voice was almost earnest, as though he thought this was actually a helpful suggestion.

Andi shook her head at him. "What did I say about poking the yeti?"

"What?" Boston said. "Construction workers can make a ton of money. . . ."

He trailed off as he noticed York's red face and clenched fists.

I stepped between the boys, leaning into York's line of sight, and smiled.

"You sound like an architect to me."

He glowered and didn't respond.

"I mean . . ." I hesitated, not sure whether I, too, was poking the yeti. "You know about the stonework and arches and—"

"Whatever." York turned and stomped toward the cabin. "Let's just do what we came here to do."

I stared after him, trying not to feel wounded. He was a jerk and a stranger and possibly a drunk. What did I care what he thought?

Boston followed York, and as Andi and I fell into step behind them, she leaned in to whisper to me.

"What exactly *did* we come here to do?"

16

"IT'S NOT HERE." York cursed and prowled around the cabin's front door, reaching into a mailbox and lifting up tiny stone statues of frogs and raccoons.

"It's here," Boston said. "Just keep looking." He joined the search, feeling along the top of the door frame and searching behind the bushes that flanked the entryway.

Finally, both boys stepped back with their hands on their hips—an identical pose that made them look, for the first time, like brothers.

"Shit," Boston said.

"Oh my God," I said. "Please tell me you're not looking for a key."

"No." Andi seethed. "They wouldn't drag us all the way up here unless they already *had* a key." She glared at the boys. "Right?"

Boston looked sheepish, but York just pushed roughly past her and circled around to the side of the cabin. We followed, stumbling as the ground sloped down toward the lake and the pine needles beneath our feet gave way to mud. I used the moonlight to sidestep small puddles of water, but Andi wasn't as careful. I heard a squelch as she tugged one of her boots from a mud hole.

"Hey!" she cried, holding up her mud-covered foot for the boys to see when they turned around. "Look at this! Do you know how much these cost?"

"Oh, did you actually pay for them?" I said.

Andi's head snapped in my direction, and the surprised look on her face was so satisfying. *That's right*, I silently reminded her. *You and me? Not friends.*

Her face melted into a smile. "Nope. Doesn't mean they're not worth something."

"The sooner we find the key, the less time you spend communing with nature," Boston said, poking behind a rolled-up hose. "Not here, either."

York checked a few windowsills. "I can't see for shit. It's too dark."

Andi huffed and fished something out of her messenger bag. "Why didn't you just say so?"

And the world erupted with light.

Boston and York held their hands up against the glare, and I had to squint, even though I wasn't in the path of the searchlight.

At least, it was bright enough to be a searchlight. But it was actually much smaller—almost small enough to hook onto a key chain, and light enough that Andi could hold it between two fingers. She lowered the beam to spare the boys' eyes, and the ground all around us glowed as if it were broad daylight.

"What is that?" York gaped.

"Uh . . . a flashlight. Obviously," Andi said, but her voice had lost some of its edge, and in the glare the light was casting all over, I could almost see her cheeks turning pink.

"That's not a normal flashlight," Boston said. He leaned in to inspect the tiny metal cylinder. "It's even brighter than an LED. What's it powered with?"

"How should I know? You said you needed light. Here's light." She backed away a step and aimed the beam at the wall. "Now, let's go."

She doesn't know because she probably picked it from someone's pocket.

"But where did you get it?" The way Boston was ogling the flashlight, you'd think Andi had pulled an ancient dinosaur bone out of her bag or something.

Andi gritted her teeth. "My dad got it off an infomercial, okay?"

"An infomercial?" York laughed.

"Yeah!" Andi shined the light directly in York's face. "An infomercial. As in, 'Here's the one-eight-hundred number. Call right now for this exclusive one-time-only discount.'" Andi's voice grew shrill, and she was practically spitting. "'Buy one, get one free, and we'll even throw in this nifty carrying case for just five dollars more!' SUCKERS!"

The last word came out as a screech and echoed through the trees, hanging in the air as the rest of us stared at Andi in gaping silence.

Guess I'm not the only one who's prone to outbursts.

Andi was breathing heavily, and the outrageously bright light shook in her hand.

York blinked stupidly in the vibrating light, his mouth hanging slightly open. Then he held up a hand, and something silver glinted between his fingers.

"Found it."

No one said much after Andi's explosion. The boys set to work turning on the lights and the air-conditioning in the cabin, and Andi and I hauled in the bag from the back of the SUV, at Boston's request. He was paranoid about leaving a bunch of drugs just sitting around outside the cabin. Never mind that the SUV they were sitting around in was stolen.

This busywork only kept us actually busy for about ten minutes, and too soon we were all crowded around a massive island counter in the kitchen, staring at a pile of heroin. Or, more accurately, we were watching Boston measure the heroin. He had laid out all the bricks of tightly wrapped plastic in neat rows on the island, and he was checking the dimensions with a tape measure, taking notes on a little pad about the size and the quantity.

"We want to be able to give an accurate description of the evidence," he explained when he finally pushed the pad away and settled back on his kitchen stool. "We'll include the dimensions in our statement. And I got the plate number off the car, too. The more details we give them, the more legit our claim sounds."

Dimensions? Plate numbers? *Legit?*

I looked over the stacks of drugs at the fifteen-year-old boy planning our escape route from this ridiculous night, and I suddenly wanted to laugh.

"This is stupid," I blurted. "I'm sorry, but what the hell are you talking about? You're just a kid."

"Oh please," he shot back. "You were my age, like, five minutes ago."

"I'm old enough to know I can't just explain my way out of this." I stood up and pushed away from the counter, feeling more like screaming now than laughing. "I'm such an idiot for coming here—for not bailing the second we found this garbage." I swept an arm over the drugs and ended with a finger pointed at Andi. "And I'm an idiot for following you."

I expected a swift comeback, but Andi only stared at me blankly. She'd hardly said a word since her fit outside, and it looked like she had fallen into some kind of eyes-open coma.

"Hey." York punched Andi lightly on the arm. "Snap out of it. Did you hear? Good news. You still have followers!"

His attempt at levity was lost on absolutely everyone, and we fell into a terrible, awful stillness. The quiet just screamed that no one in this room had any idea how exactly we'd ended up here or how to get out.

It was music that broke the silence.

Someone's phone was ringing. I reached instinctively for my purse where it rested on the counter, but I knew the song was not my ringtone. A second later, York had yanked his cell out of his pocket. He glanced at the screen and silenced the song.

"Mom and Dad. Curfew."

"Shit." Boston dropped his head into his hands. "What do we do?"

"Ignore them," York said.

"No, call them." Andi had finally woken up, and I was relieved to hear the calm in her voice. "Everyone call your mommies and daddies and tell them you're staying over at a friend's house."

Great idea. If you're the kind of person who has friends.

My hand twitched over my purse. It had to be midnight now. Where was *my* phone call?

"I don't know—" York started, but Andi cut him off.

"They're just going to keep calling. You have to tell them something."

York still hesitated, and Andi leaned in, threatening. "Don't make me throw yours out the window, too."

"Fine." York tipped his phone to the side and started texting.

"What about me?" Boston said. "I bet my phone is ringing, too." He shot Andi a dirty look. "Wherever it is. They'll be more worried about me."

"Uh, I'm sitting right here," York said, pointing to himself. He grinned like it was a joke, but the smile didn't quite reach his eyes.

Boston flushed. "I just mean—you're *always* with friends on the weekends. You're never home."

"And if it wasn't for me, you'd *always* be home."

"They're probably freaking out," Boston said, stricken.

York smirked. "Oh, they're definitely freaking out." He went back to texting and spoke as he typed. "Went. To. A. Movie. Staying. At. Jordan's. Boston, too."

He finished the text and then powered down the phone and pocketed it. "What about you?" he asked Andi. "You going to call your mommy and daddy?"

Andi pressed her lips together for a moment, then seemed to collect herself before biting back. "You don't hear my phone ringing, do you?"

Mine, either.

I dragged my phone from my purse and stared at the blank screen. Everyone was watching me, so with a little bit of shame, I pretended to send a text message. Something small and sharp twisted in my gut. So many nights I had spent worrying about Mama. But apparently she couldn't be bothered to worry about me.

17

"THE NEXT PHONE that rings goes in the toilet," Andi said.

She sounded like she meant it, so with a deep breath, I powered down my phone, watching the screen go completely dark.

"And if you answer it," York said, mimicking her serious tone, "*you* go in the toilet."

He waited for a laugh, but I couldn't even muster up half a grin. I pulled off my cap to run my fingers through my hair, digging for the smooth lumps of scar tissue underneath. I tried to retrace my steps over the last few hours, to figure out which decision, which turn, had been the point of *no* return. No doubt I should not have gotten into the SUV, but even before that, I should never have set foot in River City Park. I should have let the violin go.

But I wasn't really chasing the violin so much as a piece of Mama. I couldn't let that piece fly away, not when so much of her had already been stolen from me over the years. I was robbed of her smile when meth took three of her teeth; I lost her soft hugs when heroin sapped her will to eat and turned her body to bones; I'd even lost things I never had, because the thief of time kept Mama behind bars and left me with so many months of memories unmade.

I couldn't reclaim those things, but now that Mama was done breaking apart, I could help put her back together. I took comfort in the fact that some of Mama's stolen pieces could be tracked down. At least when those pieces were locked up in pawnshops, I knew where to find them. So even though I knew running after the violin was my first mistake, I couldn't say I would have done things any different.

My eyes strayed toward the violin, now spilling half out of Andi's messenger bag and onto the counter, alongside my purse and the drugs and the keys to the SUV—the whole story of our night on display.

I unthreaded my fingers from my hair and reached for the instrument. Andi made no move to stop me, giving me an almost apologetic smile instead.

"Bet you wish you'd just lifted that thing when I told you to," she said.

For once, we agreed.

As I pulled the violin free of the bag, I liberated more of its contents than I intended. A spiral notebook slid out of the open flap, followed by the flashlight and what looked like 3-D glasses. Andi hustled to shove it all back in her bag, but York was quicker. He snatched up the glasses.

"What the hell are these?" He slipped on the chunky plastic wraparound bands and tipped his head this way and that, looking through the lenses, which protruded like eyepieces on a microscope. "Whoa! They're like binoculars you can wear. Cool."

Andi yanked the glasses off his face and shoved them back into her bag. "They're not cool. They're lame."

"Did you steal them?" I asked.

She slapped the flap of the messenger bag closed. "Oh my God, will you just get over it? I didn't steal everything I own."

"It's another infomercial thing," Boston observed. "Like the flashlight."

Andi rounded on him. "So?"

He flinched. "So . . . you can't steal from infomercials."

"Oh," she said, placated. "Right."

"You don't have a laptop in there, do you?" Boston asked.

"No; why?"

"We need to type up our statement, and we need the Internet to figure out where to send it. I'd use my phone, but . . ."

Geez. Let it go, dude.

"You can use mine," I said. I tucked the violin under my arm and grabbed my purse, but Boston waved me off.

"Not yet. Let's write it all out first, then we'll—what's that?" He was staring at the purse in my hands.

"Uh, it's a purse. What about it?"

"Not that." He stretched across the counter to peel something from the bottom of my bag. "This."

When he pulled back, a small slip of paper was in his hands. I inspected my purse to confirm nothing else was stuck to it, then set it down again. Boston shoved a few of the plastic packages to the side and set the palm-sized scrap on the counter in front of him. It was lined paper, torn from a spiral notebook, and someone had written on it in black ink. I walked around the counter to read over his shoulder and found myself crowded in close between the boys as we all hunched over.

I had only a second to register that one of them smelled like spice before I was distracted by the words on the paper. I choked at what I read.

Forest Road 6
Trail to old launch
9 pm

York snapped upright, and the faint aroma of spice went with him.

"That's the spot . . . that's the—the SUV—the cops—"

"Coordinates for the drug drop," Boston supplied.

"Coordinates?" I leaned away from Boston, in case his nerdy jargon was contagious.

"Call it whatever you want." Boston snatched the paper off the counter and shook it. "But this is the exact time and place."

"Where did it come from?" York asked.

"From the bottom of her purse." Boston pointed at me.

"No, before that, genius."

"Well, that's obvious," I said. I lifted one of the heroin bricks from the table and let it fall back with a thud. "We dumped out an entire bag of this stuff. The slip had to be in there."

Boston pushed the block I'd dropped back in line with the others. "We didn't 'dump' the bag," he said. "We unpacked it very carefully."

"Point?" York asked.

"The *point*," Boston said, "is that I checked every inch of that bag, and every one of these . . ." He waved a hand at the drug pile. "Whatever they are."

"It's small," Andi said, pulling the paper from Boston's hand and letting it flutter back to the counter like litter. "You just didn't see it."

Boston looked her steadily in the eye. "I don't miss things. I promise you, it wasn't in there."

I shook my head. "But if it didn't come from them, that means—"

"It came from one of us," York finished.

Boston exhaled through his nose. "Exactly."

No.

Andi echoed my thought. "No way."

York grabbed the paper and held it up accusingly. "Whose is this?"

I stared hard at the slip in his hand, at the college-ruled lines cutting through the black ink, at the jagged edge where it had been ripped from a notebook.

From a notebook.

My heart skipped as I glanced involuntarily at Andi's messenger bag—the one stuffed with strange glasses and obnoxiously bright lights and one very normal-looking spiral notebook.

"I know whose it is," Boston said, his voice low and serious.

I nodded and swallowed hard. I knew, too.

I looked at him to confirm that our suspicions were the same, but when I caught his eyes, they were fierce, drilling straight into mine.

"It was you."

Me?!

"Whoa." I held up one hand, the other holding tight to the violin still tucked under my arm. "I followed you guys, remember?"

"You tried to ditch us, though," York said.

The paper was crumpling in his tightly clenched fist. I stared at it as if it were contaminated. And everyone else stared at me as if *I* were contaminated.

"That note was stuck to your purse," Boston accused.

"It must have already been on the table," I insisted.

Boston pressed on. "And you knew this stuff was heroin. Who knows that?"

"No!" I said. "I've never seen that paper. It's Andi's!"

"Hey!" Andi reeled. "You don't know that. Why would you say—"

"You're carrying a notebook," I said, pointing wildly at her messenger bag. "And who knows what else."

"She's right," Boston said, chewing his lip.

"Oh please." Andi looked genuinely insulted, and she grudgingly yanked her notebook out of the messenger bag. "Take a look. No torn pages."

She dropped the spiral onto the counter and flipped through the pages. She wasn't lying. The pages were intact. And they were beautiful. Colors flew by as Andi thumbed the edge of the notebook, letting the pages fall one by one for inspection. I saw a flash of a red-and-yellow dragon sketched in colored pencil; a bright-green frog in midhop, looking like he might leap right off the page; and a dancing leprechaun that matched the one on Andi's back.

But the most important thing I saw was that Andi's notebook wasn't lined at all. It was a spiral-bound sketch pad. Of course, it *could* still be her piece of paper, but I couldn't deny the lump of shame I felt rising in my throat.

Andi plucked the paper from York's hand. "If this belongs to anyone, it's you two. You're the ones who couldn't wait to get to the dock."

Hmm. Good point.

Andi went on, "You're the ones who hopped into an SUV that just *miraculously* had keys in the ignition."

Holy shit.

"That's crazy," York said.

Beside him, Boston had fallen quiet. He looked up at York, his eyes hooded, and whispered, "You swear the keys were in the ignition?"

"I swear!" York threw his hands up. "Boston, come on! You can't listen to this—this—*bullshit*. Please!" Then his voice dropped so low I almost couldn't hear him. "Please."

Andi cocked her head to one side. "Sounds like the yeti left you out of the loop, little bro."

Boston didn't respond at first. He studied York's face, letting his brother's unanswered plea hang in the air for a few more seconds. Then, with his eyes still on York's, he told Andi, "I believe him."

York let out an audible sigh, and I felt my own tension release with his.

I believed him, too. I believed them all.

So then, how . . . My eyes crawled over the bricks that Boston had insisted were alone in the bag, past the unlined spiral sketch pad that exonerated Andi, and landed on my purse.

"Guys," I said. "My purse . . . the car . . . that's probably where I picked it up."

Boston propped an elbow on the counter and rested his chin in his hand. "You think it was in there and somehow got stuck to your bag?"

I held my breath while he pondered the possibility.

"Makes sense," he finally admitted.

York just looked relieved that no one was pointing at him. He fingered the torn edge of the paper scrap. "Maybe. Dumbasses just had this sitting in their car? Not exactly a professional job if you can't remember a few simple directions."

Andi grinned. "Hey, don't complain that our enemies are amateurs."

I studied the faces around me, nodding together now instead of hurling accusations at one another—smiling instead of shouting—and I felt something warm feathering in my chest.

If we had enemies, did that make us friends?

BEFORE

I KEPT MY head low as I rounded the corner into the junior wing. The end of the school day was always the best and worst part of my day. In a few short minutes, I would be out the door and embracing the next seventeen hours of freedom, but first I had to go through the daily torture ritual known as J-wing—navigating the crowd of juniors, whose favorite hobby was razzing underclassmen who passed through their territory. Usually, it was the freshman boys who got called out, but a sophomore girl wasn't off-limits.

I patted the wool of my slouchy beanie hat to make sure it was firmly in place, then did my best to push through the crowd without actually touching anyone. That got tricky halfway down the hall, where traffic came to a sudden stop.

I heard what was going on before I saw it. The tinny sound of Michael Jackson's "Billie Jean" was straining out of someone's phone, and people at the front of the pack were whooping and whistling at something I was too short to see.

The crowd shifted, opening up a slim gap between a couple of kids to my left. I moved to squeeze through it, but only succeeded in pushing myself to the front of what I could now see was a semicircle. A line of boys in football sweats lounged against a row of lockers, cracking up at the one-man dance-off in front of them—one man, but lots of girls. That boy York was moonwalking from one side of the space to the other, pulling girls out of the crowd one at a time to take a spin on his impromptu dance floor.

The confident girls showed off their moves to rounds of applause, while the more timid ones gave a little shake, then ran back to their friends, flushed and giggling.

"Seven!" York called after one dance partner twirled away. A less graceful girl got a "Three!" and her face crumpled in embarrassment while York's friends snickered.

His eyes scanned the edge of the ring as the music shifted to a more modern club beat. I tried to press myself back into the crowd, my eyes on my feet and my brain screaming, *Not me! Not me!* Fumbling around in front of dozens of your classmates is not the way to be noticed.

"Hey, you," York called over the music.

Not me!

"Hey, Hat Girl."

Oh shit.

My eyes were still cast downward when York's hand stretched into my field of vision, an invitation to humiliation. But I was spared a second later by a boy pushing in front of me, knocking York's hand out of the way.

"Excuse you," York snapped.

The boy deliberately crossed through the center of the space. "Some of us have places to be," he said.

"Yeah, like cheerleading practice," York called after him. He reached into his pocket, and the music abruptly died. "Nice outfit."

The shift in tone caused a shift in the crowd, and bodies pressed on me from all sides as kids, more interested in fun than a fight, suddenly realized they had better things to do than linger in the hallway after school.

The boy turned around at York's taunt, and I noticed he was, in fact, wearing the unfortunate spandex tank top and shimmery track pants of Jefferson's male cheerleaders.

"You got a problem with my uniform, Flint?"

The crush of moving students opened up a little, and I took a grateful step forward, hoping to slip around the boys, but they backed away from each other, their standoff stretched across my path, and I hesitated, not wanting to be caught in that line of fire.

York held his hands up in mock conciliation. "No problem at all. I especially like your sparkles. Very pretty."

His footballer friends roared, save for one who tugged at York's elbow, saying, "Let it go. Don't waste your time."

I inched toward the wall opposite the footballers, my eyes on a narrow space between the cheerleader and the lockers behind him.

York shook off his friend. "No, seriously, where can I get some threads like that? Do I have to join the squad, or—?"

"At least I'm not cheering for you anymore," the boy snapped.

A split second later, fancy pants and spandex were smashed up against a locker, so close to me that I got hit with York's spit as he cursed in the kid's face.

This was my moment to move, to step around them before they spread their fight back out across the hall, taking up too much space and making themselves big with as much effort as I put into making myself small. But I couldn't move.

I was transfixed by the heat in York's face. His fists and his words all spelled out rage, but the way his eyes drew down at the corners and the strange quiver in his lower lip that only his victim and I were close enough to see smacked of something worse than anger—something closer to shame.

York was either too focused or too furious to notice me, but the other boy slid his eyes to mine.

"Take a picture," he grunted.

I ducked my head out of habit, angry at myself for letting my shield of invisibility crack, and scurried the rest of the way down the hall. I didn't care one way or the other what happened to that not-so-cheery cheerleader—and as for York and the other junior-wing vultures, well, I hoped they choked on spandex.

18

THE STACK OF drugs on the counter made us all a little jittery, but we couldn't agree on where to stash it. I wanted to bury it in the woods where no one—not even the cops, crooked or otherwise—would ever find it. Heroin came from the ground; why not put it back there? Dust to dust and all that. I got shot down by the others, who agreed we would need it as evidence. Andi said we should just put it back the way we found it, but the boys had torn the zipper on the bag when they'd unloaded the stuff. We ended up shoving it all into three small backpacks York collected from a cabin closet, then we piled the packs in a corner of the kitchen and tried to forget they existed.

The stack of drugs was soon replaced by a potpourri of food scavenged from the cabinets and the fridge. Bags of pretzels, jars of salsa, and about a dozen pudding cups were now spread over the kitchen island. It wasn't exactly dinner, but we were all too hungry to complain.

Boston picked at a pile of M&M'S until all the red ones were gone, while York single-handedly finished off a box of stale crackers and some suspicious-looking cheese-in-a-jar, then started pawing the rest of the snacks.

"I want something sweet," he said.

I held up the yellow pudding cup in my hand and offered him a spoonful. "These are sweet."

He sneered at the blob on the spoon.

"What?" I said. "It's tapioca."

"I don't eat foods that jiggle."

I shook the spoon back and forth under his nose to make the tapioca wobble. "Beggars can't be choosers."

He closed his hand over mine on the spoon to keep it from reaching his mouth and winked. "I never have to beg."

I felt a flush of something warm and tingly zip from our hands all the way up my arm and into my face.

He's a jerk, I reminded myself. *And this is no slumber party.*

But his eyes were locked on mine, and there was something almost kind there—something meant for me. I couldn't help it. I smiled.

"Ugh," Andi mumbled through a mouthful of pretzels. "Stop flirting."

York and I both dropped our hands so fast the spoon clattered to the counter, spraying little blobs of pudding on the granite. Tapioca shrapnel.

Boston rescued us from any awkward silence by announcing that he was going to start writing up our statement. He shoved the remains of our late-night binge aside and settled in with a notepad and pen at the counter. No one really responded when he asked for input. It was as if time had slowed down inside the cabin, and we were all dragging our feet, putting off the inevitable. Something about this place felt very far away, and for the first time tonight, very safe. I, for one, was no longer in any hurry to turn myself in.

York must have had the same thought, because he escaped with an excuse about finding us some blankets and pillows so we could all sleep in the cabin's great room.

Maybe it's a slumber party after all.

"What are you saying about the drugs?" I asked Boston.

He shook his head without looking up from what he was scribbling. "I don't know, the truth? We found them?"

"Don't say it's heroin," I blurted. "It might seem suspicious that we know that."

Andi raised an eyebrow. "That *you* know that."

"Whatever. Just keep it short and sweet," I said. "But, y'know, don't leave anything out, either—"

"I think I got this," Boston interrupted, waving me away.

"Come on." Andi motioned for me to follow her out of the kitchen. "We'll check his spelling later."

As we retreated, I heard Boston mutter something about being the River City Regional Spelling Bee champ for three straight years.

We found the great room in the center of the cabin, bookended by the floor-to-ceiling glass walls. The back wall opened up to a view of the lake. The water was as still and slick as ice, belying the heat outside, and a long dock stretched quiet and steady over the water. The serenity was almost unsettling after the turbulent night we'd had.

"It's beautiful," I breathed, touching a hand to the glass wall as if I could reach right out into the moonlight.

"Yeah, it's a regular Bob Ross painting," Andi grumbled.

I turned away from the window in time to see her flop down on a giant leather couch. "Who's Bob Ross?" I asked.

"Some painter my dad watches on TV."

"Bob Ross and infomercials," I said. "Exciting television over at your place."

Andi pursed her lips.

"That's where that stuff came from, right?" I said. "The flashlight and the binoculars. From infomercials."

Andi sat up to make room for me on the couch. "You mean the Sun Shot and the Super Zooms?"

We both let out a laugh, but hers sounded bitter.

"You guys buy a lot of stuff off TV?" I asked.

"Yeah. If it's 'As Seen on TV,' it can probably be seen lying around our house somewhere."

"Or in your bag."

Andi narrowed her eyes at me. "It's not stealing if you take it from home."

"I didn't—I wasn't saying—"

"My dad doesn't even use those things. He just buys them, okay?"

"Okay."

I hadn't meant to imply that she'd stolen anything, but since she brought it up . . . I glanced over at Mama's violin, resting where I'd dropped it in an armchair. "Why did you take it?" I asked.

Andi followed my line of sight. "Because I could tell you wouldn't."

"So?"

"So it seemed like you really wanted it. And I got it for you. You're welcome."

She wasn't getting off the hook that easily.

"If you got it for me, why did you run away from me?"

Andi smirked and propped her feet on a wide wooden coffee table. "Because you seemed like you needed a little something else, too."

"Like what?"

"I don't know. Fun?"

"This night is the opposite of fun," I said.

"Is it?" She caught my eye and let the question hang in the air for a second. Then she shrugged and looked away. "Anyway, I didn't know all of this would happen. I was just messing with you. I would have given it back."

"And my money?" I pressed.

"That's payment for the violin."

"How did you do that, anyway?"

Andi laughed, and this time it sounded genuine. "It's just a little trick I picked up."

I know a trick, too. It's called wait until you're asleep, and then take my cash back.

Andi yawned and stretched her arms to the sides, her tree tattoos stark against the moonlight. I scooted down the couch and caught one arm in the air. I did it without thinking. The second my hand closed around her wrist I expected her to yank it away, but she only leaned forward to give me a better look.

"Did they hurt?" I asked.

She shrugged. "Not as much as I wanted them to."

My fingers strayed to the scars half-hidden under my hat. I couldn't imagine *wanting* to feel pain. I was pretty sure I had blocked out memories of my own. It had to hurt when my hair burned away and my flesh literally bubbled and split open, but all I could remember was how itchy my scalp had been as the hair grew back, prickling against tender, pink new skin. That itch was the worst of it. The rest was a black hole in my brain. One second, heat and flame and a straight blond ponytail; the next, scratchy scalp and funny new orange-colored curls. Grandma used to say I carried the fire in my hair as a constant reminder, but who the hell wanted to be reminded of that?

"This is all I could find." York stomped into the room with one arm full of pillows and the other wrapped around two small rolled-up sleeping bags. "Our mom strips the beds at the end of the summer to do laundry."

"Speaking of tattoos," Andi drawled, rolling her head back to peer at York over the couch, "Sam says you've got some chick's name on your chest. How much is that gonna cost to laser off?"

York dumped the pillows in a pile at our feet and switched on a lamp, shifting the room from moonlit silver to warm amber.

"It's never coming off."

I felt an unexpected twinge of disappointment.

"Who's the unlucky girl?" Andi quipped.

"Your mom."

I started to laugh, but choked on it when I remembered Andi's mom was dead.

A shadow crossed her face, but she didn't play the pity card with York.

"Dibs on the softest pillow," she said, kicking the pile.

Who could sleep? My body was exhausted, but my brain was buzzing. It felt like we'd lived five years in the last five hours. I probably wouldn't rest until the police had our statement, bought it, and started hunting down those crooked cops instead of hunting us. Then I would sleep for a year.

But a little part of me—a part I'd just been introduced to that night—hoped to delay that moment. Yes, this was an awful nightmare. Yes, I was scared, and Mama was alone, and we were all in deep shit, but there was something else in the air, too—something that felt more real than the intangible fear and the invisible police chasing us. Something almost . . . exciting?

Ridiculous . . . and yet true.

I watched York unroll the sleeping bags on the floor and Andi push the coffee table back to make room. I wasn't even sure I liked them, but in this moment, inside this cabin's strong, safe walls, with the drugs and the SUV out of sight, I felt like I knew them. And it was nice to know someone other than Mama.

"Hey, Worms," York called, tilting his head at me. "Help me lift the couch."

Or maybe I don't want to know them after all.

"Hey, Douche Bag," I replied, my voice ice. "Lift your own damn couch."

York dropped the end of the sofa he'd picked up and held out his hands. "What'd I do?"

"I don't think she likes her nickname," Andi said. She nudged me aside and helped York move the sofa back a few feet.

"It's not my nickname," I said. "It's not my any name."

York shrugged. "Well, I didn't mean anything by it. Nicknames are cool . . . *Hat Girl*." He grinned and dropped a few pillows on top of the sleeping bags. Our communal bed was complete.

"What's your nickname?" Andi asked him.

He hunched forward with his arms out and flexed his muscles. "Danger."

In that ridiculous pose, he looked about as dangerous as a dung beetle. I said so out loud, expecting him to be offended, but he just laughed, full of confidence.

"So what's it mean, then?" he asked. "Worms?"

"It's your scars, right?" Andi stepped up close and squinted at my hairline.

Instinctively, I reached up to tug on my cap, but Andi caught my arm. "That hat doesn't hide as much as you think it does."

"BOOM! Done!" Boston roared into the room, holding up his notepad in triumph, but the celebration was short-lived. His socks slipped on the wood floor, and he slammed into the back of the couch, somersaulting over it, bouncing off the cushions, and landing spread-eagled on the sleeping bags.

There was the smallest moment of shocked silence until Boston, eyes wide open in surprise and fixed on the ceiling, uttered quietly, "Ow."

Andi and York exploded in laughter, and I pressed a hand to my mouth to keep from joining them. I started to ask Boston if he was okay, but when he sat up dazed and shook his head like a wet dog, I was undone. All that came out was the snicker I'd been trying to swallow.

He spun on his butt and goggled at the couch. "Was that always right there?"

That sparked fresh hysterics, and after one more head shake, even Boston joined in.

York begged his brother to go back into the kitchen and do it again, and Boston obliged, reenacting his fall in dramatic slow motion, complete with cartoonish facial expressions. York fell to his knees, applauding, while Andi and I leaned on each other to keep from collapsing in a fit of giggles. God, it felt so good to laugh—so *normal*—as if this night was about fun instead of fear. And, for just an instant, I pretended coming here was a choice, not a chase.

It was a moment before I noticed the wet on my cheeks. Through my howling I reached up to swipe at my face, and was startled to see my fingers come back damp.

Huh. Maybe I can cry after all.

19

WHEN THE LAUGHTER finally died down, Boston tore off the top page of the notepad and waved it with a flourish.

"Kind of genius, if I do say so myself."

"And you always do," York said.

Boston gave the paper to York to read. "It would make an awesome college admissions essay prompt: 'Try to convince the cops you're innocent of a crime.' Way better than 'What's your favorite word?' or 'Who is your political hero?' Those kinds of questions are so pointless. But this—this is real."

"Doesn't get any realer," Andi agreed.

Actually, I thought it was all a little *un*real. I kind of wished Boston hadn't finished the statement so quickly. It shattered my happy illusion that none of this was really happening.

"Maybe I could go rogue with my essay," Boston mused to himself. "Ooh, 'rogue.' That's a good favorite word. I could draw a line from the X-Men to the outlaws of the Old West to my own predicament."

York finished reading and passed the statement to Andi. "Dude, the only thing you have in common with outlaws and X-Men is that nobody likes you."

"*Everyone* likes the X-Men," Boston scoffed.

I leaned in to read over Andi's shoulder. The statement was straightforward enough, with only a few embellishments like "gross misunderstanding" and "disturbing discovery." His explanation that we took the SUV because we thought it belonged to someone else was a little weak—stealing is stealing—but he did his best to make hitting the officer sound like exactly the accident it was. Then he described in detail how we were shot at by police and later discovered drugs in the car. He finished by offering our full cooperation in tracking down the real criminals.

Points for calling them criminals instead of cops, I thought. But otherwise, I wasn't sure what Boston was so proud of. The statement was well written, but all the proper grammar and spelling in the world wasn't going to get us completely out of trouble. Accident or not, we still mowed down a police officer. There would be consequences.

Boston took the page back from Andi for a final review. "I should change 'wrongly persecuted' to 'wrongly pursued.' What do you think?"

York picked at the laces on his tennis shoes. "Is it okay that you left out the fact that I was drinking?"

Boston lifted one shoulder in a shrug. "I think it would have gone down the same either way, and it doesn't help our case to add a DUI to the mix."

York finally lifted his eyes and offered a tentative smile. "Then I think it's good—a nice copulation of info."

Boston laughed. "Compilation, not copulation."

"Oh, screw your SAT words," York said. "I was trying to give you a compliment."

"I wish that was an SAT word. 'Copulation.' Right next to 'coitus' and 'cunnilingus.'"

York clapped his brother on the back. "Now you're speaking my language!"

I made a gagging motion with my finger and mouth. "Yuck. I hate the word 'coitus.' It sounds like something wet and squishy."

"Well, it *is* kind of wet and squishy," Andi pointed out.

"You would know," York said.

"And you wouldn't," she countered.

I wouldn't know, either, but if it *was* wet and squishy, I was willing to wait a while longer to find out.

Boston slid our statement onto the coffee table and stretched. "You think Mom and Dad will buy it?"

"I think Mom and Dad will buy anything as long as you're the one selling it," York said.

Andi cleared her throat. "If you guys are done congratulating yourselves, I have a question. That bit about our full cooperation—does it have to be *our* cooperation? Can it just be yours?"

"What do you mean?" Boston asked.

"I mean," Andi said carefully, "maybe—just maybe—Sam and I aren't here right now. Maybe we were just a couple of girls you picked up at the party before all of this went down."

I tilted my head at her. *Where are you going with this, Andi?*

Boston scrunched up his face and scratched his head. "But you are here."

"But what if we weren't?"

"Your hair." Boston pointed to her dreadlocks. "That witness saw you."

"Maybe you let us out of the car as soon as we left the park, and we went home," Andi pressed. "Maybe you don't even remember our names."

Oh! I like this idea.

"Besides," Andi said. "Look at me. I'm not exactly helping your case." She held out her tattooed arms as evidence. "Maybe it will be better for you if I'm not involved."

Boston frowned. "Maybe."

"Maybe *not*," York snapped. "But nice try."

Andi dropped her arms and shook her head. "Look, I just don't want my name attached to any of this."

"Who does?" York argued.

He was right. As appealing as Andi's idea was, it wasn't fair.

"We're all in this together, remember?" I echoed Andi's words from the parking lot of that broken-down taco shop. It seemed like ages ago.

She leaned away from me, unmoved by my camaraderie, but I was rewarded with a small smile from York. I wondered if he really did know about sex and whether it was wet and squishy. Then I spoke, if for no other reason than to shut up my wandering thoughts.

"So what's next? How do we get this thing to the police?" I pointed to the paper on the coffee table.

"Well," Boston said, glancing sideways at York, "we could have Mom and Dad give it to them."

York opened his mouth to protest, but Boston charged ahead.

"We're going to have to tell them everything anyway. Why not go to them first and have them take our statement to the police? It will look better that way. People respect them."

York raised an eyebrow.

"Okay, people who aren't *you* respect them," Boston amended.

"I know we have to tell them," York said, sounding defeated. "But they won't go for this. They'll tell us to shut our mouths, and then they'll call in an army of attorneys."

"They're not wrong about that," I said.

Mama probably would still be in prison, round one, if she hadn't had the best lawyer all her country-music money could buy.

"Are your fancy parents going to get fancy attorneys for all of us?" Andi asked, sounding bitter.

Boston's blush gave away the answer. Maybe we weren't all in this together after all.

"I thought not," Andi said.

"We'll find another way," York said. "We need the Internet to figure out who to—"

"Don't turn your phone on," Andi interrupted. "I don't trust you not to call your parents."

She pulled her own phone from a back pocket, and Boston snagged it from her hand the second it was out.

"Hey!" Andi scrambled after it, but Boston was already on his feet, clicking it on.

The glow of the screen waking up illuminated his face, and in the faint blue light I could see his expression shift from a question mark to fear to fury. Whatever he saw on Andi's screen, he didn't like it. There was a beat of silence as Andi froze halfway to reaching for her phone, and Boston turned it slowly so York and I could see it.

I took one look and rounded on Andi. "You said nobody tried to call you!"

A stack of missed-call alerts on Andi's cell phone screen told a different story.

Andi stood and brushed some invisible lint off her tank top. "No, I said you didn't hear my phone ringing. And you didn't."

She swiped at the cell, but Boston held it out of her reach.

We were all on our feet now, and I stretched my arms wide in front of Andi, half to hold her back and half to protect her from York, who looked ready to level her.

"Just because we didn't hear it doesn't mean it wasn't ringing," Boston said.

Andi shrugged. "That's the magic of the mute button."

"It's not a mute button," Boston said. "It's a silencer."

"No." York shook his head. "A silencer is something on a gun."

I couldn't stop the annoyed groan that escaped my lips. "Am I the only person in this room not suffering from extreme ADD?"

"You're suffering from extreme stupidity," Andi spat.

It startled me enough that I dropped my arms. "What's that supposed to mean?"

"We can't trust them." Andi waved a hand at the boys.

"What's this 'we'?" I pointed back and forth between us. "You and me? We're not a 'we.'"

Even if it felt for a second like we were.

"You're the one we can't trust," York said. He took the phone from Boston and scrolled down the screen. "Who's blowing up your phone, Andi? All these numbers are the same."

Andi smiled, but her voice dripped poison. "It's my boyfriend. Jealous?"

"There are texts, too," Boston said.

York read the messages out loud. "'Andi, where are you?' 'Andi, call me now.' 'Call me, or I will end you.'" He glanced up. "Nice boyfriend."

"It's complicated," Andi deadpanned.

I gave her a sidelong look. This time I hoped she *was* lying.

"That's messed up," York said.

"That's none of your business," Andi snapped back. "But since you're completely violating my privacy, you'll notice I didn't respond to any of those texts or calls. Isn't that what matters?"

The boys shared a look, then turned to me. I shrugged in response. They'd probably jumped to the same conclusion I had—that Andi was trying to work a way out of this for herself on the side—but my suspicions had expired with the text messages. If I had an asshole boyfriend like that, I wouldn't tell anyone about him, either.

"Fine," Boston said. "But you might want to text your psycho lover boy back to let him know you're okay."

"Hey, tell him you're spending the night with two dudes," York said, his mood suddenly lighter. "He sounds like the kind of guy who'd totally have no problem with that."

"Actually," Andi said, plucking her phone out of York's hand, "I'll tell him I spent the night with Sam. *That* he *will* like."

She moved to sling an arm across my shoulders, but I dodged her. "Don't make me part of some sick sex fantasy with your creeper boyfriend."

Something like hurt flitted across her features, but it was gone a second later as she buried her face in her phone.

"What am I even searching for?" she asked.

"The River City Police Department," Boston said.

"No kidding. I mean specifically. There's not exactly a link for criminals to submit a confession."

"It's not a confession," Boston corrected. "It's a statement."

Tomato, tomahto.

"Look for the tip line," York suggested. "The one they give out on TV. It's, like, one-eight-hundred-NARC or something."

I would have laughed, but it seemed like we had left funny behind about ten minutes ago.

"Oh shit," Andi breathed.

"What?" the rest of us asked in unison.

We crowded in behind her to see the screen, but she lowered her phone and tipped her head back, her eyes closed.

"Don't worry about telling your parents, boys. They already know."

20

"EVERYONE KNOWS," ANDI said.

Boston pulled the phone from her hand, and she didn't fight him.

My first reaction when I saw the screen was shock; I'm ashamed to say my second reaction was a rush of relief. Three photos blazed across the River City Police Department's "alerts" page.

Just three.

I looked around at the faces next to me—they were older than the faces in the photos, since the pictures looked like they'd been pulled from our last yearbook, but unmistakably the same.

"How did they get these up so fast?" Boston asked.

"My car," York groaned. "We left it there. They probably ran my plates or whatever the hell they do."

"I'm sure you're not the only one who left a car behind after that bust," Andi said. "I guarantee they got our names and that

God-awful photo"—she punched a finger at her picture—"from someone at the party."

"But no one gave them my name," I said.

The others exchanged quick glances, and Boston shifted from foot to foot.

"Well," he said, "it's just—you know . . . I don't think a lot of people *know* your name."

Oh. Right.

"*I* knew it," Andi piped up, sounding proud of herself.

"I didn't," York admitted, and the apology in his voice stung.

I looked from York to Boston to Andi and saw the same misplaced pity in all of their eyes. It caused an angry flush to creep up my neck. So what if no one knew my name? I had made it that way. I was the architect of my own anonymity—hiding under my hats and keeping my head down, speaking the minimum in class and not at all in the hallways. I *wanted* invisibility. I chose it.

Didn't I?

"I mean, I think I recognized you," York rushed to add. "Kind of. The hats . . ."

I spun toward Boston. "You knew people called me—" I couldn't bring myself to say it.

He shrugged. "I remembered from when we were kids, before we switched schools."

Worms.

Hat Girl.

All this time, I hadn't been invisible so much as unimportant. Noticed, but not worth knowing.

A strange lump rose into my throat then, and I forced myself to swallow it back down.

Really, I was lucky nobody knew me. It meant that instead of my face also being splashed across the police department's website, there was just a box with a question mark holding my place. I should have been grateful.

"At least they're not looking for you," York said.

No one was looking for me—not even Mama. My hand went involuntarily to my pocket before I remembered we'd turned off our phones. Maybe she *had* called by now. Then a thought occurred to me.

I turned to Andi. "How come nobody's called your phone besides your boyfriend? It's been on this whole time. If the police know your name, they've probably been to your house. Shouldn't someone have called you?"

Andi looked uncomfortable. "My dad . . . doesn't have this number."

"How can your dad not have—" I stopped, understanding. "It's stolen."

"I didn't steal it," Andi rushed to say. "It's kind of a loaner."

I raised an eyebrow, inviting her to explain.

"It's not in my name," she said. After a pause, she added, "Sometimes I do favors for people in exchange for stuff."

York leered. "What kind of favors?"

"Not like that, perv!" she snapped. "I'd get my own, but my dad can't be bothered to get off the couch to set up cell service."

"Can he be bothered to answer the door for the cops?" York asked.

Her eyes flashed, and she almost smiled. "Maybe?"

I didn't know why she made it sound like a question, or why her whole face lit up with hope, but I suddenly felt inexplicably sorry for Andi.

"But it's not like he'd know where to find me," she said, then her eyes opened wide. "Hey, what about *your* parents? Won't the police be looking for you at your house? At *this* house?"

"Oh shit," I said. I craned my neck to peer through the front wall of glass, expecting lights and sirens to break up the utter blackness outside at any second.

When I looked back, the boys were staring at each other, having one of their silent eyeball conversations. Boston twisted his hands together, and York cricked his neck back and forth.

"What?" I demanded. "What is it?"

Boston sighed. "The only way they'll find us here is if our parents tell them to look here."

"Which is totally possible," York said.

"If they thought we were here, they'd call," Boston argued. "There's a landline in the kitchen, so—"

"Guys!" Andi said. "I've got news for you. The police can find you here with or without your parents' permission. They'll have a record that you own this—"

"That's just it," Boston interrupted. "We don't own it."

I smacked a hand to my forehead. *Awesome. We already ran over a cop, left the scene of a crime, and evaded police. Why not add breaking and entering to the list?*

"So whose cabin is it?" I asked.

"It belongs to a family friend." York shrugged like it was no big deal. "They let us stay here for a few weeks at the end of every summer, because my mom strips the beds and locks the place down for winter."

Andi gaped at the boys, and there was a slight smile in her otherwise shocked face. "I'm sorry, are you saying your mom is the *maid*?"

I bristled at the mirth in her voice. Mama had worked more than one cleaning job. What of it?

"Hey," York said. "Who wouldn't take something for free if they could get it? Just because our parents make it their business to give other people money doesn't mean they aren't stingy."

"Actually," Andi said, "that's exactly what that means."

"The point is, we know the owners," Boston rushed to say. "It's totally okay that we're here. We've been coming here since we were kids. It's practically ours."

A sense of calm settled over me. "You're saying we're safe here," I said.

We could stay; maybe not forever, but definitely for now.

"Maybe they can't trace us to the cabin," York said, "but they can trace that phone." He pointed to Andi's cell, still in Boston's hand. "I don't care whose name it's in. *Somebody* has your number. Eventually the police will figure it out. You should turn it off."

"Wait," Boston said. He scrolled past the yearbook-photos-turned-mug-shots to a short paragraph below, saying four teens were wanted for questioning regarding an attack on a police officer. Below the paragraph, there was a phone number and an e-mail address for people to contact with information. Boston pulled a pen from his pocket and jotted both down on the palm of his hand.

"Okay, now turn it off," York insisted.

"One more thing." Boston tapped the screen quickly, pulling up a Google search about the incident in the park. A long list of news articles flooded the screen.

"We don't have time to read all that," I said. If York was right that Andi's phone could eventually be traced, I was as antsy as he was to shut it down.

"Just one," Boston pleaded. "I want to see if our parents are quoted."

But they weren't. The article he pulled up included just one interview.

Andi ripped the phone from Boston's hand so fast I thought she'd tear his arm off.

"I knew it!" she said. "That bitch!"

21

TEN MINUTES LATER the cell phone was dark, and we were sprawled across the great room—Boston and York stretched out on the sleeping bags, Andi curled up on the couch, and me tucked into an armchair, arms wrapped tightly around Mama's violin.

"She's a worthless piece of garbage," Andi said.

She had already used up her entire arsenal of curse words and was now inventing more colorful insults.

Georgia Jones had given a reporter from the *Daily River* an earful. She was quoted as saying York Flint and his little brother, Boston, had wandered away from the party and left their car behind, and that two girls may have gone with them. In an especially gleeful-sounding quote, she described Andi as a "degenerate with greasy dreadlocks." The article was quick to point out that the dreads matched the description of one of the suspects.

The suspects! Since when are people wanted for questioning "suspects"?

Georgia had told the reporter all about how much York had to drink and exactly what Andi's tattoos looked like. Then she'd vividly described a creepy girl—most likely Andi's girlfriend—who had crashed the party. This girl, according to Georgia, was the kind of person you had to keep an eye on, in case she came to school with a gun one day and opened fire.

That quote stole the air from my lungs. Is that what she thought? Is that what other people thought? Did being a loner automatically make me someone so despicable?

Sadly for the poor reporter, Georgia couldn't recall the girl's name—only that she went by the "street name" of Worms.

Of course, it was the reporter who used the term "street name," but why not? Georgia had painted a perfect picture of a disturbed teenager headed for a life of crime. Naturally, I had to have a street name.

But there was some good news in the article, too. The officer we'd run down was expected to make a full recovery, despite having been knocked unconscious. Other police, who'd been helping to bust up the party, had raced down to the dock after hearing gunfire. There, they'd found an officer down, tire tracks, and a single bullet lodged in a tree. They'd also heard a motor out on the water, but they couldn't yet say whether any of the suspects had escaped by boat.

That was good, Boston had pointed out. It supported our claims about being shot at. Now there was just the small matter of convincing the police that their fellow officers were the ones doing the shooting.

"She's an attention-seeking whore," Andi said. "She's a rat."

"She's a hot rat, though," York said. Then, under Andi's steely glare, he amended, "But she's a shit kisser."

York kissing Georgia. There's a visual I didn't need . . . or want.

"Yeah, she is," Andi agreed.

My head whipped in her direction, surprised, but she offered no explanation. Instead she fell back on the couch, still muttering insults. The boys lapsed into a private conversation, talking in low voices and occasionally glancing my way. I strummed Mama's violin like a guitar and pretended not to notice.

Probably just trying to remember my name.

Finally, York cleared his throat. "We have a new idea."

"Does this idea involve stringing Georgia up by her toenails over a pit full of crocodiles?" Andi snarled.

"Sure," Boston said. "Right after Sam gives our statement to the police."

I stopped strumming the violin. "Say what, now?"

Boston held up his hands as if to ward off any protest. "Hear me out. They don't know what you look like . . . or even your name," he added apologetically. "You're the only one of us who could walk into a police station right now without being arrested on the spot. You would have time to hand in the statement before they jumped to conclusions. You could speak for all of us."

He said this last bit like it was some great honor to be the orator of the group.

More like the scapegoat.

"What happened to e-mailing our statement?" I asked. "Or letting your parents or a lawyer do it?"

"It might be more convincing if you go in person," Andi said. She sounded a little too eager, and I suspected she was on board with any idea that didn't involve her commingling with police.

"It will," York agreed. "We won't seem so much like we're hiding."

"Except you *will* be hiding," I pointed out.

"Just for a minute," Boston said. "And if you go in person, you'll be able to turn in the drugs along with the statement."

"What?" I propped the violin on my knees like a shield that could protect me from all their crazy. "You want me to walk into a police station with a hundred pounds of heroin?"

"It's not a hundred pounds," Boston said. "Closer to twenty-five. No more than thirty."

My jaw dropped.

"I'm good with numbers," he said.

"I don't give a shit about the numbers," I spat. "You're trying to set me up!"

"I swear we're not," York said. "Scout's honor."

I seriously doubted he was ever a Boy Scout, but I only *hmph*ed and sat back in my chair. It felt like they wanted me to take the fall—but then again, they weren't asking me to lie or hide their names. They just wanted me to walk into a building and hand in a piece of paper.

And a shitload of drugs.

In a way, it made a sick kind of sense to send me—the invisible girl—the one nobody was looking for because nobody noticed. Still, I was unsettled, and I felt our night coming to a close much too quickly, like a brick wall rushing up at a speeding car.

"I'll think about it," I said.

The others didn't look convinced.

"We're not going anywhere tonight anyway. It's dark, it's late, and we could fall asleep at the wheel on the way home."

"I'm not tired!" Andi said brightly.

I shot her a look.

"Wait—" Boston started to protest, but York put a hand on his arm.

"That's fair," he said. "Take the night to decide."

Then he offered me another one of those smiles, but this time it seemed calculated to make me swoon, and I wasn't feeling very swoony.

"How much do you think those drugs are worth?" he said, deliberately changing the subject.

"Why?" Andi asked. "You think we'll get a reward if they're worth a lot?"

York leaned back with his hands on the floor behind him. "I was just curious. But a reward wouldn't suck."

"Our reward will be not getting arrested," Boston said with a pointed look at me.

Back off, dude.

"I bet it's thousands of dollars," York mused.

Mama used to hand over hundred-dollar bills for stacks of ten tiny bags filled with the sandy brown substance—one hit each. The heroin was the easiest to identify, because it always came in those semisheer envelopes stamped with colorful logos that could fit in the palm of your hand. I know, because I palmed one once when I was five, and Mama lost her shit over it. She started keeping all her drugs in locked drawers after that. It wasn't quitting, but I guess it was something.

Other drugs were trickier to name. They came in bags or vials of powder or pills. I had a hard time telling the difference between ecstasy and acid or cocaine and crushed-up pharmaceuticals, and I had no idea what meth looked like, because Mama never let me near it, except that once.

I tried to picture how many of those itty-bitty ten-dollar envelopes just one of the bricks of heroin we had could fill up. And how many bricks were there? Fifteen? Twenty? The calculations rapidly exceeded the limits of my mental math, and I gasped inwardly.

Not thousands of dollars. More like a million.

BEFORE

THE LINE OUTSIDE Mrs. Doyle's classroom after school was ten students deep, all of them no doubt there for the same reason I was—to explain why they hadn't done their geometry homework. I hoped the others wouldn't wear out her sympathy before I could tell her I'd attended an emergency NA meeting with Mama last night. That excuse had served me well freshman year, but the sophomore teachers seemed to have less patience with my family drama.

I decided to avoid the line and spend a couple of minutes in the bathroom across the hall instead. I practiced my story in the mirror, wishing I could work up a tear or two—even just watery eyes—to really drive it home. When that failed, I folded myself inside a stall, enjoying the quiet in here for once. No girls gossiping or trading lip gloss or generally moving in pairs the way they all seemed to do—just me and a fresh roll and the scrawl of Sharpies on the stall door.

Most of the door graffiti had been edited, with comical results.

A faded "Jessica loves BJ" now had the word "giving" inserted after "loves" and an "s" added to "BJ."

Someone had also crossed the word "freshman" out of a large "Freshman Barbies were here!" proclamation and changed it to "Sophomore." Below that, a red marker corrected the text once again, turning "Sophomore Barbies" into "Sophomore Sluts."

I flushed and pushed through the stall door. That's what happened when you let yourself be seen. If even the girls we were all supposed to like the most were hated, what hope was there for the rest of us?

Back out in the hall, the line outside Mrs. Doyle's door had disappeared, and my footsteps echoed down the empty corridor. School was creepy after hours—too dim, too quiet. I could hear the hum of every pipe in the wall, the discord of the intro-level concert band practicing a floor below. I could even hear the last student in line in Mrs. Doyle's room pleading his case.

"But if I don't test out of geometry, I can't take precalc until next year."

"And that's still a grade ahead of—"

"You don't understand!" the boy cut off Mrs. Doyle. "This messes up my whole timeline. I need calculus on my transcripts next year!"

He sounded like he might be crying. Damn, why couldn't I do that?

"I *do* understand—"

"That means I need to be in precalc now!"

"Calm down." Mrs. Doyle's words were soothing, but I could hear tension simmering underneath. "I told you at the start of the year that you could only take the bypass test once."

"But it's not my fault. It's my O-C—"

"I'm aware."

"They made me sit with the window on my left. The practice tests were in study hall, with the windows on the right."

Mrs. Doyle sighed. "And that issue is something that will not be accommodated at the college level. Just take the time now to get a handle on this—"

"I've *got* a handle on it," the boy interrupted. "I was just distracted by the—"

"By the windows, I know. Look, even if I let you take the test a second time, and even if you pass, you would be starting precalculus months behind the other students, and I don't want to set you up to fail."

"I don't fail!"

"I understand you're disappointed—"

"I'm not disappointed, I'm pissed off!"

I slumped against the wall outside Mrs. Doyle's door. This kid couldn't have picked any other day to cuss out a teacher?

"And I'm done!" Mrs. Doyle snapped. "Out!"

Yep, that did it. The little overachiever in there had broken Mrs. Doyle, and now I had no chance. I hitched my backpack over my shoulder and slipped quietly past the door, vowing to come back tomorrow with a better excuse than "My mom's addiction ate my homework."

22

I KEPT MY mouth shut about the value of the drugs, afraid if I told the rest of them, they'd not only pressure me to be their mouthpiece but also disappear the second I took the fall. Grandma would have flushed it all straight down the toilet, no matter how much it was worth or how much we needed it as evidence. Aunt Ellen wouldn't have touched it. She'd leave it all right where it was and draw the police a map. Then she'd blame Mama, because somehow, to Ellen, everything was always Mama's fault.

For a long time I agreed with her. It was easier that way. Trouble making friends? *Well, her mom's a drug addict, you know.* Not doing homework? *Who can blame her, with the mother always away.* Everyone pointed the finger at Mama, and I'd just learned to point in the same direction.

Now I wasn't sure who to blame.

"I can't sleep," York groaned, punching a pillow into shape.

"Me, neither," Boston said.

Andi stared past me toward the cabin's back wall of glass, overlooking the lake. "Let's go swimming."

I snorted.

Yeah, right—we'll just take a dip in the middle of all this. Totally normal.

York shared my derision. "We're not getting in the lake in the middle of the night, wacko."

But Boston sat up straight, his interest piqued. "Hmm."

"Oh, come on!" York shoved his brother's shoulder. "Stay focused."

Boston ignored him and got to his feet. "What if it's our last chance to swim before we're locked up?"

"We're not getting locked up," I said, more out of habit at this point than conviction.

Boston shrugged. "Still better than sitting around in here freaking out."

"I'm not freaking out," York said.

I am.

"But you're not sleeping, either," Andi pointed out, and she stood up next to Boston. "Do these people have any spare swimsuits?"

Boston frowned. "Oh. No, Mom took all of that home with their laundry."

Well, that settles that.

Andi clapped once and rubbed her hands together. "Skinny-dipping it is, then!"

I opened my mouth to protest, but suddenly York was up off the floor, standing with the other two crazies. His eyes slid to me, curled up in the chair. "Maybe a swim would help clear our heads."

Boston gaped at him. "Really? But you never go in the—"

"Shut it," York said. "One more word, and you'll end up like my car keys—at the bottom of the river."

Boston's jaw closed with a snap.

Then they all turned to me, waiting for their fourth. I wanted to tell them to go on without me, but I could see in their eyes the same feeling I had in my gut—that it was an all-of-us-or-none-of-us kind of night. I'd always been one of the none. Tonight, I couldn't deny it felt good to be part of the all.

"Fine," I grumbled. "But I'm keeping my underwear on."

The lake was surprisingly cold, despite the steamy summer air. Goose bumps erupted all over my body the instant my feet touched the water, making all my arm hair stand on end like the prickles of a startled porcupine. I shivered and crossed my arms over my chest. I wished I was wearing something cuter than gray grandma panties and a plain beige bra. The moon had done me a small favor by hiding behind a cloud so no one could get a good look at my ugly undies and hat hair, but that cloud was moving, and in a second, both the moon and I would be exposed.

Get in the water, I commanded my body, but the goose bumps prickled in protest.

"What are you waiting for?" Andi shouted from farther out in the lake. She had done a running jump off the end of the dock and resurfaced screaming and laughing all at once, her wild hair spraying water. Now she was splashing around like a mermaid, totally at ease.

I wanted to be wild and brave like Andi. I wanted to be at ease.

The first shot of moonlight hit the water as the curtain of clouds above parted. I took a deep breath, ran three long strides into the water, and dove.

The freeze of a thousand icicles stabbed me all at once, shocking my body in that crazy way that makes you feel like you're gasping even though you're holding your breath. It demanded all of my senses, stealing attention from the parts of me that were focused on fear and worry. Baptism by icy lake water.

By the time I came up for air, I was in a different place on a different night under different circumstances. I let out a *whoop* of exhilaration, and felt something more than my trapped breath release with it. I felt light for the first time all night, and it wasn't just the water buoying me.

Andi answered my cry with one of her own, and within seconds, we were both howling like wolves.

"Keep it down!" Boston called from the dock, but a second later he matched our volume with the earsplitting crack of a belly flop onto the lake.

"Ow!" Andi winced. "That sounded like it hurt."

It did, judging by the pained look on Boston's face when he broke the surface.

"Next time," he gasped, "cannonball."

I laughed, and Andi waved at the shore where York was standing in his boxers, his toes barely in the water. "What are you waiting for?" she called.

"Yeah, York!" Boston cried, and his voice was mocking. "What are you waiting for?"

York flipped up both of his middle fingers in response.

"He can't swim," Boston said as the three of us waded back into the shallows.

I raised my eyebrows. "Really?"

"Screw you," York said. "I can swim."

As if to prove it, he took a few tentative steps into the lake, but he froze at ankle depth. Andi and I splashed up to meet him, while Boston stubbornly stayed waist-high in the water.

"Let's see it, then," Boston taunted.

They stared each other down in a silent face-off, as Andi and I stood on the sidelines.

"You can't, can you?" I asked.

York twitched but didn't look at me.

"How can your parents bring you to a lake every year and not teach you to swim?" I said, appalled.

Not that I'm in any position to point fingers at irresponsible parents, but still.

"They taught us," Boston said. "But one of us had a little incident, turning upside down in a kayak, and suddenly forgot how."

"We shouldn't have been fishing from a kayak in the first place," York snapped back.

"It was ten years ago! Get over it!"

My head swung back and forth between the brothers, not sure who to side with.

"So, wait," Andi said slowly. She propped a hand on her hip, where a tattoo of a three-headed snake slithered out from under her black lace thong and up her side to her rib cage. "Are you telling me all those kids you push around have to do to get away from you is jump in a pool?"

"I don't push anyone around," York said. Then he grinned. "But if one of them did jump in a pool, I'd go in after them."

"Come in after me, then," Boston said, and this time his voice was inviting, almost pleading. "Just to here, where you can still stand."

I decided then that I was with Boston.

"It's warmer once you get all the way in," I coaxed, motioning for York to follow me deeper into the water. "It's the air that feels cold now. Look." I held out one arm. "I have goose bumps."

York took a few tentative steps toward me. "I can't see."

I matched his forward steps with backward ones of my own. "Come closer, then," I teased.

He smiled. "Oh, I see the game now, player."

I laughed. "Come on. All of us or none of us."

He hesitated, then step-by-step he worked his way in, so close I could almost read the cursive name inked over his heart.

Amelia? Adrienne, maybe? I tried not to look long enough to be obvious.

We waded deeper until we were level with Boston, who smiled and glided a few feet farther away from shore.

"Don't mess with me," York warned.

"She did it." Boston pointed at me.

"She's cuter than you."

They probably couldn't see me blush in the thin moonlight, but I ducked my face in the water anyway.

"Just a few more feet," Boston coached his brother.

"If you're up to something, so help me, I will drop you."

Boston raised his arms in a gesture of peace, then lowered them, palms up, to the water's surface in front of him. "You don't drop me, I won't drop you."

It was an invitation to learn to swim the way we'd all learned—on our stomachs in the water, cradled in trustworthy arms so we wouldn't sink. York inched closer to Boston, then paused to cast a sidelong look at Andi and me.

Oh.

Of course he didn't want to be cradled in front of a couple of girls. I turned my back on the boys and moved toward the shore, dragging Andi with me by the elbow.

"But," she protested, "I want to watch the yeti swim!"

I tugged harder on her arm and didn't let go until our feet touched grass. We sat huddled there, wrapped in some towels Boston had managed to scrounge up, and watched the boys in the distance. York was prone on the water, with Boston giving orders like "head up" and "kick your feet" and "think of your arms like a propeller."

Apparently, swimming was a little like riding a bike, in that you never really forgot how to do it, and soon York was treading deep water on his own, laughing and splashing Boston.

"Is that normal sibling behavior?" Andi asked, leaning back on the grass.

I wouldn't know. I'd only ever been around Aunt Ellen's kids, and they were too little to compare. One spent all his time on the floor playing with Legos, while the other cuddled the stuffed animals in her crib.

I pointed at myself. "Only child."

"Me, too," Andi said. "Just me and my dad."

"Just me and my mom," I echoed.

"Where's your dad?"

"Don't know." *Don't particularly care.*

"Divorce?" Andi asked.

"They never married. I think it was a one-night stand or something. He's probably back in Nashville, where I was born."

"Nashville? Cool. You should go visit him."

"Ha," I barked. "I'm pretty sure I'm not invited."

"So you're not close," Andi observed.

"He's just some guy who used to send me Christmas and birthday cards."

"Used to?"

"He stopped."

When I was six years old, and Mama went to prison for the second time.

I'd always figured he was probably scared that the courts were going to try to shove me off onto him when Mama went away. The way Grandma told it, he'd signed a bunch of legal documents waiving his custodial rights forever and ever, and I'd never heard from him again.

The boys waded up out of the water, splashing us with freezing droplets, and collapsed on the ground next to us.

"Told you I could swim," York said breathlessly, a huge grin on his face as he pulled on his shirt. It stuck to the wet skin of his chest, leaving his lean stomach exposed. He sure was *shaped* like a swimmer.

York caught me looking and winked. "Maybe I should go out for the swim team," he said, cocky.

Boston laughed. "Yeah, like you play any team sports anymore."

York sat up suddenly, and there was a crackle of tension between the two boys as Boston shrank back, his face stricken. "I'm sorry. I didn't mean—"

"Oh yeah!" Andi interrupted Boston's weak apology and squinted at York. "You used to be all about soccer and football and shit, right? What happened to that?"

York ignored her and stomped to his feet, glaring down at Boston cowering on the grass. "You suck," was all he managed to say.

Boston's voice shook, and he put his palms up in a pleading gesture. "I just meant if you're going to get back into sports, football was always—"

"Don't pretend like you want me back on the team—like you miss the days when they ignored *you* and acted like *I* was the golden child."

I didn't have to ask who "they" were. It sounded to me like two parents might be just as complicated as one.

Boston stood, his pleading hands now rolled into fists. "You think I like them climbing up my ass about everything all the time? Monitoring my grades, my college applications, my extracurriculars?" He propped his fists on his hips and scrunched up his face in an impression of someone. "'Boston, drama club won't get you any points at Yale unless you major in theater.' 'Boston, join the Mathletes. It's practically a requirement at MIT.'"

I whispered to Andi, "We have Mathletes at our school?"

She shrugged.

"Oh, how *terrible* for you!" York cupped his hands over his heart in an exaggerated gesture. "It must suck so bad to be the smart one."

Boston let out a sound of disgust. "They didn't even notice I was smart until you started acting so stupid."

"So I quit the team, so what? What do you—"

"You quit *everything*!" Boston yelled. "You quit on me. You quit on yourself." He threw out his skinny arms in a challenge, and I thought for a second that he was going to invite York to hit him. "You could have had a scholarship—a free ride! You could have had everything! But what? *Bart* can't play football, so *you* can't play football?"

The words exploded from him uncontrolled, and he literally slapped his hands to his mouth as if to push them back in, but it was too late.

Bart who?

York pulled back a fist and lunged as if to strike, but at the last second, he pulled up short and dropped to the ground instead, crouching with his head in his hands.

"Wait," Andi said quietly. "Bart Abernathy? That was you?"

Abernathy. I rolled the name around in my head. It sounded familiar somehow, but I couldn't say where I'd heard it. Though as I pictured it spelled out in my mind, I knew exactly where I'd *seen* it. York tugged at the neck of his shirt and touched the tattoo with the tips of his fingers, and Boston turned away, shame in his face. Somehow, it looked to me like Boston had been the one to throw the punch.

"Who is Bart Abernathy?" I asked.

Without lifting his head, York muttered, "Was."

"Sorry?"

He looked up finally, and I was stunned to see his eyes ready to spill over with tears. "Who *was* Bart Abernathy."

I lifted a shoulder, confused.

York locked eyes with Andi for just a second, taking in her startled expression. Then he stared for a long time at the back of Boston's head, as if willing him to turn around. Finally, his eyes came back to me.

"Bart Abernathy is the guy I killed."

23

FOR ONE WILD moment, I thought York meant the officer in River City Park.

"But he's not dead."

Everyone turned to look at me like I had an extra head growing out of my neck.

"Oh." I stood up, suddenly preoccupied with adjusting my towel around me. "Right, you mean someone else."

"How do you not know who Bart Abernathy is?" Andi gawked at me.

Boston backed up her gaping with scorn. "He was only the number-one topic at school for, like, a year."

Well, how nice for Bart Abernathy that he's so memorable, while all you can recall about me is that kids used to call me Worms.

I crossed my arms and stared back at them.

York uncurled from his crouched position, but even standing he looked limp, deflated.

"First home game of sophomore year," he started. "Bart had moved over the summer and was playing varsity for Washington

High. He never would have made varsity at Jefferson—too small, too slow. But Washington had a weak team."

I gasped, remembering. I was a freshman at the time. I hadn't been at the game—I'd never been to *any* game, *thanks anyway*—but I'd heard about it. A boy from the opposing team had taken a hard hit, but then got back up to play, no harm done. Ten minutes later, he collapsed on the field for no apparent reason. Two days after that, he was dead. I couldn't remember why.

"He was such a punk," York said. "We all hated him on JV—where he should have stayed." There was a hitch in his voice, and he coughed to cover it up. "He was so pumped for that game; he really wanted to show us what he could do—kept trash-talking. . . . We just wanted to knock him down a peg," he finished quietly.

"It was an accident," I offered. "A freak accident. That's what they said on the news. I remember now."

York only shook his head, and Boston tentatively gripped his big brother's shoulder.

"Sorry I brought it up, man. I'm really, really sor—"

York shrugged out from under Boston's hand and swiped at his cheeks.

"It was an accident that Bart got hit in just the right place to make his brain bleed," York said. "And it was a *freak* accident that the bleeding was delayed, so he didn't get help fast enough. But it was no accident that he got hit that hard in the first place."

"York—" Boston started, but York held up a hand and kept talking. The tears were gone now.

"I hit him hard. I *meant* to hit him hard. There's nothing else to say."

I studied York for a minute, thinking there was probably a *lot* more to say—about whether one bad move made you a bad guy, about whether accidentally taking someone's life meant you should throw yours away, too.

"I hung out with Bart at a party once," Andi said quietly. "He was a decent guy."

"He was an asshole," York said. "But he didn't deserve that."

Andi walked away up the slope, unwrapping her towel as she went. Halfway to the cabin, she spread the towel in a patch of moonlight and lay down on her back. "Let's sleep out here," she said.

Boston scrambled after her and eagerly put down his own towel, looking grateful for the change of subject. "Is it too late for sleeping? What time do you think it is?"

With our phones off it was impossible to tell, but I guessed it was around 2:00 a.m. Boston and Andi lapsed into a conversation about cell phones versus watches and the meaning of time—the kind of philosophical stuff that only seems to come to mind when you're delirious from lack of sleep.

I moved to join them, but York caught my arm and held me back. His hand was still cold from the lake, and it sent a shiver up and down my skin.

He waited until I looked up at him, then said quietly, "I made a mistake. I own it."

I shook my head but kept my eyes locked on his. "Kind of sounds like it owns you."

I left him standing there and went to stretch out next to Andi and Boston, who had moved past their musings on time and were now indulging their hunger pangs with a food fantasy.

"Filet mignon with mushroom sauce and blue cheese," Andi said, licking her lips. "And a heaping side of mashed potatoes—the chunky homemade kind. Not that stuff from a box."

"Spicy tuna rolls from Sushi Street," Boston countered. "And a bottomless bowl of edamame—extra salty."

"Ugh," I said. "Raw fish. Nasty."

"Have you ever tried it?" Boston asked.

"I don't have to try it to know it's disgusting."

He rolled onto his stomach and knit his eyebrows together. "Didn't you used to eat your scabs?"

Oh my God, enough already with the total recall of all things awful.

"No!" I said, my voice a touch too shrill.

"Yeah," he plowed on. "Yeah, you did. You used to pick your scabs and eat them!"

"You *ate* your *scabs*?" Andi gagged. "Sick!"

"Okay, yeah, maybe!" I spat out. "In kindergarten or something. Who cares?"

"No," Boston said. "It was, like, first and second grade, after—" He faltered, and his eyes lifted past mine, up to my hairline. I leaned back out of the moonlight and ran a hand over my head. My wet hair was plastered to my skull, probably showing a lot more of my scalp than usual.

"What about third grade?" Andi teased. "Fourth? Oh my God, you still eat them, don't you?"

She and Boston rolled on their towels, laughing at my expense. Part of me wanted to punch them both in the face, and part of me wished my towel would suddenly turn into a magic carpet and carry me away. All night I'd been doubting my decision to not play with my peers, but this moment—this one right now—reminded me why I'd chosen a long time ago to just hang out with myself.

York finally joined us, lured by the laughter. "What's so funny?"

"Sam used to eat her scabs," Boston twittered.

York's face started to twist in disgust, but then his eyes landed on mine, and whatever he saw there caused his expression to morph into a smile. "Oh yeah?" he said, laying his towel down next to mine and settling in. "I can beat that."

"Please do," I said, eager to turn the attention to anyone else.

"I got into my dad's toolbox when I was a kid and ate a fistful of washers."

"Washers?" Andi asked.

"You know, the flat metal discs with holes in the middle." He held up his hand and curled his finger and thumb to make a tiny circle. "I got, like, twelve of the really little ones down before I started gagging or something."

"I don't remember that," Boston said.

York shrugged. "You were too young."

"Sorry," I said. "That is not nearly as gross as . . . what I did." Though I appreciated his attempt.

"Not as gross on the way *in*," he agreed. "But guess how I got those things *out*?"

"Surgery?" I said.

"Nope. The ER docs said they were small enough to come out the old-fashioned way."

"Okay, *that* is gross," Andi said.

York played it up. "They made this awesome *plink-plink* noise when they hit the water."

"Ew," Andi and I said in unison. We laughed, and York laughed right along, with a deliberate wink at me. He was showing me how it was done.

"That's not even the sick part," York said. "I wanted to keep them as souvenirs, so my mom had to fish them out of—"

"Ugh! Stop!" Andi retched and laughed at the same time, a horrible but hilarious sound, which set us all off again.

"And *that*," York finished with a flourish, "is how I got my abs of steel."

We laughed until our stomachs hurt, and it was amazing how the howling sound shifted from painful to playful once I'd joined in.

When we finally settled into breathless sighs and just the occasional stray giggle, Andi reached across her towel to yank my hand away from my head. I hadn't even realized that I was working my fingers along my scalp again, making knots in my wet hair.

"Picking your scalp is as bad as picking your scabs," she said.

"But not as bad as eating them," I joked.

"Do you think you could have OCD?" Andi asked.

"She doesn't," Boston piped up. "Trust me."

"He would know," York agreed.

"What about borderline personality disorder?"

I pulled my hand back and laughed. "I don't think so, Dr. Dixon."

Andi rattled off a few more mental diagnoses, then sat up, excited. "Oh! I've got it! Could you be a sociopath?"

York shook his head and pointed at Andi. "Nah, we took a vote and decided you're the sociopath."

She smiled and flopped down on her stomach. "Well, better a sociopath than boring."

"I'm sure no one ever accused you of being boring," I said.

She tipped her smile up to me. "You, either."

24

THE MOON DISAPPEARED behind another canopy of clouds, and we ended up lying on our backs in a kind of circle with our heads together, counting stars through the breaks in those clouds. At least, *I* was counting stars. The rest of them had gone back to counting our troubles.

"I hate that we even have to haul that shit back to town," York said. "What if we get pulled over and they find all those drugs in the car?"

"We could leave them here," Andi said. "And just tell the police where to find them."

"That would look shady," I said. I hadn't agreed to speak for the group yet, but it was making more and more sense by the minute—even the part where I would drag three backpacks full of drugs into a police station.

"Do you think there are even enough drug addicts in River City for all that heroin?" Boston mused.

"Drugs addicts are everywhere," I said.

They're your mailman, your math tutor, your mom.

"Everyone I know just takes their parents' Xanax," York said from my left. He shifted on his towel, his shoulder bumping mine. Then he shifted again, more deliberately, and this time our shoulders stayed touching. "Vicodin, too, and Oxy, if they can get their hands on it. Oh, and Ambien. If you push past the part where it makes you sleepy, you get some crazy high."

"That's stupid," Boston muttered.

"I'm not saying *I* do it," York said. "I'm just saying at least it's not heroin. If you can get it out of the bathroom cabinet, it's probably not that dangerous."

Mama used to keep nail polish remover in the bathroom cabinet. I saw her take a swig of it once when she ran out of alcohol. That seemed kind of dangerous.

"My dad has a pharmacy in the bathroom," Andi said.

I tipped my head to the right and studied the profile of her face. "Like what?"

"Antidepressants. You name it, he's got it."

"You ever try any of it?"

She grinned into the night. "Do I look like I need uppers? No way."

I felt an unexpected inner sigh of relief.

"But he needs them," she said, her smile melting. "And he won't take them."

"What's he need them for?" Boston asked.

If he'd been next to me in our circle instead of across from me, I would have elbowed him in the ribs to let him know what a rude question it was. But Andi didn't seem to mind.

"His brain got all scrambled after my mom died. I mean, he's always been scrambled eggs to me, because I was so little when it happened, but everyone else says he used to be normal—fun, even. And funny. Now he's just a lump of mold growing on our living room couch."

"Watching infomercials," I prompted.

She nodded. "Not that he uses any of that shit he orders. He just lets it pile up all over the house, like his meds, all shiny and new and totally unused. If it wasn't for companies delivering stuff to our door every week, I swear, he wouldn't get up for anything but bathroom breaks."

"Doesn't he work?" York asked.

"No. He got some huge life insurance payout when my mom died. Everything's paid for—for, like, ever."

"Forever?" I whispered.

"And then some. I think he buys that seen-on-TV junk because he feels obligated to spend what she left for him—to get some enjoyment out of it. But it's kind of hard to blow through cash when you're comatose."

She steals, when she could buy the whole store.

"At least you don't have to worry about paying for college," Boston said. "Right?"

"Not really sure I'm going to college, but if I decide to, then I guess I'm covered."

"Cool."

I swear, I'm going to get up and kick him.

"Yeah, cool." Andi's voice dripped with sarcasm. "Who cares if your dad refuses to celebrate holidays or take you on vacations or make you dinner or even *look* at you, as long as *college* is paid for."

When Boston spoke again, he sounded small. "I just meant, y'know—at least you can get away from him, right?"

Okay, that's it!

I moved to sit up, but before I could, York's arm was flying backward over his head. There was a *crack* as his palm met Boston's forehead.

"Ow. Sorry," Boston muttered, and I hoped his "sorry" was meant for Andi.

"You know, for a smart guy, you're really pretty stupid," I said.

"Well, my GPA says otherwise," he retorted, sounding smug. Then he answered the question no one asked. "Four-point-six."

"On a four-point-oh scale," York said before Boston could. "We're all very impressed."

"The average unweighted GPA of incoming freshmen at Harvard is three-point-nine-four," Boston said. "And you know most of them got AP credit, so the weighted GPA average is probably more like four-point-five."

I thought of my own measly two-point-nine grade-point average. *Guess Harvard's out.*

"Did anyone else understand that gibberish?" Andi asked.

York sighed. "Unfortunately, yes."

"He gets kind of tired of hearing about it," Boston said.

"More like tired of hearing Mom and Dad go on and on and *on* about it. You'd think they were the ones picking a college. It's all they ever talk about."

The closest Mama and I ever came to talking about higher education was the time she pinned up a pamphlet for River City Community College on my bulletin board. I covered it with a postcard of the canals of Venice in silent protest. I had every intention of going to college, but it wasn't going to be within a thousand miles of River City.

"Drag," Andi said.

York was quiet a moment, then said, "I hate them."

Boston sighed. "Come on, don't say that. You don't hate Mom and Dad."

"I do. And you do, too. Everyone hates their parents a little. It's normal."

Andi stretched her hands up to the sky, inspecting her black fingernails. "I don't *hate* my dad. I just wish he'd wake up." She lowered one hand to poke me. "Do you hate your dad? For bailing on you?"

"I think we kind of bailed on him," I said.

"So you hate your mom, then?"

"I love my mom," I said reflexively. "But . . ."

God, I sound just like the kids from family therapy. How many of them had I had to listen to at those mandatory sessions when Mama was in the halfway house? It was always the same with the children of addicts. *I love them, BUT . . .*

I gave myself a beat to really think about it. I thought of the two of us curled up on the couch watching scary movies while she shielded my eyes during the parts she knew would freak me out the most. I thought of hour-long road trips for Whitey's Ice Cream, which we both agreed was worth the drive. I thought of late nights listening to her stories of life on the road; but then again, the moral of those stories was always to stick close to home. Mama's constant message was how much she needed me—how I was her rock. And the subtext of that flattery was that I couldn't leave her behind. By giving me all the credit, Mama also gave me all the responsibility. And as much as I loved her, sometimes I hated her for that.

"She used to be . . . kind of messed up," I said.

"Messed up how?" York asked.

"Infomercials?" Andi suggested with a laugh.

I bit my lip, not sure I wanted to share the way Andi had. I tested the water with a single word.

"Drugs."

"What kind of drugs?" Andi asked.

Boston answered for me. "Heroin, right? That's how you knew what that stuff was."

"Yeah, heroin," I confirmed. I fought to keep my voice from shaking. "And meth. And coke, pills, pot . . ."

"And a partridge in a pear tree," Andi sang.

I tried to laugh, but it came out as a shudder. York must have felt it ripple through my shoulder to his, because he reached over to steady my arm with a squeeze. Then, slowly, he slid his hand down to find my fingers and wrap them in his own. I was glad it was dark and everyone was flat on their backs with only a view of the sky. I opened my hand to his and then closed it again with our fingers laced together.

"My mom was a country star . . . almost," I said, bolstered by the support of York's hand in mine. "She was a singer-songwriter."

"That explains Nashville," Andi said.

"Yeah. And she was a musician, too—an amazing fiddler. She could play all the strings—banjo, cello, violin . . ."

"Oh," Andi said quietly, and to my surprise, she whispered, "I'm sorry."

"You didn't know," I said.

"What's her name?" York asked. "Maybe we've heard of her."

"Trust me, you've never heard of Melissa Cherie. She played with a lot of the big names, though—on tour, at the Opry—and country's no different from rock and roll. A lot of drinking, a lot of drugs. She says she was on top of the world and at the bottom of a bottle all at once."

"What happened?" Andi asked.

"She got busted buying something off an undercover cop— like, a lot of something. Went to prison. Got out and couldn't get any gigs. Then she got knocked up with me and came home."

"Geez," Boston said. "That's heavy."

"No wonder you're so weird," Andi teased, but her elbow gave me a reassuring nudge.

"Not nearly weird enough," Boston said. "It's kind of amaz-ing you're not completely screwed up."

I rolled my eyes. "Not everyone whose parent is an addict is screwed up."

"I don't know," York said with exaggerated slowness. "Andi's dad sounds like an infomercial addict, and she's pretty screwed up."

"Hey!" Andi cried with feigned indignation, and we all laughed.

When the laughter died, we settled into a comfortable kind of silence, broken only by the occasional *crack* of a tree settling or the rustle of something small scurrying through the woods. The clouds gathered, and our circle of stars grew smaller and smaller until there was no clear sky left to be seen.

25

AS THE LAST star winked away, Boston said quietly, "Guys, how did we get here?"

"In a car," York answered.

"An SUV," Andi corrected.

"A *stolen* SUV," I perfected.

Boston sighed. "No, I mean, how did we *get here*?"

York's hand reached up to ruffle Boston's hair, and with our heads so close together, he tangled all of our tresses as one. "We know what you meant, buddy."

"The bigger question is how we're going to get *out* of here," Andi said.

The group fell silent, and I shifted uneasily, knowing they were all wondering whether I would stand for them—whether I would use my power of invisibility to be their hero. I still wasn't sure I was the best person for the job. Sure, my anonymity would get me through the front door of the police station without getting handcuffed, but then what? It wouldn't be as easy as handing over a piece of paper and a few backpacks full of drugs as "evidence." I would have to sell our story, and while I'd had more experience talking to cops than the rest of them, I couldn't help but think I'd sell it better with Boston's brains or Andi's guts or York's sense of humor.

"When I—*if* I take our statement to the police," I started, my speech halting, "how close will you guys be?"

"Close!" Boston answered hastily.

"Very close," York promised.

"But not too close," Andi said, and the boys groaned. "What? I'm just being honest. We're not going to park our stolen car in the front lot, right?"

"Don't listen to her, Sam," Boston purred. "It's like you said earlier: all of us or none of us. We'll be right around a corner or something."

Or something.

The fingers of my free hand threaded through blades of grass at my side, and I closed my eyes, imagining the grass growing on a rolling hill in Ireland . . . *where I am lying under the sun, tasting salt on the wind as ocean waves try to scale cliffs in the distance. Everything is emerald green as far as the eye can see, and there are bagpipes playing, though I can't see any bagpiper. I can't see anyone at all. As always, when I go away like this, it's beautiful, but I'm alone. And I'd rather be in trouble than alone.*

I shut my eyes to the Irish sky and opened them to the inky blackness floating above northern Illinois.

"Like I said," I told the others, "I'll think about it."

Boston started to push, but York urged him to drop it.

"Police shouldn't be so scary," Boston said. "Maybe instead of becoming a judge, I should go into law enforcement."

York chuckled. "You want to be a police officer now?"

"Not an officer. A chief. Or a commissioner. Or a sheriff! I could weed out all the crooked cops."

"I could never be a cop," I said. "It would be too hard to bust people like Ma—like my mom."

"Plus, the uniforms are really unflattering," Andi added. "No flair."

"You could be a flamenco dancer," I suggested. "They have flair."

Andi laughed. "What about you?"

Me? All I'd ever wanted to be when I grew up was somewhere else.

"I just want to travel."

"Travel where?" York asked.

"Everywhere."

"That's not really a job, though," Boston pointed out.

Party pooper.

I pictured my corkboard at home, a menagerie of exotic sunsets and towering mountains, a postcard of Hong Kong's neon lights overlapping a full-page spread on Bora-Bora torn from a magazine. The article was written by a self-proclaimed Gypsy traveler who spent every last penny he had on a one-way plane ticket, then begged his way into a job cleaning toilets at some resort. He'd seen half the world that way, staying in one place just long enough to save up the money he needed to get to the next place.

I told the others about the Gypsy, but they weren't as enchanted by the idea.

"So you're saying he's homeless," Boston said.

"Well, when you put it that way . . ."

"You could teach English overseas," he said. "Our cousin does that."

"Or join the Peace Corps," York offered. "They travel."

I had actually looked into that one. But the Corps usually required a college education, and Boston's admission statistics had given me new doubts about whether any school would even take me. I vowed in that moment to spend more time studying this year and less time wandering around downtown.

As I thought about it, the familiar scene of downtown River City unfolded in my mind, its storefronts lit up with neon, the shelves of Pete's Pawn packed to the rafters with junk. Well, what if it wasn't junk?

"Maybe I could open a store," I said. "You know those guys in Iowa who go all over the country buying cheap antiques at flea markets, then sell the stuff for a bazillion dollars?"

"You want to sell antiques?" Boston asked.

"Not antiques," I said, the vision coming together even as I spoke. "More like exotic imports. I could travel the world buying hand-printed fabrics or statues carved from bone or spices you can't find in any grocery store. And then I could open up a little store somewhere."

"I'd shop there," Andi said.

"Great," I deadpanned. "So I'll need to install some surveillance cameras."

She laughed. "I promise to pay for anything I take from your store. But you have to give me the friends-and-family discount. *Friends and family.*

I smiled up at the clouds. "Deal."

"Nice." York squeezed my hand. "You've already got your first customer."

"What about you?" I asked him, a teasing note in my voice. "What do you want to be when you grow up?"

York let go of my hand and said pointedly, "Apparently not an architect, right, B?"

Oh yeah. I'd forgotten about that little spat.

"Oh fine!" Boston sighed dramatically. "You can be an architect!"

"Gee, thanks." York stretched, and I found myself wishing he would reach for my hand again, but he didn't. "I don't care what I do for a living, as long as I'm not doing something lame when the apocalypse hits."

"The apoca-what now?" Andi asked.

"The apocalypse," York said. "The end of the world. The big ka-boom! I don't want to be, y'know, caught with my pants down when it happens."

"I heard you got caught with your pants down in the girls' bathroom once." Andi snickered, and I felt a twinge of irritation when York didn't deny it.

"Yeah, and what if it had all gone to shit right then and there? Or worse! What if I'd been taking a dump?"

"Dude," Boston said. "What the hell are you talking about?"

"Think about it," York insisted. "How many people are sitting on toilets right this minute?"

"Thousands?" I suggested.

"No," Andi said. "Probably hundreds of thousands."

"More like millions," Boston said.

York waved his hands in the air over our heads. "It was a theoretical question."

"A rhetorical question," Boston corrected.

"Whatever." York sighed, losing patience. "The point is, if there was some sort of apocalypse right now, not everybody is going to be standing in the street watching it all go down like in the movies. Somebody—probably a lot of somebodies—are going to be squatting on porcelain." I felt his shoulder shrug into mine. "I just don't want to be that guy sitting on a toilet at the end of the world."

26

A COOL BREEZE started to blow in off the lake, chasing us inside. The cabin didn't have a washer and dryer, but the boys pointed Andi and me to a bathroom with a hairdryer to help get the damp out of our underwear. Andi was disgusted to find bits of dirt and twigs clinging to hers.

"Forget it," she said, tossing the black thong into a trash can. "I'm going commando."

She focused instead on fixing her eyeliner while I diligently dried my own gray undies and pulled on the rest of my clothes.

"What about your hair?" she asked.

I peeked in the mirror and instantly wished I hadn't. Where my hair wasn't flat against my scalp, exposing the scars on my forehead, orange curls were starting to sprout in places as they dried. "It will just frizz," I said, frowning at my reflection.

"What do you use?"

"For the frizz? Hats."

"No, for the color. It's crazy cool—kind of orange and pink at the same time."

When I didn't say anything, Andi's eyes opened wide. "Is it natural?"

"It is now. I used to be blond."

Andi tipped her head—a question—but I didn't elaborate.

"Blond is boring," she said, breezing past my silence. "This is better. And I can help with the frizz."

She reached toward my head to run her fingers through my hair, but hesitated when she felt the lumps underneath, letting out a little breath of surprise. "Oh!"

"Yeah, they're everywhere," I said.

"Do they—"

"They don't hurt."

"Okay."

Her fingers moved again, gingerly at first, then faster when she could see in my face that it truly didn't hurt. She picked through the knots and separated what curls she could, but it was no use. I was looking more Little Orphan Annie by the minute.

Finally, she settled back against the bathroom sink and crossed her arms. "It's hopeless."

"Thanks a lot."

"I'm just saying, you need product and tools for that mop."

"You don't have anything in your bag?"

Andi tugged one of her dreadlocks. "I have wax for these babies. That's all I need." She stretched a hand out and scrunched a few of my curls. "You've got great hair for dreads, actually.

I could help you do them, if you ever get tired of trying to make this mess work."

Leave it to Andi to offer to help me and then insult me in the next breath.

"I'm good with hats, thanks."

I plucked my muddy mess of a newsboy cap off the back of the toilet, where it was drying out. Somehow it had been stomped into the ground, though everyone had denied doing it. It was still half-damp and caked with dirt both inside and out.

"That's disgusting," Andi said. "You can't put that back on your head."

"I know." I sighed and dropped the cap in the trash on top of Andi's underwear. My eyes flicked to the horror show in the mirror again. "I can't go out there like this."

"Here, I have something." Andi picked up her messenger bag from where she'd dropped it on the floor and rooted around. Finally, her hand emerged holding a bright-green knit hat.

I took it gratefully and tugged it down over my head. A quick mirror check confirmed it was a huge improvement.

"Thank you," I said to the Andi next to me in the mirror.

Her reflection smiled back at me. "It even matches your eyes. Bonus!"

I nodded down at her messenger bag. "You've got everything in there."

"Yeah, I'm a regular Mary Poppins." She slung the strap across her chest and let the bag settle at her hip. "You ready?"

I checked the mirror one last time.

"You look fine," Andi said. "Trust me, he'll like it."

I took an involuntary step away from her. "He who?"

"The yeti."

I sniffed. "Yetis aren't my type."

"Whatever you say," she laughed, and swept past me out of the bathroom.

We found the boys in the great room, stringing a line of rope between the fireplace and a heavy floor lamp. They appeared to be back to their bickering, with York complaining about the wet towels in his arms getting heavy and Boston insisting that the lamp would tip over from the weight of those towels.

"Fine; tie it up somewhere else, then," York said.

Boston unwound the rope from the lamp and crossed the room, looking for a new anchor, but he and York moved at the same time, and the rope caught York in the neck. He made a choking sound and dropped the load of towels.

"Oops," Boston said.

York grabbed the line with both fists and yanked on it so that Boston stumbled. "*Oops?* You almost castrated me!"

Andi snorted. "I think he'd have to aim a little lower for that."

Boston dropped his end of the line and inspected his palms for rope burns. "He means decapitated."

"I can speak for myself," York snapped. There was a sneer on his face, but I saw more behind it. He knew he'd said something embarrassing, but he wasn't sure exactly what. "I meant you almost took my head off."

"Yeah," Andi said. "That's decapitation."

York looked pained. "Okay, fine. So what's the other one?"

"Castration?" Andi laughed. "Google it."

York caught Boston's eye, seeking help, but Boston only grumbled, "Thought you could speak for yourself."

I cleared my throat. "It means to cut off your—"

"Never mind," York interrupted with a wave of his hand. "I knew what I meant."

I busied myself with collecting my purse and the violin and setting them together on the couch, so no one would see how much that stung. This boy with the scowling face and clenched fists was not the same boy who had held my hand in the dark.

Boston abandoned the rope and collapsed on the other end of the couch, yawning.

"We need music," he said. "Or I'm going to fall asleep."

I wasn't sure when we'd collectively decided to pull an all-nighter, but it definitely felt like we'd silently agreed somehow. All of us or none of us.

"I want to hear some of Sam's mom's music," Andi said.

York stepped over the mound of towels on the floor and perched on the coffee table. "Yeah, you got any?"

I didn't meet his eye. "I have a few songs on my phone," I said. I pulled my cell from my purse and looked around for permission to turn it on.

"It's fine," Andi said.

But Boston hesitated. "Just for a second."

"A song takes more than a second, stupid," York said.

I was suddenly afraid of what might happen if I turned the phone on—not just because there could be messages from Mama, or, worse, the police, to drag me back into the real world, but also because . . . what if they didn't like Mama's music? After what I'd already told them about her, I didn't think I could stand to hear them put her down.

"Maybe we shouldn't risk it," I said.

I started to slide the phone back into my purse, but Andi moved like a cat and swiped it from my hand. She was powering it up before I could protest. I couldn't see the screen from this angle, but I knew it was on when it started vibrating and dinging in Andi's hand.

"Hey, Sam," Andi said. "Your mama called."

She held the phone out for everyone to see, and my cheeks pinked to see "Mama" stretched across the screen over and over again.

York laughed and imitated a mechanical doll's voice. "Ma-Ma. Ma-Ma."

"Shut up," I said. I wanted to wipe off the hand I'd let him hold, to scrub it free of the lie that he might be a nice guy—or at least anything above an asshole. Instead, I used that hand to snatch my phone back from Andi.

"Aw, hey, Hat Girl. I was just kidding." He sounded sincere, but I didn't care.

I scrolled through the calls until I lost count. It looked like Mama had started trying to reach me sometime after one in the morning. Why had she waited so long? And what was she doing right this minute? My thumb hovered over the missed calls, an impulse away from pressing the screen to call her back, but what could I say that would make this any easier on her?

*Hey, don't worry, I'm not missing! I know right where I am—
running from crooked cops who may or may not be selling the garbage that
ruined your life and hiding from the good police because I was accidentally
involved in running down an officer.*

I backed my thumb away from the screen and moved it to
the power button instead, shutting the phone back down.

"We still need music," I said, just to fill the silence that had
settled.

York jumped up in response. "I'll get you music." He swayed
on his feet for a moment, trying to catch my eye, but I stubbornly looked away. Finally he stomped out of the great room
and started banging around in the deeper recesses of the cabin.

"What's his problem?" Boston muttered.

"Maybe he's PMSing," Andi said, but she gave me a sly wink.
"Way to keep him on the ropes."

Boston tilted his head, confused. "I was the one who caught
him with the rope."

Andi dropped onto the couch next to Boston and patted his
hand. "Don't worry, little one. You'll understand someday."

I smiled at the pair of them—the sassy former queen bee
and the clueless genius. I didn't really know them, but I knew
enough to decide they didn't deserve this trouble.

I perched on the edge of the sofa, my hand straying to Mama's
violin to finger the strings.

"I've made my decision," I said.

Their heads swiveled in my direction.

"I'll do it." My voice cracked when I said it, so I repeated
myself more surely the second time. "I'll do it."

Boston's face broke into a wide grin, but Andi looked uncertain.

A voice behind me said softly, "You don't have to."

We turned to see York frozen in a doorway, a radio cradled under his arm.

"You don't have to go in by yourself," he said. He moved into the room and dropped the radio on the coffee table. "I'll go with you."

Finally I looked him in the eye. His offer only solidified my resolve.

"I know my way around a police station," I said. "I'm not afraid to do it alone."

Because I didn't feel alone at all. Everyone in the room was looking at me—*really* looking at me—like I mattered. And for once the looking didn't make me want to hide.

"We'll be close by," York promised. He turned to Andi and Boston. "Right?"

Boston nodded eagerly. "Totally!"

Andi didn't answer right away. She was still wearing that critical expression, and I could tell she was holding something back, but she finally forced a smile. "Sure."

A sense of relief went around the room, and I was happy to be the cause of it. I may have been an accessory to a crime—*or two, or three*—but I hadn't really done anything all that terrible. I would explain our situation and get us all out of this, and then maybe we'd come back to this cabin someday under different circumstances, as something other than accidental fugitives.

Or maybe I was delusional. But the only way to find out was to trust them—to take the fall and pray they'd be there to catch me.

"Everything's going to be fine," Boston promised.

"Because we're innocent," York said. "Mostly."

I agreed. Everyone agreed.

We were feeling less and less like bad guys by the minute.

York turned on the radio and clicked a button, flipping through static and fuzz until he found a clear signal.

Boston nixed it right away. "No metal music."

York clicked again.

"Ugh. I hate country," Andi complained. Her eyes flicked to me. "No offense."

I shrugged. "None taken."

The next station pounded out the opening beats of an old punk-rock anthem.

"These guys are poseurs," York said. "But this song's all right."

"Yeah, I like this one," Andi agreed.

"Me, too," I said, and Boston nodded his consent.

We all smiled. It was nice to have something in common besides a felony.

York cranked the volume, and I lost myself in the pounding drums and three-chord guitar riffs. The song was an angry love letter to an ex-girlfriend, but I'd always pulled a different meaning from the lyrics.

I've never felt a need like this
How can so much bad feel like so much bliss

It's my unfortunate addiction!
I know deep down you're ugly
But all I see when I'm with you is your beauty
You're my unfortunate addiction!

When I was old enough to understand Mama's disease, I'd played this song on repeat more times than I could count. It had just the right amount of despair and fury, and was just loud enough to drown out anything but feeling.

The line between love and hate wears thin
But I'll die—I'll DIE—if I don't see you again
It's my unfortunate addiction!
You're my unfortunate addiction!

As the chorus swelled, York played air guitar, and Andi drummed her knees.

Boston is right, I thought, feeling it all the way to my bones. *Everything* is *going to be fine.*

But because it's just my luck, seconds later, everything was absolutely, completely, most definitely not fine.

27

THE SONG HIT a crescendo with a blaze of light.

And I don't mean that as a metaphorical compliment to the music.

I mean the cabin literally exploded with light, blasting through the front glass wall and bouncing around the room, glaring off every reflective surface, until it finally settled into two solid beams shining on us like laser pointers.

Headlights.

Instinct dropped me to the floor behind the couch, and a split second later, Andi and Boston were rolling over the back of it to join me. Only York had the presence of mind to shut off the radio and kill the few small lamps we had on in the great room. Then he crouched down next to us, breathing heavily.

"It's Mom and Dad, isn't it?" Boston whimpered. "We're in so much trouble."

"Maybe it's just a neighbor," York said. "We were being kind of loud out on the water. Someone at a cabin farther down the lake might have heard us."

"Can you get rid of them?" Andi whispered.

York held a finger to his lips, then tiptoed toward the front door, avoiding the beams of light. I could barely make out his shape in the dark, but I heard the slow soft click of the dead bolt locking into place and saw a tiny sliver of light open up next to the door as he moved aside a curtain.

Car doors slammed. An engine died. But the lights kept blazing.

"Fuck," York breathed. It was the smallest of whispers, but it carried the weight of doom.

"Oh God, it *is* them," Boston cried. "Our parents. They're going to kill us."

In a flash, York skidded across the floor, landed next to us on his knees, and clamped a hand over Boston's mouth.

"Shut. Up."

I shivered. Something was very wrong.

"It's not your parents," I whispered.

York shook his head, his eyes somber and scared. "Get your shit," he said. "We're going out the back."

"What about the backpacks?" I asked. The corner of the kitchen where we'd stashed the drugs suddenly seemed very far away.

"Leave them!" Andi said, and we all hushed her. She lowered her voice but not her urgency. "Leave them all here. Let the police come find them."

"Which police?" York asked, a sharp edge to his whisper. "The ones outside?"

Every muscle in my body tensed, bracing the way you would in a car wreck milliseconds before impact, and it made sense. We definitely seemed headed for a crash.

Andi's hands went to her throat, as if physically choking back a cry of fear. Boston was slower to catch on. I saw it happen in his eyes, above the hand York still held firmly pressed over his mouth. They grew wide, and then swelled up with tears.

The crash of shattering glass outside made us all jump. Literally—we jumped to our feet and moved as a single unit to the front door. I had only enough time to grab the violin and my purse. Andi took the instrument from my hands in the dark foyer and slid it silently into her messenger bag, and this time I let it go willingly. I had a feeling I might need my hands free.

"Are you sure it's them?" I whispered to York.

"I didn't see their faces before," he admitted in a low voice. "And they're not in uniform. But two guys, right size . . ." He hesitated, daring another peek past the curtains. "With guns."

Outside there was another smash of glass, followed by shouting.

"It's not here!" a man's voice boomed.

"They're busting up the car," York said. "Shit, they're coming!" He flinched back from the curtain. "Go!"

Chaos. Blind stumbling. Stampeding feet.

I let myself get herded into the kitchen, let someone loop a heavy backpack over my shoulders, and let them push me toward a side door, all with that one command screaming in my head.

GO!

I was vaguely aware of a heavy rhythmic pounding at the front door. It wasn't a knock. Someone was trying to smash their way in.

"Follow me," York whispered fiercely. He threw open the side door and leaped out into the night. We were only steps from the cabin when a voice off to our right cried, "Here! Got 'em!"

I turned at the sound, tripping over my own feet and falling hard on my hip.

It's done, I thought as the shadow of a man crept toward us, one hand up like a warning to stay still. His other hand hung loose at his side, holding a gun pointed harmlessly at the ground.

We'll throw ourselves on their mercy and pray that while they may be crooked, they're not killers.

But a second later the man was crying out, shielding his face from a disturbingly bright ray of light aimed directly at his eyes. In the glow, I could see the familiar lines and angles of the face I'd recognized back in the bowels of River City Park. Strong hands grabbed me under my armpits and lifted me off the ground as I followed the damaging line of light back to its source—Andi's flashlight.

And just like that, we were running again. The hands that picked me up—York's—now grabbed me by the arms, forcing me to move. Andi pounded the ground right beside us, aiming the light wildly over her shoulder.

"Sun Shot, motherfuckers!" she cried.

The pack pounded against my back, and my legs ached, but still I ran. The boys led us at top speed toward the lake, then made a sharp right at the shore, into the trees. Needle-like branches lashed at my arms, and traps made of weeds tried to tangle my feet.

Go!

About twenty breathless paces into the woods, the trees suddenly opened up around a rough shack, open on one end like a tiny barn. The boys gave no instructions, possibly because they were too winded from carrying their own heavy packs, but they motioned for us to hurry. Inside the shack, two mud-caked ATVs sat side-by-side.

We climbed on without question, me behind York and Andi behind Boston. Just before the engines of the little four-wheelers roared to life, I heard the thudding sound of feet moving through the trees. We shot out of the shed at the exact moment the men broke into the clearing. This time their guns were raised, but if they planned to fire, they didn't have time. York nearly ran over the familiar one—I swear he swerved on purpose—and then we were rocketing up a narrow trail, leaving a cloud of dust in our wake.

Boston and York were shouting at each other, but their words were lost to the thunder of the ATVs. The dirt path narrowed, and we fell into single file, York and me in the lead. He refused to slow down, even when the forest floor became uneven, pitching the ATV from side to side and bouncing it right up off the ground. I had my arms wrapped so tightly around York's chest he was probably struggling to breathe, but I didn't loosen my grip.

York let go of one handlebar to motion to Boston, and the ATV rocked dangerously on two wheels. Every muscle in my body clenched as I wondered whether it would be worse to be shot or crushed under a four-wheeler. York leveled us off at the last possible second and finally slowed to a stop. He inched the ATV to the side of the path so Boston and Andi could pull up alongside us.

"The road!" York hollered over the idling motors.

Boston killed his engine and motioned for York to do the same.

"The main road?" Boston whispered, though it sounded like a shout in the sudden silence. "They'll see us."

Tears streaked his face, and I didn't know whether it was from driving into the wind or out of danger. I unlocked my arms from around York's chest to feel my own cheeks. Dry, as usual. But inside—inside I was more than crying. I was screaming.

"Just across it," York said. "We have to get to the deeper part of the woods."

"They'll check the house first," Andi said with some certainty. Her dreadlocks stuck out in every direction, some of them looking torn apart, like they'd snagged on branches.

"You think?" I said.

She only replied, "I told you we should have left that shit behind."

I saw her point now.

They would search the cabin, and when they failed to find their loot, they'd come after us. Again.

"It's our evidence," Boston said, almost apologetically. "I thought we'd need it."

"Well, we have it now," York said. "And we can't just sit here."

Boston's shoulders sagged, but he offered no alternative. He turned the engine over and readjusted his perch on the ATV. "No lights," he said, turning off the four-wheeler's headlights.

York powered up and did the same. When we moved again, the pace was much slower, which scared me more than the high speeds of before. We were driving in pure darkness, barely faster than I could walk, making a racket that screamed *Here we are!*

I held my breath and closed my eyes as we reached the road, but we crossed it quickly, with no sign of the crooked cops. Once we hit the trees on the other side, the boys turned on their lights and picked up speed again, racing deeper and deeper into the forest. We passed several forks in the trail until they found one that went left and took it. Now we were flying south toward River City, leaving the cabin behind.

I wondered if the ATVs could carry us all the way back to town. I no longer feared the idea of walking into a police station. At this point, I would bang on the door and demand to be let in.

Hurry, I urged the engine underneath us. *Take us home.*

The ATV answered my plea, but it wasn't the answer I wanted to hear.

It slowed, sputtered, and then died.

York swore and banged the handlebars with his fists. "Out of gas," he said as Boston and Andi chugged up. I kept my hands locked around York, my face buried in his back, and tried very hard to cry.

28

"SCREW THIS!" BOSTON said, killing his engine and climbing off the ATV. "I'm done playing cops and robbers!"

Andi swung a leg around and sat sidesaddle on the ATV. "You realize they're the cops and we're the robbers in that scenario, right?" The words had all her usual sarcasm, but her voice was flat.

"I'm calling the police," Boston barreled on. "The *good* police. Someone give me a phone."

York and I both reached for our cell phones simultaneously. I got to mine first and handed it to Boston. Forget best-laid plans— we should have done this from the very beginning.

Boston clicked the power button with one hand while he looked at the palm of the other. "Shit!"

"What?" York hopped off the ATV and held out a hand to help me down.

Boston raised his palm to show us a smear of black ink. "I sweated off the number, and the website won't load. The

Internet's not working! Your phone sucks." He tossed my cell back to me.

"Forget the Internet," York said, powering up his own phone. "Let's just call nine-one-one."

He dialed and held the phone to his ear, but after a second he made a face. "Nothing's happening."

"What do you mean nothing's happening?" Boston grabbed the phone from York and dialed again himself. "There's no signal!"

I checked my own phone. No bars. I tried 9-1-1 anyway. Silence.

"I thought nine-one-one was supposed to work no matter what," I said.

Andi shook her head. "It's supposed to work even if you don't pay for cell service. But if there's no tower . . ." She gestured at the woods around us. "No tower, no signal, no nine-one-one."

We were truly alone out here. I knew a little something about being alone, but this was different. I clutched a hand to my chest and knotted it in my shirt. If I squeezed tightly enough, maybe I could get my heart to slow down and beat normally.

Boston stomped this way and that into the trees, holding up York's phone like an antenna. "Nothing!"

"Calm down," York said, though he sounded tense himself.

"Calm down?" Boston said through gritted teeth. "CALM DOWN?!"

He hurled York's phone into the trees, and there was a very final-sounding crunch of metal and glass on bark.

Two phones down, two to go.

"You scum!" York yelled.

"You're the scum!" Boston pointed a finger at York. "If it wasn't for you, I wouldn't be here. *None* of us would be here."

That's not fair.

"Drunk driving—you." Boston held up a second finger, then a third and a fourth. "Stolen car—you. Running from the cops—you. Nearly killing a police officer—*you!*"

Huh. Maybe he has a point.

"You're right!" York exploded. "I'm the reason you're here, because if it wasn't for me, you'd never go anywhere. You'd sit in your room hugging your college brochures and jerking off to the slutty animated bimbos in your computer games. I'm the reason you're here, because if it wasn't for me, you'd still be back in that cabin pissing yourself behind the couch while those guys busted down the door. I'm the reason you're here, because despite the fact that you're an ungrateful prick, I never leave you behind."

Boston opened his mouth, then closed it again.

"And I won't leave them behind, either," York said, pointing at Andi and me but keeping his eyes unwaveringly on his brother. "But you—you would bail in a heartbeat, wouldn't you?"

Boston's silence unnerved me.

Would he?

York found his answer in the quiet. "Yeah, exactly. You and me got nothing in common."

"You and I," Boston said finally.

York shook his head. "You're an asshole."

Our little group walked in tense silence down the path, the boys talking only enough to assure us that the trail dumped out in a field alongside the main road. Andi and I each held our cell phones out in front of us, keeping a keen eye on our bars in case one of us got service.

I hated the quiet. It gave me too much space to think, and I was thinking I'd been a fool. That's what Grandma would have called me, and she always called 'em like she saw 'em. Boston's own brother thought he was a traitor, so maybe I was a fool to agree to his plan. I had most certainly been a fool to believe we were safe at the cabin. I tried to ask the others how the cops could possibly have found us, but Andi only shrugged, like she didn't care, and York muttered something noncommittal about "parents" and "narcs" and "I told you so." His face seemed folded into a permanent frown.

As the trees grew thinner, we spread out along the path, each walking as far from the others as possible while still keeping everyone in sight. The gaps between us made me uncomfortable, and I closed the distance to York.

"You okay?" I asked him.

Lame. Of course he's not okay. None of us are.

York shrugged. "You know how it is with little brothers."

"I don't, actually."

"He's a punk most of the time, but he was really there for me after . . ."

"Yeah," I said, so he wouldn't have to finish the sentence.

"He was the only one I could talk to. I blew off a lot of my friends for a while. Most of them were on the team, and I just—I couldn't face them."

"That's why you used your brother's locker," I said.

York cocked his head at me. "What?"

It was strange. Boston's locker had been across from mine all of freshman year, but the only person I'd ever really noticed using it was York. I guess I wasn't the only invisible person at Jefferson.

"I saw you in the freshman wing. It must have been right after it happened." I looked down at my feet and added quietly, "You didn't see me, I guess."

York tipped my chin back up with one finger.

"I see you now." His eyes met mine, unblinking, for the length of a breath, then he shrugged. "Anyway, that whole year was a downward spiral. I didn't know who I was to my friends without football, so I had to, I don't know—find another part to play."

Is that what everyone else was doing in school? Playing their parts? Some got starring roles, while the rest of us were just extras.

"What part are you playing tonight?" I asked.

His smile returned. "The dashing hero."

I thought about how he'd hustled us out of the cabin. The ATV wasn't exactly a white horse, and York's armor was more smudged than shiny, but yeah, he was kind of a hero.

29

THE WOODS FINALLY parted, and we stepped into a brown field, awash in the first glow of a new day. The sky had turned from black to deep blue while we'd trekked through the woods, and the dark was slowly lifting from the world.

We passed through low rows of soybean plants, keeping the road back to River City on our left but staying a safe-enough distance away that we could duck out of sight at the sound of a car. Not that the beans would provide much cover. A cornfield would have been better.

"Anything yet?" Boston asked from a few paces behind me.

I checked my phone, but I already knew if I'd had service, I'd have heard it ring. Mama had probably broken her finger hitting redial all night. I felt a little bit of shame that I'd doubted her concern, and a whole lot of guilt for making her worry. I vowed to answer the next call that reached me.

"Nothing," I said.

Andi didn't even look at hers. I wondered if she was less eager than I was to start getting calls again. Her boyfriend sounded like a real prick. For all I knew, that's what she was really running away from last night.

Maybe we were all running away from something more than the cops.

Rays of sunlight started to break over the horizon, turning the brown field to glowing amber around us. Illinois was having an extra-early harvest season, thanks to the long, hot summer, and all we could see for miles in every direction were flat expanses of gold backed by deep-green tree lines. It was the kind of scene I liked to see captured on a postcard, so I could pin it up on my bulletin board and imagine myself there. Who knew there was this kind of beauty so close to home?

Our phones woke up at the same time as the fields.

Mine beeped, Andi's buzzed, and we all froze in our tracks.

"I've got a bar!" I said.

"Shit, I just lost mine." Andi spun in circles with her phone held to the sky, trying to reconnect, while the boys ran to my side.

"Call nine-one-one," Boston said immediately.

Forget 9-1-1. "I'm calling my mom."

Mama always told me she'd gotten *out* of a lot more trouble than she'd been *in*. Maybe she would have a way out of this as well. It rang three times before her phone finally picked up, and then all I heard was dead air.

"Mama?" I cried into the phone.

Still no answer. I checked my screen. We were connected, but maybe the signal was weak. I was afraid to move in any direction in case the call dropped altogether.

"Mama, can you hear me?"

"Sammy?" It came out slow and groggy.

"It's me!"

"Where are you? I was so worried about you." But it sounded more like *Wherer you? Izo word bow you.*

I felt a chill slip down my spine despite the warm morning sun.

"Did I wake you up?" I said hesitantly—hopefully.

Not that it was okay to sleep while your child was missing, but it was better than the alternative.

"Whashoo been doin'?" she slurred.

No.

Boston started to snap at me to just call the police, but I held up a warning hand, and York dragged him away with a concerned nod in my direction. Andi filled their space, parking in front of me with her hands on her hips, listening.

"What have *you* been doing?" I said into the phone.

"Mussa fell 'sleep." There was a bang and a scuffle on Mama's end, then: "Whoops. Dropped a phone." She giggled.

Damn it. Goddamn it!

Then I spoke God's name in earnest, begging him silently, *Please. Please, not this. Not now.*

"Wha' time'sit?" Mama mumbled.

My voice sounded hollow to my own ears. "It's early on Saturday."

"'S my unnversary," she said brightly.

Well, it would have been.

The handle of Mama's anniversary gift glimmered in the sunlight where it poked out from the corner of Andi's messenger bag. I reached for it, and Andi handed it over with a quizzical look on her face. I held the violin by the neck, letting it rest on my forearm, cradled in the crook of my elbow. The hand holding my phone shook.

"Mama, I have to go."

But Mama was starting to wake up. Her words still slurred together, but there was urgency in her voice now. She said something mostly incoherent about curfew and scared to death and, again, *Where are you?* . . . and then she started to cry. I wished I could, too. "Good-bye, Mama," I whispered into the phone, and then I turned it off—all the way off—and let it drop to the ground at my feet.

I swayed for a second, rocking in the sun, the only moving thing in this whole sleepy field. Andi reached for me, but I stepped out of her grasp.

"No," I said.

She reached instead for my phone.

"No!"

"O-kaaay." Andi backed away slowly with her palms out. "Sam, what just happ—"

"No." I said it over and over, stomping a foot on my cell phone every time. But the soil was too soft, and I was only burying the phone, not breaking it. I began to sweat with the effort, and the violin slid in my grip.

Yes.

I twisted the violin so the body was aimed away from me and wrapped both hands around the neck as if it were a baseball bat. I swung it high over my head, and then brought it down hard. It made direct contact with the phone on the first try. The glass screen cracked, and a seam on the violin opened with a pop. Another direct hit, and the phone's screen turned into a black puddle, as if leaking ink; the violin's lower trim splintered away. I aimed again.

For making me afraid.

And again.

For making it always all about you.

And again.

And again.

For leaving me alone.

For my HAIR!

My hands lifted the violin and slammed it down with increasing force each time. The phone was long past destroyed when the violin's strings snapped with a satisfying *Ping! Ping! Ping! Ping!* Still I pounded. Until my arms ached, I pounded.

The body of the violin finally separated from the neck, skittering away from me. I chased it through the field, using the neck as a club to bash away at it until there was nothing left but slivers.

I stood up, chest heaving, and surveyed the damage. Bits of blond wood were scattered all around me, and with the sun lighting them up, they blended in almost perfectly with the rest of the field. I twirled the neck in my hand, ready to aim at something new, but there was nothing left to destroy. Instead I chucked the final piece of the fiddle as far as I could into the soybeans and out of sight.

When I finally looked up, three faces gaped at me. I paced like a cat: a warning—don't come too close.

"Is she done?" Boston asked in a stage whisper.

"I think she needs more stuff to smash," York answered.

Andi rooted around in her messenger bag and emerged with something that shined bright white in the sunlight.

She held it out, cupping it in her palm the same way she'd done back at Pete's Pawn.

The snow globe.

She lifted one corner of her mouth in a tentative smile. "Go crazy."

AFTER

MAMA LOOKS DOWN at the handcuffs with shame all over her face. But with Mama, shame sometimes looks an awful lot like self-pity, and I'm tired of seeing it. I wave her off when she tries to explain.

She already made her excuses, and I haven't decided yet if I believe her. If she's lying, I can't bear it, and if she's telling the truth, then my temper tantrum looks foolish.

I remind her that visiting hours are short and my story is long. It's difficult to get Mama to focus on anyone other than herself, but she makes an effort to stay still and listen. I appreciate it.

"I told you not to thank me yet," I say. "For the violin."

"You must have been in a lot of pain."

She's making excuses for me, as always, but she's not wrong.

"I was in a lot of *trouble*," I say. "I needed you, and when I heard you . . ."

"I know."

My voice cracks. "I was so mad at you."

"I know."

The chain of the handcuffs scrapes the table as Mama stretches her hands toward me and I pull mine away.

"But I am sorry about the violin," I say.

"Oh, Sam."

Mama is crying now. Whimpering, really. It's pathetic, and I feel sick to think that about my own mother, but even the other inmates and their families are looking away uncomfortably. The visitation room is very crowded today, and I wish she would keep it together. It's not good to show weakness behind bars. She's the one who told me that, after all.

"I just hate being here again." Mama sniffles and looks around at all the gray. "This place . . ."

"*You* hate being here?"

"I know, honey, I know. I'm sorry." She flaps her hands to settle me down, as if I'm the one making a scene here. "Of course you hate it, too. Of course you do." She cries fresh tears.

I know in this moment that I'm stronger than Mama. And not because I don't cry, but because after everything life has thrown at us—or, more accurately, after everything Mama has thrown at our lives—I'm not so breakable. Mama is glass that shatters too easily. I am stone that doesn't crack easily enough.

We're both screwed up that way, but sometimes—like right now—I'm glad to be me, if only because it reminds me that I'm not her.

30

IT'S MY FAULT.

The words kept repeating in my head. *My fault, my fault, my fault.*

I said it inwardly with every weary step. We'd been walking for an hour and had covered almost no ground, the soft soil working our calves until they screamed for relief, forcing us to move at a crawl.

After I'd destroyed my cell phone, Andi had held up her own and dealt the deathblow. "Battery's dead."

"How can it be dead?" Boston had cried.

"Because I never turned it off! And because some idiot made me keep it on for the last hour, searching for a signal."

"Only because some *other* idiot threw mine out a window!"

"Okay, so it's settled," York had said. "You're both idiots."

I had said nothing but *My fault, my fault, my fault.*

And so we walked.

The boys wanted to head to the place they called Pit Stop, but by the time we saw signs for Pitson the traffic on the freeway was heavy, and we all agreed our "friends" might be there waiting for us. There was a small argument about whether it was worth it to get inside a building with a phone and call 9-1-1, but then we would have to wait who-knows-how-long for sheriff's deputies out here in the boonies. It was too risky, someone had argued, and whoever it was had won the fight.

I hardly paid attention. I was too busy thinking about Mama, wondering if she was in a bar right this minute—or, worse, in some drug dealer's filthy living room, buying God-knows-what to kill her worries. Little did she know I was carrying all the drugs she could ever want on my back. I was Mama's compass for sobriety, her true north, and when I hadn't come home last night, she'd lost her way.

My fault.

"I need to stop," Boston panted. He shrugged off his backpack and dropped to the ground next to it.

We all collapsed in response, lying down right in the dirt.

"How long is it going to take us to walk all the way home?" Andi asked.

"Years," York said.

Boston sat up and rested his forearms on his knees. "Sixteen hours. Give or take."

"Give or take what?" Andi asked.

"An hour. But that's only if we keep up our pace."

"Our snail's pace," York complained.

"How do you know it's sixteen hours?" I said. My throat was dry, and it came out as a croak.

"Hey, look, it speaks!" Andi scooted over to me. "Thought maybe you were going the way of those monks or whatever, who take a vow of silence."

"It can't be sixteen hours," I groaned.

Boston scratched his head. "Well, it's an hour to the cabin in good traffic, at a driving speed of sixty-five miles per hour, so at a walking speed of—"

"Spare me your calculations," I said. "I meant *we* can't go sixteen hours. We'll die of dehydration."

Not to mention lack of sleep.

"Obviously," Boston said, looking wounded. "We'll find a phone or a bus stop before then."

"A bus stop on the highway?" York said. "I know every inch of this road, and there's no bus stop. There's no *nothing*. We should have gone into Pitson, like I said."

"There are houses," Boston countered. "Farms and stuff. We'll knock on a door, use the phone, and wait for the police." He stood and kicked his backpack-load of heroin. "I'm sick of running, anyway."

Me, too.

"Uh, guys?" York said.

"Forget running," Andi said. "I'm sick of *walking*."

"Guys?"

"I can't walk one more step," I agreed.

Boston stretched. "Well, if we want to stop running, we *have* to start walking."

"GUYS!"

York was on his feet, shielding his eyes against the sun and looking up the highway from the direction we'd come. He dropped his hand to reveal pure panic on his face, then he turned to us and shouted a single word.

"RUN!"

I didn't ask questions. The last time York told us to run it had saved our lives, for all I knew, so I stood and stumbled blindly after him. Andi and Boston were faster, and I panicked when I realized I was bringing up the rear. I had no idea what we were running from, but I didn't slow down to look. Mama and I watched a lot of horror movies, and the person in back of the pack always bit it. Monster bait, Mama called them. And then she would tell me, *If you're ever in trouble, you only have to be faster than the slowest person.* Parenting, by Melissa Cherie.

Just when I thought my legs were going to fall off from pumping so hard, York dove behind a low stack of round hay bales. I landed on my stomach, dry-heaving. Everyone was prone on the ground except York, who crawled up enough to peek over the top of the hay. Thank God for harvest season, or this field would have provided no cover.

But cover from what?

I crept up next to York and saw a pickup with huge wheels stopped on the side of the road, just yards from where we'd been resting.

"That looks like the truck that was at the cabin," York said.

"Did they see us?" Boston whimpered in panic.

"Did they see us running and flailing around like idiots?" Andi huffed, still out of breath. "No, I'm sure they didn't notice a thing."

"Are we sure it's them?" I asked.

Andi joined our peekaboo position and pulled her binocular glasses from her messenger bag. "Super Zooms say affirmative," she said.

"This isn't a joke!" Boston snapped.

"You're the joke," Andi said, passing him the Super Zooms. "But take a look. They're leaving."

Boston slid the funny glasses onto his face, but I didn't need binoculars to see the truck begin to roll forward. I heard gravel under the wheels as the pickup pulled back onto the highway, then it pulled an abrupt U-turn and zoomed back up the road the way it had come.

"Where are they going?" I asked. "Why would they leave?"

"Maybe they don't want to murder us in broad daylight," Boston said.

"Or they decided we're not worth the trouble," Andi offered.

I watched the truck's bumper disappear into the tunnel of trees where the woods swallowed the road. I hoped Andi was right.

York stood up the second the truck was out of sight. "Okay, let's go."

"Go where?" Boston stood too and threw his arms out.

"I don't know," York said. "But we can't sit here with our heads in the hay like a bunch of dumb ostriches who think that if you can't see your enemy, your enemy can't see you."

"That's not why ostriches bury their heads," Boston said. "They dig for pebbles to help with their digestion, and——"

"Wow, dude, we *so* don't care right now," Andi said.

"Let's just start moving." York nudged Boston. "You said there'd be a farm with a phone. Here's the farm. Let's find the phone."

I got to my feet and spun in a circle. I saw nothing but black soil and butter-colored hay for miles in every direction. More than likely, we were sitting in the middle of a corporate farm, which meant hundreds, if not thousands, of acres of corn or soybeans, and zero farmhouses.

York snatched the Super Zooms from Boston's face and put them on his own. "There are buildings back there." He pointed deep into the fields, away from the road.

Anything away from the road sounded good to me. I started walking in the direction York had indicated, but a cry from Boston stopped me.

"My backpack!" he said, his hands scrabbling at his back. "I left it by the road!"

I reached for my own pack, still firmly in place. No wonder I had been running so slowly.

York still had his, too, and he hiked it higher on his shoulders. "It's fine. Just go get it and come right——"

"No," Andi said vehemently. "I told you guys to leave that shit alone from the beginning. Leave it now."

Boston protested, "But it's evidence——"

"It's not worth it!" she shouted. "We have enough evidence right here." She pointed at the bags York and I were carrying.

"She's right," I said. I knew we were mostly innocent, but it *felt* more true if we weren't all hauling heroin on our backs. Less is more seemed to apply here. I looked at Boston. "They might be waiting for us just up the road. If they come after you, your dead body might be the evidence."

"Don't be so dramatic," York said. "They're not going to kill us."

"Not alongside a busy highway, anyway," I muttered. "But I'd rather not take my chances, thanks."

"But they didn't even shoot at us back at the cabin," York pointed out.

"Well, then they're practically good Samaritans!" I cried.

"I just meant—"

"Look," I cut him off. "Let's go see what those buildings are back there—see if one has a phone. You can keep an eye on the bag with the mad-scientist glasses."

"Super Zooms," Andi corrected.

York peeked through the glasses to confirm that he could see the pack in the distance, then propped them on his head and reluctantly agreed. "One of those buildings had better be a house."

No such luck.

It was a three-mile hike at least to the cluster of buildings, but the Super Zooms told us a mile in that there was no reason to keep walking.

"Tractor storage," York said, passing the glasses around the group so we could see for ourselves. Long, low garages, wide-open on one side, housed lines of green-and-yellow John Deere machines. Next to them, a barn-sized warehouse was also open—and completely empty.

The only other building within view was a tall metal cylinder off to our left—a grain silo.

"Great," Boston said. "Now—"

"Don't say 'now what,'" York warned. "The next person to ask that gets clocked in the face."

"I'll tell you *now what*," Andi said deliberately. "Now, we rest."

"Right here?" Boston asked.

"No." Andi pointed at the silo. "In there."

The inside of the metal tube was hot, the air choked with the dust of old hay. It took a few sneezes for my nose to adjust, but then I gratefully parked my butt on the dirt floor and leaned against the curved wall.

No more walking, no more looking. Let someone come find us instead. Hell, let the crooked cops come find us.

I was past caring.

My eyelids slipped closed, but popped open again when Andi snapped a finger in my face.

"Rest!" she ordered. "But don't sleep."

York dropped to the ground in defiance and rested his head in my lap. "Can I use you as a pillow?" he asked.

I was past caring about that, too.

"Whatever," I said.

"Not whatever," Andi said. "No sleep—sleep—sleeee—" Her words were choked off by her own deep yawn.

Boston was already curled into a ball on the other side of the silo, and Andi looked around at us, defeat on her face.

"Fine," she said with another yawn. She stretched out on the floor. "But just for a few minutes."

The sun had moved to the other side of the sky by the time we woke up.

31

I WAKE UP on a soft leather couch, comfy but confused. I'm used to the scratchy motel-room sofas and the busy buzz of the Cartoon Network on TV. It's too quiet here. I rub my eyes and remember we have a house now—or, what did Grandma call it? An apartment.

I'm hungry, I realize, and pad off to the kitchen in my pink footie pajamas. Mama promised pancakes every day in this new place. Mama is not in the kitchen, but something is cooking on the stove. It does not smell like pancakes. It does not smell like anything good at all. I don't want to eat that, whatever it is. I need to get rid of it so Mama doesn't make me.

I stand on my tiptoes, but my fingertips only brush the handle of the pot—just like in my kindergarten class, where all the other boys and girls can reach the top toy shelf except for me. The smell from the pot is making my tummy hurt. I pull out the drawers next to the stove one by one to make a set of stairs, but on the second stair the drawer breaks, and I trip forward.

"Sam."

I am falling toward the stove in slow motion. My face is going to hit the pot. No, no! I don't want to smell it. I thrust my tiny arms in front of me to push the pot out of the way, and then it's all flames, flames hot on my face.

"Sam!"

I grab at the air, but there is nothing to hang on to, nothing to save me from the fire. I turn my face just in time, and my ponytail turns to ash.

"SAM!"

Rough hands shook me awake—many rough hands. I came to with a jerk to discover that Andi and York each had me by an arm, and Boston was actually sitting on my feet.

"Get off me!"

I squirmed until they let go, and Andi sat back with a thump against the silo wall. "Jesus, that was some kind of nightmare." She picked something up off the dirt floor, dusted it off, and held it out to me—the green knit hat.

My hands went instantly to my hair, where I felt a matted knot of curls.

"You took it off," York said quietly. "You were pulling your own hair out. We had to . . ."

I snatched the hat from Andi's outstretched hand and tugged it on, yanking it down as far as it would go. "Got it," I said, and then, because it seemed like the not-weirdo thing to do, I added, "Thanks."

"Thanks?" Boston scoffed, climbing off my legs. "That's it?"

"Yeah, that's it," I snapped.

"But—but—what were you dreaming about?" he pressed.

York gave him a backhanded smack to the chest that practically knocked him over. "What do you think she was dreaming about, asshole?"

"Sam," Andi said quietly. "What the hell happened to you?"

I wiggled my fingers up under the hat, feeling my scars. They seemed hot to the touch, but maybe that was just because the silo was now sweltering in the afternoon heat.

"You used to be blond," Boston said, staring at the hand digging into my scalp. "In kindergarten, right? Blond, and then . . . then you went away."

That's one way to put it.

"And you didn't come back until first grade, and then you . . ." He trailed off, but I saw the memory coming to him, saw how his eyes slid from questions to compassion. I'd rather be interrogated than pitied.

"And then I wore wigs," I finished for him.

That was all I was going to say, but the three of them were watching me intently, sitting in a little semicircle around my legs. I stretched, then contracted my body, pulling my knees to my chest.

"I wore wigs to cover my scars," I began. "But they were worse than scars back then. They were . . ." *Still oozing, still red and raw like meat.* "Still healing."

"But what happened?" Boston asked. "Why did you go away?"

"I didn't go away, exactly. I was in the hospital for a really long time. My—I lost my . . . There was an accident, and my hair caught fire."

"What kind of accident?" York asked.

I rested my chin on my knees and stared at the floor. My next words came out in a rush. "The kind that happens when a drug addict attempts to cook her own meth and leaves a pot of poison sitting on an open flame with her curious six-year-old unattended in the next room."

"Whoa," Boston breathed.

"I don't really remember it—not the bad bit, anyway. I just know I was falling, and there were flames, and that's it. Then I was in the hospital." *And there were lollipops and ice chips and clean sheets and cartoons.* "Honestly, I'm lucky I didn't pull the pot off the stove and dump it all in my face. I'd probably be blind or something. My mom knows all about taking drugs, but she doesn't know shit about making them."

"What did they do to her?" Andi asked.

"Not as much as they could have." My voice was rough, scraping the rust off words never used—a story never shared out loud. "She was wasted, but seeing your kid's head on fire will wake you up pretty quick. She took me to the hospital herself and called my grandma on the way. Grandma got rid of everything—I mean *everything*—in our apartment. As far as the police were concerned, I'd set myself on fire trying to reach a pot of boiling water."

"So she got away with it?" Boston said, his eyes bugging.

I looked up from the floor. "Oh no; she went to prison."

"But, you said—"

"I told you, she'd already been busted once. After that, they don't let you off easy for anything. They got her on neglect and probation violation. They probably suspected drugs were involved because she had a history, but they couldn't prove it. So she only got nine months that time." I twirled one of my orange curls around a finger. "And I got new hair forever and ever."

"And scars," Andi added.

"And scars," I agreed.

"I think I laughed at your wigs," Boston said. "I'm sorry." He looked miserable about it, and I tossed him a forgiving smile.

"Hey, at least you didn't try to pull my wig *off*."

"Someone pulled your wig?" York said. He punched a fist into the silo wall, causing a metallic ring to reverberate all around us. "That's messed up."

I turned my smile to him. A punch thrown in my honor seemed more valiant than violent.

"Some girl," I said. "Marla or Marlo or something. I can't remember now. She moved away. But she pulled it off at recess, and everyone could see——" I circled a hand over my head.

Boston swallowed. "And that's why we called you . . ."

"Worms. Yeah," I said. "Because my scars are kind of shaped that way."

Boston started to apologize again, but I held up a hand to let him know he didn't have to. Then we fell quiet, which was sort of awful, because I knew the quiet meant they all felt sorry for me and didn't know what to say. It's funny how people feeling bad for you can make you feel more like an outcast than people being cruel to you.

Andi was the first to break the silence. She pulled one of her long dreadlocks forward and inspected it. "*I* should be called

Worms, with this hair." She waved the twisted lock at me, and I laughed gratefully. "My offer stands," she said. "I could turn your curls into dreads. Cover up some scars—give people a new reason to call you names."

"Don't cover 'em up," York said. He lifted a hand to my face and gently tugged up the front of the knit hat so the ends of my "worms" were exposed on my forehead. "Scars are cool."

"Cool?" I asked.

"Yeah—mysterious. Kind of . . . sexy. Like your hats." He smiled. "Hat Girl."

I knew I was turning pink, and a pink face always made my scar tissue turn white, but I didn't pull the hat back down.

On my other side, Andi snickered. "Way to take someone's childhood trauma and use it to hit on them."

"Too bad Andi wasn't around back then," York said to me. "You needed a friend like her to kick that wig puller's ass."

"Nah," Andi said. She plucked a small rock off the ground and tossed it back and forth in her hands. "I would have been one of the girls pulling the wig. I was a real little bitch back then."

"Uh, sorry," York teased. "But if you were a bitch back then, what are you now?"

Andi chucked the rock at him and laughed. "Fair enough."

"What changed?" I asked her. "You used to be . . . different."

"You mean I used to be like Georgia?"

"You were never *that* bad," I said. Not that I knew.

"I was worse," Andi promised. "Much worse."

"You guys were joined at the hip," York said.

"And at the lips." Andi's voice was heavy with meaning.

"You guys made out?" Boston gaped.

"And then some."

"So, not just a phase?" I asked.

"Not for me. I thought—I don't know, that it was me and her against the world. Nobody liked us, so—"

"Um, excuse me," Boston interrupted. "Since when does nobody like the popular girls?"

"Since you have to do some pretty unpopular shit to stay one of those girls," Andi said. "Just because people want to *be* you doesn't mean they *like* you. But Georgia and I . . . we liked each other. That was enough."

"You *like* liked each other," I said.

"Just me." Andi traced patterns in the dirt with her fingers. "It really was a phase for Georgia. Or an experiment or something. She got freaked out. And then I got freaked out."

"And then you . . ." I waved an arm wide around her, not sure how to put it.

"Got a new look?" she supplied.

"Yeah."

"That was part of it, I guess. I just didn't want to keep being what everyone expected me to be."

"But you have a boyfriend now," I said. "The nice guy on your phone, who left you all those charming text messages."

Andi looked up, one eyebrow raised. "What, a girl can't keep her options open?" She winked.

"Speaking of options," Boston said, standing to stretch, "what are ours?"

I would rather have shared ten more disturbing childhood memories than discuss the answer to that question, but I dragged myself to my feet and stumbled out of the tin tower with the others. The air outside was cool and fresh compared to the sweat lodge that was the inner silo. I held out my arms to feel every bit of the light breeze blowing around my body.

Maybe we don't have to go anywhere. Maybe we can just stay right here and start one of those communes like old hippies. Maybe we can have a new beginning.

"Maybe we should hike back to Pit Stop," York said.

Or that.

Boston eagerly agreed, but Andi repeated her warning that the crooked cops might be waiting for us there. Always the voice of dissent.

My head said she was right, that trouble could be parked in Pitson, but my sandpaper throat and screaming calf muscles didn't care. We needed water. We needed rest.

"I'm with the boys," I said. "We'll call the police from there and let them come to us."

I didn't add that I was secretly relieved I wouldn't have to march into a police station all by myself.

"What do we tell them?" York said, tightening the straps on his backpack.

Boston shouldered the second pack. "Everything."

"You all sure you don't want to come up with a different story?" Andi asked. "I like the one where you just picked us up at the party and then let us out of the car. Whose idea was that again?"

"Yours," Boston and York said simultaneously.

"Oh yeah."

I tugged one of Andi's dreadlocks. "All of us or none of us," I said.

She sighed and threw her arms up in defeat. "Fine, whatever. Let's go to back to Armpit."

"Pit Stop," York said. He started the long trek back toward the highway, retracing our earlier steps, and we all fell in line behind him. "And then we go home," he promised.

I heard Mama's slurred speech in my head and imagined her sprawled out, passed out, blacked out on her bed. Home was the last place I wanted to go.

32

"I'M THIRSTY," BOSTON complained after only a few steps.

"I'm starving," Andi added.

I was both, but I didn't see the point in complaining about it.

Ahead of us, York stopped and turned, digging into the front pocket of his jeans.

"Here." He pulled out a slightly smushed package of something colorful and tossed it to Andi.

She ripped into it with her teeth, then stopped to inspect the contents. "Gummy worms?" She raised an eyebrow, but stuffed three in her mouth at once and offered the bag to Boston.

"I only eat the red ones," he said.

"I pocketed them back at the cabin." York shrugged. "Better than nothin'."

"Barely better."

Boston agreed with Andi. "You couldn't have grabbed some beef jerky or something?" he said through a mouthful of red gummies.

"And what did you bring?" I challenged Boston.

It seemed to me that he and Andi were being a little ungrateful. If it hadn't been for York keeping his wits about him, we probably wouldn't have even gotten out of the cabin, let alone with a little bit of food.

York elbowed me lightly as we started walking again. "Thanks."

"No problem. But seriously, gummy worms?" I laughed. "I thought you didn't eat foods that jiggle."

"I don't." He slipped me a sideways smile. "But I like *worms*."

My face burned so hot I thought my scalp might catch fire all over again, but I forced myself to return his smile. He stumbled when our eyes met, his feet tripping forward a few steps.

"Your eyes," he said, recovering but still not watching where he was going. His gaze was focused on me instead of on the field ahead. "I noticed them before, but in the sunlight, they're . . . wow."

I bit my lip. "Good wow?"

"I've never seen—I don't even know how to describe the color."

"Alien green?" I suggested, thinking of the little boy Mama had said complimented me by way of insult back in third grade.

He laughed. "No, but they are kind of . . . radioactive."

The cocky smile on his face said he thought this was high praise, so I decided to take it that way. But seriously? Boys don't get much better at compliments past the third grade.

"Hey, Romeo," Andi interrupted from behind us. "You got any cigarettes in those pockets?"

"You should quit that shit before it fries your face," York called back. "You'll end up looking like a little old raisin."

"I don't care how I look," Andi said. "The world has enough Georgias."

"That's for sure," I agreed. I smiled back at Andi. "For what it's worth, you can do better than her."

"And better than your douche boyfriend, too," York said.

"Thanks?" Andi sounded unsure whether she was being flattered or insulted.

"I'm just saying I like you better now," York said.

"I like me better now, too." Andi said it softly, but her voice carried over the quiet field.

"Wish we could say the same for you," Boston chirped at his brother's back.

York clutched his chest with both hands and dropped to one knee. "Oh, I'm so wounded! Whatever will I do without your approval?"

I laughed and dragged him up by the elbow as Boston and Andi caught up to us.

"He's not wrong, though," Andi said. "You used to be a nice guy—kind of a meathead and always a little full of yourself, but, y'know, nicer."

"Was that supposed to be a compliment?" York retorted, unfazed.

His muscles tensed under my fingers, and I realized my hand had been lingering on his arm since I'd helped him up. I pulled it back now, embarrassed.

"I think she means," Boston interpreted, "better a jock than a jackass."

If Andi wasn't walking between the two of them, I was pretty sure York would have answered in the form of a fist, but instead he just muttered, "*Who's* the jackass?"

"You're always trying to impress those guys now," Andi said. "Like it's your job to entertain them or something. You stopped being their teammate and started being their mascot."

Ouch. The Jefferson High mascot was an otter—not exactly a flattering comparison.

"I'm nobody's mascot," York bit back. "I make people laugh. Since when is that a bad thing?"

Since making some people laugh makes other people cry, I thought.

Except I didn't just think it. I said it right out loud, the words tumbling out before I could stop them.

"See, even Sam agrees," Andi said.

All three heads swiveled in my direction, and I turned away, staring stubbornly at the endless wash of brown field in front of us. The walk back to the road seemed a lot longer than the hike in.

"Do you?" York asked quietly, and the vulnerability in his voice made me melt a little.

"Well, I— It's just—" Images flashed through my mind: York punching a locker, York crouched by the lake with tears in his eyes, York humiliating the boy in spandex, York touching my face as he pushed back my hat to admire my scars. It was like a mash-up of two wildly different songs, but somehow they found a common beat.

"I think maybe you're nicer than you let people see," I finally said. I looked down the line at my partners in crime. Their faces were all the same as they were less than twenty-four hours ago, but they were somehow changed, too. "But maybe we're all something a little different than we let people see."

There was a moment of awkward silence that made me want to throw myself in front of a tractor, but Boston rescued me.

"Deep, that is," he squeaked in his best Yoda voice.

York followed up with a high-pitched yawning roar— a pathetic Chewbacca impression designed less to impress and more to crack us up. It worked. Boston called out another *Star Wars* character and York immediately obliged, saying some seriously filthy things in the voice of Darth Vader. It was obviously a game they played a lot, and by the end, York had mimicked everyone from R2-D2 to Princess Leia, each impression worse— and more hysterical—than the last.

When the laughter settled, the field wasn't as silent as it had been before. I could hear the infrequent *whoosh* of a car speeding down the highway, even though I couldn't see the road yet.

"It's spooky out here," I said to no one in particular. "It reminds me of *Children of the Corn*."

"What's that?" Andi asked.

"It's a scary movie. An old one, with a bunch of demonic kids living in a cornfield."

Boston shivered. "No, thanks."

York stepped closer to me and fiddled with the straps of his backpack. "You like scary movies?"

"They're okay." I shrugged. "It's just sort of a thing I do with my mom. . . ." But I didn't want to think about that—about her—right now.

York noticed and quickly shifted gears. "What about, uh, mini-golf? You ever been to the mini-golf complex over in Williams? It's got bumper cars and an arcade."

I grinned. I hadn't been to that complex since I was a kid, with Grandma and Aunt Ellen, before my cousins were born. It seemed like it might be fun to go again with someone my own age.

"You hate video games," Boston piped up, looking at York as if he were an alien.

I wish he'd fall back a few paces.

"If you're trying to ask her out, you're doing it wrong," Andi said.

Her, too.

"I was just asking what kind of stuff you like," York said to me, ignoring the others. "Besides travel."

His lips tipped up in a smile. He was proud of himself for remembering.

Cocky, I thought. *And cute.*

He almost made me forget the ache in my calves, the nagging pang of my empty stomach, and everything that had come before.

"I like music," I said. "But I can't play it or anything. Guess that skill skips a generation. And . . ." I thought of downtown River City—seedy but alive, thanks to the bar hoppers, the street vendors, the creep in the suit, and even the guy who owned the Chinese place who was always arguing with the woman in the upstairs apartment. "And I kind of like watching people."

"You mean people-watching," Boston said.

"Same thing." I could see why York got annoyed with Boston's constant corrections.

"No," Boston said. "People-watching is normal. Watching people is creepy."

"Trust him," York said. "Boston knows all about being creepy."

"You're not creepy," Andi assured me. "But you're definitely not normal."

Pot, kettle.

"Thanks a lot."

"No, I mean—God, who wants to be normal? Bleh." She turned to walk backward in front of us. "You're crazy, but I like crazy. There's a quote—I can't remember who said it— 'The only people for me are the mad ones.'"

"Kerouac," Boston said, beating me to it.

Andi snapped her fingers. "Right. Jack Kerouac. I had to read him for lit last year. I agree with him. The only people for me are the mad ones."

"From *On the Road*," I said. I had read it for lit last year, too, and it had crawled under my skin with its wild desires—to see, to experience, to just *go*.

"*On the Road*," Andi repeated with a smile. "Like us. We're the mad ones."

"He doesn't mean it in the same way you do," Boston said. "He doesn't mean crazy."

"How do you know?" Andi asked, falling back into line with us. "You ever met the guy?"

"The 'guy' is dead."

York rolled his eyes at his brother. "Well, what does he mean, then, smartass?"

"He means they're free," I said. I wasn't sure if that answer would get me an A on an essay or anything, but it *felt* right. I felt it in the warm wind at our backs and in the open stretch of road waiting somewhere ahead of us. We were mad to be doing any of this, but at least in this small moment, we were also free.

"Kind of," Boston said. "He was talking about the beatniks. He meant that they were passionate about life and art and, yeah, freedom, I guess. They made him feel——"

"Alive," York finished.

Yes.

"I stand by what I said." Andi gave my shoulder a light punch. "You're still one of the mad ones. And that's why I'm sticking with you."

I raised an eyebrow. "Because I make you feel alive?"

She grinned. "No, because you make me feel sane."

"And because you don't have any other option," York pointed out.

A few steps later, we were even with the hay bales where we'd hidden earlier that morning, and in the distance the highway rose up like a great gray snake crossing our path.

There, waiting for us like a mirage in the hazy afternoon heat waves, was the other option.

33

THE BACK WINDOWS were smashed and streams of dried mud splattered the sides, but otherwise, the SUV looked just as it had when we'd stolen it from River City Park.

We confirmed all this through Andi's Super Zooms, from the safety of the hay-bale wall.

"The backpack is gone," York said, passing the glasses back to Andi. "Do you think they're hiding inside the SUV?"

Boston crouched low behind the hay. "It's a trap!"

"It's not a trap," Andi said. "It's a gift. A way home!"

"Yeah, I'm sure they brought it here as a present," I said with mock cheer. "It practically has a big red bow on it."

"I'm going to check it out." She stood up too fast for any of us to stop her and tiptoed around the hay bales.

"Hey, Andi," York said. "Did you take candy from strangers when you were a kid?"

She answered him with her middle finger, but she didn't take any more steps into the field. "They got what they wanted," she said. "Now they're letting us go."

"Not everything they wanted." I pointed to the packs on York's and Boston's backs.

"So it could be a trade," Andi insisted. "We left them the bag, they left us a ride."

I was skeptical. "And what exactly do we get for the other two bags?"

"Only one way to find out," she said.

I stood up next to her. "Fine, but we go together."

York was on his feet as fast as I was.

"I've got your back," he promised.

"It's not my back I'm worried about," I said. "It's all of our asses."

"Or none of our asses," Boston mumbled.

Andi laughed down at him. "Hey, genius, did you just make a joke?"

But Boston wasn't laughing. The coward wasn't standing, either. He remained in his crouched position behind the hay.

Or maybe he's not a coward so much as just smarter than the rest of us.

"I'll go alone," Andi said, as if reading my mind. She held up a hand when I tried to protest. "I'm faster than you, shortie—no offense."

I was secretly too relieved to be offended. I guess I was a coward, too.

"I'll just zip up there to check it out," she said. "If the car's clear, I'll wave you in."

She tossed the Super Zooms to York, then lifted her messenger bag from her shoulder and handed it to me. It was heavy with the weight of her army jacket stuffed inside.

I took it reluctantly. "Are you sure——"

But she was already gone, racing off across the field.

York watched her through the glasses while my eyes flicked back and forth between the infinite ends of the highway. I didn't breathe until she reached the road and dropped low behind the SUV.

"What's happening?" I asked York, not taking my eyes off the Andi-shaped blur in the distance.

"She's looking in the back window."

"And?" Boston whimpered.

"And . . . she's going around the side. Shit."

"What is it?" I nearly snatched the lenses off York's face.

"I can't see her. She's on the other side of the car. Wait——"

"What?" I said, my heart racing.

"Oh my God."

"What?!"

"Oh holy shit!"

I leaned into the hay bales, willing my vision into something even better than 20/20 so I could see what York was seeing. Andi was back behind the SUV, and it looked like she was doing jumping jacks.

Finally, York pushed the Super Zooms back onto his head and turned to me and Boston with a whoop. "She's got the keys!"

I took a peek through the glasses to see for myself, and sure enough, Andi's jumping jacks were actually some kind of strange victory dance. She held the keys high in one hand and waved at us with the other.

"They left us the keys?" I said.

Maybe Andi was right. Maybe it was a trade after all.

We waved back and practically climbed over the hay bales in our hurry to join her. It was possible the crooked cops were trying to buy our silence with this peace offering, but at the moment I didn't care. All I could see were four wheels and all the places they would take us—to food, to water, to comfortable beds, and, yes, even to the police station. Anywhere was better than this middle of nowhere. Luck was finally on our side.

Or so it seemed for thirty glorious seconds.

Because that's all the time we had before the heavy roar of an engine drowned out our celebration. It came from the end of the highway that disappeared into the woods, and I barely had time to blink before a pickup truck shot into view, blasting down the road, heading straight for Andi.

The rest of us fell prostrate on the ground out of some sort of instinct, but I couldn't take my eyes off the scene in front of me. I shoved the Super Zooms back onto my face, and then immediately wished I hadn't. It meant that I could see the surprise, then the panic, then the sheer terror on Andi's face, and for one insane moment, I knew we were both thinking the same thing: the truck was going to run her down.

But at the last second the pickup slammed on its brakes, and the sudden stop seemed to shock Andi out of the paralysis that had kept her frozen on the road, her arms still up in the air. She bolted for the field. Something pounded next to my ear, and feet raced into my vision. York had gotten up to help her.

Yes, help her!

I struggled to stand, too, but it was as if I were moving through water. Everything else was happening too fast. The doors of the pickup were open. A man—I couldn't tell whether it was the cop with the familiar face or the other one—was right on top of Andi, and York was still yards away. It might as well have been miles.

The guy caught up to Andi in a second, his arms locking around her. She shouted something I couldn't make out, then twisted out of his grasp long enough to get one arm free. That arm sailed toward the sky in an almost elegant gesture—a ballerina taking a bow. The crooked cop redoubled his efforts and trapped her arm once again, this time lifting her all the way off her feet with his bear hug.

Fight, Andi! I screamed it in my mind. Or maybe I screamed it out loud.

Boston cried out for his brother from somewhere on the ground behind me, and while I couldn't blame him, I silently willed York to run faster. But it was too late. The man now had Andi's dreadlocks in his fist and was forcing her face-first into the truck.

The pickup was peeling away before York was even halfway across the field.

34

I STARED AT the cloud of exhaust left by the pickup until every wisp of it flew away on the wind. I couldn't tear my eyes away from the spot where the truck had been, where Andi had been. I stood staring for an eternity stuffed inside a few short seconds.

Behind me, Boston was wailing "Oh my God, oh my God" over and over again. Up ahead, York was on his knees, screaming, "Help me!"

It was the latter cry that unstuck my stare and got my feet to move. I flew across the field toward York, my heart pounding. Why was he on the ground? Had he been hurt, and I hadn't noticed? But when I caught up to him, winded and aching, I saw that he wasn't on the ground in pain but in panic. He crawled through the rows of soybeans, using his hands to scatter soil and crushing plants as he went.

"The keys!" He panted without looking up. "She tossed the keys!"

The ballerina's bow.

I dropped to the ground next to him, and a few seconds later Boston was there, too, the three of us sweating and searching, our nails and the creases of our skin caked with black dirt. We worked in speed and silence, each of us knowing the unsaid: the truck could be back at any moment.

"Got 'em!" Boston leaped to his feet, a set of silver keys jingling in his filthy hands.

We moved as fast as our weary bodies could toward the SUV, driven by pure adrenaline.

"Where do we go?" York panted.

"After the truck," I answered without thinking, at the same time Boston said, "To the police."

Yes, that makes more sense.

"The police already have her," York said.

"That didn't look like an arrest." I clutched at a stitch in my side. "More like a kidnapping. I'm with Boston. We call the police."

"Pitson, then?" York said. "For a phone?"

A phone.

The word brought me up short, then gave me new speed. I rushed forward, ignoring my groaning body and digging into Andi's messenger bag as I ran.

"Andi's phone!" I cried without looking back at the boys. My words came out choppy with exertion. "We can plug it in— power—the equipment—call the police!"

They said nothing, but I knew they had understood when two sets of feet pounded up behind me. We reached the road at the exact moment my hand closed around Andi's phone inside her bag.

Another second of searching, and my other hand found a cord. I yanked it out, praying, and . . . "Yes!" I cried. "Car charger!"

We could not be so lucky.

And, of course, we weren't.

The SUV was gutted. I mean, it still had seats and a steering wheel and all, but the electronics were gone. All that was left of the old tricked-out console and dashboard were a few raw wires stabbing uselessly into the air, their connections severed.

I had leaped into the driver's seat, phone and charger in hand, and now I slumped in it, deflated. For the first time in my life, I wished very hard to be in River City and nowhere else. Adventure, I was quickly learning, was much safer inside my head.

"Well, we can't sit here," York said, slamming the passenger door shut and strapping on a seat belt. At least they'd left us those.

Boston leaned forward from the back and shoved the keys into the ignition. "Drive!" he commanded.

My hand went to the ignition, but I hesitated. "I don't know how to drive an SUV."

"It goes forward and back like any other car," Boston snapped. When I still didn't move, he threw up his hands. "Fine, I'll drive."

"Oh, we so don't have time for that," York said, tapping the rearview mirror.

Under any other circumstances, I would have laughed. But right now, I just wished I could cry.

York closed his hand over mine on the keys, and when he spoke, I could tell he was fighting to keep his temper—his fear—under control. "Sam, please."

I nodded and gripped the keys, ready to turn the ignition when a familiar crackle filled the car. I froze—not just my hand, but my whole body.

"Hello, friends."

I experienced a sickening wave of déjà vu as York yanked down his visor, and the walkie-talkie tumbled out. He gripped the radio so tightly his fingers turned white. He pressed the button on the side of the walkie-talkie and barked, "We are not your friends!"

Boston gripped York's arm. "Don't talk to them!"

The boys struggled for a moment, Boston grabbing at the radio while York shook him off.

"We're not your enemies either, champ," the voice answered.

York pressed the button to respond, but he released it again when Boston shouted, "Wait!"

I had a sudden urge to throw the radio out the window the way Andi had done with Boston's phone.

"Try another frequency," Boston urged, breathless. "There has to be someone else we can reach—tell them to call police."

"Yes!" I cried. "You really are a genius!"

"Ignore us again," the voice warned, "and we'll take it out on your friend."

"Shit," York breathed. He looked at me, waiting for I don't know what. Maybe it was because I was in the driver's seat; maybe he just didn't want to be the one to make the call; but for whatever reason, the decision was apparently mine.

I nodded once.

York gave Boston an apologetic look, then held down the button. "We're listening."

"Good boy. This is simple. You have something we want, and now we have something you want. Even trade."

"No way," Boston said. "They're lying. We call the police, and we call them *now*."

"You go ahead and call the police," the voice said. "Tell them we say hi."

I sucked in a breath and smacked York's hand. He hadn't released the button in time.

"I suspect I know a little more about police work than you do." The utter calm in the voice was infuriating—and frightening. Either he was sure his word as a cop would stand up to ours, or, worse—the whole damn department was crooked.

"Better be ready to explain why your fingerprints are all over that stash," he said. "Why you're driving the car that ran over a cop; why you skipped town. And . . ." He paused for effect. "Why your friend is missing a few fingers."

I whipped the radio out of York's hand and slammed down the button. "Don't you touch her!"

"It doesn't have to be like that," the voice cooed. "Nobody wants to hurt anybody. It's not in our best interest. I'm merely trying to impress upon you the severity of our situation."

Our situation, as if we were partners in this.

"A simple trade will be good for all parties involved," he said. "We can even make that car disappear for you, too. No evidence, no crime. Everyone walks away with their hands clean."

I stared down at the dirt crusted under my nails and smeared over my skin.

Too late for that.

We all got our hands dirty. What mattered now was how we cleaned up our mess.

York reached to take the radio back, but I held it out of his grasp. "You know where we are," I said. "Bring her here."

The sick bastard actually laughed. "No, no, no. No more risks. We're not doing this on the side of the road where anyone can see."

Damn. That was exactly why I wanted to do it here.

"Now pay attention!" the voice snapped. Then he rattled off some instructions about a dirt road and a fork and a field and a left turn at the something-or-other. He talked so fast, I couldn't keep up. I struggled to yank Andi's notebook out of her messenger bag, but by the time I found a pen, he was done.

"You have one hour. Every ten minutes you're late, your friend pays for your tardiness. If I see a cop car—if I see *any* car other than that jacked-up SUV with your three pretty faces inside it—she'll lose more than a finger. Time starts now."

"Wait!" I wailed into the radio.

But the voice was gone.

BEFORE

THERE WERE TWO options for serving detention at Jefferson High: before school in the empty classroom next to the indoor pool, where the chemical smell was enough to knock you out— or get you high, if that was your thing—and after school in the east-wing gymnasium.

I always opted for the latter, since you could sit in the stadium seats and spread out rather than bumping elbows at cramped desks. Also, the odds of me making it to the morning session on time were slim, considering the only thing I ever got detention for in the first place was being late to school. It's funny; I always woke up early on weekends, no matter how little sleep I got the night before, but dragging myself out of bed to come here every day was like torture.

I climbed the bleachers, choosing a spot high on the left, away from everyone else. A few students sat together in pairs, but Mr. Wayne quickly split them up and barked something about this not being social hour. I had Mr. Wayne for sophomore health first semester, and I remembered him being pretty laid-back, but now he looked as miserable about being here as the rest of us. I wondered what teachers had to do to get detention.

He was just about to close the gym doors—once those doors closed, you couldn't get into detention and had to do double duty the next day—when one more body slipped through. From above, all I could see was a mess of long, ropy dreadlocks on top of a tall frame.

"You're late, Dixon," Mr. Wayne said before sealing the doors behind her.

Dixon?

Now I noticed her army jacket and the messenger bag she carried in place of a boring backpack like everyone else, but her signature—that luxurious mass of long hair—was gone. She was almost unrecognizable.

Almost.

Some things you just couldn't change, like the confident way she breezed past Mr. Wayne and dismissed him with a flick of her hand, or the way her very presence commanded attention from everyone in the room as she stomped up the bleachers.

"That's far enough," Mr. Wayne called out, and Andi stopped two rows directly below me. Her eyes flicked upward as though she could feel my stare, and I immediately buried my face in my homework. She turned to sit, and the movement sent a wave of stale cigarette smoke spinning up in my direction.

The second her butt was on the bench, a boy to her left leaned sideways and hissed, "Nice hair."

Andi ignored him and pulled a notebook from her bag. Over her shoulder, I could see several lines of equations, but she wasn't doing math. Her hands worked quickly, filling up the margins of the page with sketches of flowers wrapped around daggers, a snake eating a rat, and a caricature of Mr. Wayne and his oversize jaw that was so good I almost laughed out loud.

When Mr. Wayne retreated to a desk in the far corner of the gym, the boy down the row from Andi tried again.

"Did your head get stuck in a washing machine?" he whispered.

Andi cricked her neck back and forth but still didn't answer.

"Stick your finger in a light socket?"

"Quiet!" Mr. Wayne bellowed.

And the boy was quiet, bending over a binder and hastily scribbling a note. He folded the note neatly and slid it down the bench to Andi. She caught it with one hand and, without looking up, pulled a small yellow Bic lighter from her pocket. She flicked the wheel and held the flame to the still-folded note. It burned silently in a matter of seconds, and Andi shook the last little bit of paper to cool the embers, then swiped the black ashes from the bench, scattering the evidence.

The boy sneered. "*Dyke.*"

My gasp was covered up by the sound of Mr. Wayne slamming a hand down on his desk. It echoed around the gym, and all eyes turned toward it except mine. I was the only one who saw Andi's shoulders finally sink, saw her curtain of dreadlocks fall forward as she ducked her head, saw the ink bleeding into the paper where her pen had stopped moving.

I wished I could share my invisibility with her in that moment, but some people will always be seen, whether they want to be or not.

35

"I GOT IT, I got it!" York said, to calm my panic.

I had desperately scribbled everything I could remember of the directions onto a page of Andi's sketch pad, but I'd missed at least three turns.

York snatched the pen away to stop my frantic scratching. "I know the area he's talking about. Just drive."

I turned the key without hesitation now and threw the car into gear.

"Wait, wait!" Boston cried as I hit the gas. "Let's talk about this for a second!"

"Can we get there in an hour?" I asked York.

He nodded. "Yes, if we don't stop, but . . ."

"But what?"

"This is way beyond—it's more than . . . maybe we should just call the police."

"They *are* the police!" I shouted. "Didn't you hear him? He was practically bragging about it."

"So what?" Boston pulled himself into the space between York and me. "Not every cop is crooked."

These guys were more than crooked. They were completely broken. Drugs did that to people. It didn't matter whether you were a user or a seller; somehow, you got messed up either way. I knew one end of the spectrum was waiting for me back home, but that problem seemed hopeless. I couldn't fix Mama, but I could do something about this.

"The police will believe us now," Boston insisted. "This is too crazy to make up."

"I know they will," I admitted. I adjusted my mirrors without slowing down. "But that's not the point anymore."

"Sam," York started, his tone urgent but gentle. "We could be driving into some damn serious danger."

"Could be," I echoed. "But Andi is *definitely* in danger."

Both boys started to talk at once, but I cut them off. "All I know is this: if we go to the cops, and *if* they believe us, and *if* they go straight to check this place out, we'll still have wasted time, and by then, Andi could be . . ."

I didn't want to think about what Andi could be.

There was a hitch in my voice when I spoke again. "But if we just do this now—*right now*—there's at least a chance to get her out of there. And *then* we go to the police," I promised.

"Slow down," York said.

"Just listen to me!"

"No, slow down! This is the turn!" He pointed up ahead at an unmarked road, and I hit the brakes, making the tires squeal.

We were thrown to the right as I skidded left onto new, uneven blacktop.

"York, what are you—" Boston started.

"Listen, B." York turned to face his brother square. "If something happens to her, it's my fault."

"How is it—"

"*I* took the car. *I* hit that cop. *Me.*" He gave Boston a sad smile. "That's what you said, right? That none of us would be here if it wasn't for me."

"I didn't mean . . ."

"Sure you did. And it's okay; you were right. But it's on me, not you. So you don't have to come."

"What?" I jerked the wheel in surprise. "But they said all three of us—"

"I don't care what they said," York growled. "I screwed up, and I owe it to Andi to help, but I'm not risking my brother's life for her or for anyone. If he wants out, we let him out."

I slowed the car to a crawl. I didn't like it, but the compromise seemed fair, and I would rather have at least York with me than no one.

Boston took an unsteady breath and rubbed a hand over his face. Then, to my eternal surprise, he looked York straight in the eye and shook his head.

"I stay with you," he said. And he flopped back in his seat and didn't speak again.

Turn by turn, York directed us to a spot about ten miles downriver from where this had all begun. The fastest way to get there would have been to drive straight into River City and follow the well-traveled highways that snaked along the riverbanks, but the directions seemed deliberately designed to keep us on back roads instead—a circuitous route meant to help us avoid police.

Help us? Or help them?

"We never figured out how much the drugs are worth," York said during one long straightaway between turns. "It must be a lot, for them to . . ."

He didn't say "to kidnap and possibly torture a girl," because he didn't have to.

I gripped the wheel tightly as I navigated around a pothole. "I think it's—I mean, I'm not sure, but—it could be close to a million dollars."

The boys shot up straight.

"Wow."

"Seriously?"

I worried the high stakes would change their minds, but York only said, "We should ask them for a cut."

"Yeah, right." Boston rolled his eyes.

"No, really. Promise not to go to the police if they deal us in."

His halfhearted smile said he was only kidding, just trying to lighten the mood to help us through this drive into hell, but I suspected there was something legitimate behind the joke.

I glanced over long enough to catch his eye. "You know money won't keep you from being that guy on the toilet at the end of the world."

He laughed. "Yeah, but maybe if I invest it right, the toilet will be made of gold."

York twisted in his seat to look at Boston. "And you can go to Harvard."

"Yale," Boston answered.

"You decided?"

"Best law school in the country." Boston's voice was monotone. "So I can send guys like them to prison."

York nodded. "I hear bad things happen to cops in prison."

"I hope so," Boston said.

I set my lips in a thin line. It was hard to wish that kind of thing on anyone, but the only people who had ever treated Mama worse than the cops were the lowlifes who sold her drugs, and the people waiting for us were both—the lawmen and the lawless.

"Bad things happen to just about everyone in prison," I said. "Trust me."

The boys were quiet for a moment, then York said, "That phone call. Your mom . . ."

"Yeah."

"Was she . . . ?"

"Yeah."

The SUV bumped along on the uneven blacktop as the wind rushed in through the windows, a few of them broken and the rest rolled down because the assholes had somehow taken our air-conditioning, too.

"I thought she was clean now," York said. "When you talked about her last night, I thought—"

"She is." I bit the inside of my cheek. "She was."

"You think she fell off the wagon because she was worried about you?"

"If she was struggling, she should have gone to a meeting," I said. I hoped the conviction in my voice hid the guilt.

Boston leaned forward. "Like an AA meeting?"

"NA."

"What's that?"

"Narcotics Anonymous."

The boys waited for me to say more, but I just shrugged. "They take the same twelve steps."

"Drag," York said. "How long was she clean?"

"Four years today."

It hit me then—just *bam!*—hit me so hard I had to slam on the brakes to keep from driving off the road. The SUV skidded to the side, and I heard a twin *thunk-thunk* as the boys slammed back into their seats.

I barely heard their shouts of "Whoa!" and "What the hell?!"

Zero days clean. Four years wiped out in one night.

I opened my car door and leaned out to retch.

"Gross," Boston said behind me. His comment was followed by a yelp of pain and the sound of a car door opening and closing.

My eyes were still on the sick I'd left on the pavement, and York's shoes suddenly appeared in my field of vision. He crouched down in front of me, careful not to step in my mess.

"You want me to drive?" he asked, pushing a curl out of my eye and tucking it up under my hat.

I nodded and shimmied over to the passenger side so York could climb into the driver's seat.

"You're probably dehydrated," Boston said. "When's the last time any of us had water?"

Dehydrated, devastated. Both good reasons for losing your lunch. Not that we'd had any lunch. And now it was well past dinnertime, too. The leftover sick taste in my mouth begged for food and water.

"We're close now," York promised as he pulled back onto the road.

"How do you know?" I asked.

"I detassel corn every summer. I've worked these fields."

The farmland soon fell away, replaced by unplanted stretches of land, wild with overgrown weeds and speckled with occasional trees. The forest loomed in front of us, and beyond that was the river, where an *X* marked the spot we were speeding toward.

36

THE LAST TEN minutes of the drive were almost unbearable.

York hummed "Unfortunate Addiction" as he drove, while Boston played with the buttons for the back windows—up up down, down down up, up up down, down down up. It was maddening, and I interrupted as often as possible to ask York when we would get to the next turn. Soon we were rolling through a narrow break in the woods, the SUV aimed directly at the river.

The first signs of life were draped over low-hanging tree branches. Damp shirts and shorts, towels, belts, and gun holsters hung like limp welcome signs as we pulled into a small clearing along the water.

"What's with the laundry?" Boston said.

"Uh, what's with the tents?" York pointed at the makeshift camp around us.

Small pup tents ringed a fire pit built up with rocks. Between the tents, broken-down cars in various stages of repair sat rusting, their hoods studded with beer cans. More cans and other trash littered the site, stretching from the fire all the way to the water's edge, where a long speedboat had been dragged halfway onto the shore. More laundry was draped across its nose, drying in the last rays of sun as evening turned to night.

"What is this?" York said. He parked the car but kept the engine running, his hands tense on the wheel.

"They're camping out, I guess," Boston said.

I peered through the windshield at the mess in front of us. "For how long?"

"Longer than just since last night," York observed.

"Where are they?" Boston whispered.

I opened the door to find out, but York grabbed my elbow. "Be careful."

We left careful back in that broken-down taco shop lot outside River City Park. Every decision since then had been crazy. *Mad.*

I pulled out of York's grasp, and he killed the engine and followed me out of the SUV with Boston close behind, each of them shouldering a pack with our half of the trade.

"This doesn't feel right," he said.

No shit.

From the center of the camp, with the fire pit at our feet, everything became a little clearer. The cars weren't being repaired so much as stripped for parts. Various pieces of metal were divided by size and shape into individual piles, and a fold-out camping table held an array of electronics similar to the ones that used to fill the SUV.

"That's a cop car," Boston said, pointing to one of the rusty vehicles. "A real one. Not undercover."

I had no idea what to make of that. Did they steal it from their own department? Or maybe it was a discontinued model? It was hard to think with my nose full of the sickly sweet smell of old beer warmed by the sun. This place was disgusting, and it had clearly been this way for a very long time.

York spoke, his voice low. "I'm starting to think these guys are more criminal than cop."

"Where's Andi?" I said, kicking a beer can in frustration. "Where's *anyone*?"

"Maybe they didn't expect us to get here so soon," Boston said. His voice sounded small, and I noticed he was standing very close to his brother.

I jerked my chin toward the water. "You think that's the boat they had at the dock?"

We walked as a group toward the speedboat, and as we drew closer, I realized with a start that the clothes drying on the bow were not your average duds. They were all black—pants and button-down shirts, the collars pierced through with small gold stars, thick patches stitched onto the short sleeves.

River City police patches.

"This is wrong," I whispered.

I didn't care where these guys did business—or their laundry, for that matter—but I doubted this was how any cop, crooked or not, took care of his uniform. The edges of the pants were frayed; some of the shirt seams were pulling loose; and the gold plating on the stars had worn thin in places to reveal plain, dull metal underneath.

Grandma always said things were clearer in the light of day. She was usually referring to Mama sleeping off a bender, but it seemed to apply here, too.

"Very wrong," I said again. "We need to get out of——"

A car engine cut me off—or, more accurately, a truck engine.

We turned to see the pickup that had found us at the cabin and had sped away with Andi emerging from the trees. The driver maneuvered deliberately, parking the truck at an angle that blocked our road out of the campsite.

I felt the boys' shoulders bump into mine as our group instinctively pulled together.

The truck doors opened and closed, and three men hopped out, all of them long and lean, with smirking, unshaved faces. But only one of those faces was familiar.

He stepped forward as the other two circled carefully to either side until we were surrounded. The familiar face motioned for us to come closer, and I saw he was beckoning not with a hand but with a gun.

"Welcome!" His voice was booming and almost buoyant, but no smile touched his lips. "Welcome to my office. Please, have a seat."

He gestured around at the various tree stumps and broken lawn chairs that had been stationed by the fire. His words were inviting, but when none of us took him up on his offer, he pointed his gun and turned it into a command.

"Sit."

Boston and York hustled to share a length of log, but I didn't move.

"Where is she?" I asked, grateful that my voice was steady.

The smiling face turned quizzical.

"Do I know you?" he said.

I know you, I thought.

I was kicking myself for not probing deeper for the memory before. But seeing a familiar face in uniform, I just assumed . . .

He used the business end of his pistol to scratch his chin, and I found myself willing the gun to accidentally go off.

"I do," he said. "I know you from somewhere. Did I sell you something?"

"I'm not one of your clients," I said with venom. "And you're no cop."

37

THE FAMILIAR FACE laughed. "Who said I was a cop?"

I reached a hand back toward the boat, and he steadied his gun, aiming straight at my chest. "Careful now," he said.

Slowly, I lifted my hand, and gripped in my fist was the shirt half of the officer's uniform. "You were wearing this. In the park."

Now the other two guys were laughing. I noticed that neither of them had guns—not in their hands, and nowhere else I could see on their bodies, which was pretty much everywhere, since they were both in jeans and dirty tank tops.

"We ain't no pigs," one of them said. "But those *are* kind of our uniforms."

"You kids thought we were the real deal? This whole time?" The leader lowered his gun but kept a tight grip on it. "She didn't tell you."

She who?

"My mom?" I asked, at the same time York said, "Tell us what?"

The gun lifted again.

"Whoa, whoa. I'll be asking the questions here. What's this about your mom?" He leveled the gun at me. "Did you go crying to your mommy about all this?"

"I don't cry," I said through gritted teeth. "And you already know my mom."

"You know him?" York said, gaping at me. Next to him, Boston was whimpering.

"I recognized him. I thought he was a cop who arrested my mom."

"Well, now I'm curious," the creep said, stepping closer to me. "Who is your mom?"

I didn't hesitate. "Melissa Cherie. And you were her dealer."

"I doubt that," he said. "I don't deal anymore." He spread his arms to indicate the campsite, smiling as he lorded over his kingdom. "I'm more of a behind-the-scenes guy now. Dealers answer to me."

"Well, I don't answer to you," I said.

"Oh my God," York groaned. "Just sit down."

"Nah, let the lady speak," the gunman drawled. "What's on your mind, little girl? You mad at your mom and taking it out on me? Sorry, but I'm not your guy."

"It was years ago," I said. "She's clean now."

It was a lie, but just a day ago it would have been the truth. I wanted him to know he had lost one to sobriety.

"Melissa Cherie, you said?"

I nodded.

"She used to be a country singer or something?"

The bottom dropped out of my stomach. I knew I was right—knew it the moment I heard his slimy voice in person and finally saw his scum face lit up with the last gasps of daylight—but having him confirm it made me physically ill.

"Yeah, I remember her now." He chuckled. "No way is that bitch clean."

I wanted to scream at him not to call her a bitch, but a logical part of me remembered he had a finger on a trigger, and a deeper part of me felt ripped open by the truth. He was right. As of this moment, she wasn't clean.

My fault.

No.

His fault.

"Careful with that," he said, aiming his gun at my hand.

I looked down and saw that I was crumpling the police shirt in my fist.

"Did you really think these would fool real cops?" I asked.

One of the sideline guys called out, "How 'bout you just shut your mouth and sit down like the man said?"

"Sam," Boston's voice was pleading and racked with tears. "Just sit!"

I ignored everyone except Mama's dealer.

"Those uniforms aren't for the cops' benefit, sweetheart," he said. "They're to keep the other riffraff away while we're doing business."

He turned his head to the side to spit, and a thick brown glob hit the ground. The sight of it twisted my stomach. "Most folks in River City Park at night don't want to be anywhere near police," he said. "All hookers and dope-heads and trash." He spit again. "Like your mom."

"Fuck you," I said.

The logical part of my brain had apparently just gone on vacation.

His smug look turned vicious now, and he aimed his weapon right at my face. "You may not answer to me, honey, but you will answer to my gun."

York stood up then, and the dealer turned his gun on the boys. York instantly put his hands up, and, not taking his eyes off the weapon, he said to me, "Sam, come on. *Please.*"

The fear in his voice shook me awake. That's what I was supposed to be feeling—fear. The rage had chased it all away, but it was seeping back in now. I shuffled over toward the fire, and by the time I had dropped onto a low stump, my whole body was trembling.

"Finally!" The dealer lowered his gun and rotated his shoulder. "My arm was getting tired. Now, get the other one out here."

The sideline thugs—who looked more like meth-heads than bodyguards, with their skinny frames and gray teeth—backtracked to the truck and returned with Andi between them.

My heart pounded. She had a dirty gray cloth stuffed in her mouth and bruises on her tattooed arms, but I counted ten fingers and exhaled with relief. The goons threw her into a lawn chair and then took up posts on either side of the campfire. They twitched with nervous energy, reminding me too much of Mama at her unpredictable worst. The man in charge dropped into a chair next to Andi and pulled the cloth from her mouth. She gagged as it came out.

"She's a screamer, this one." He winked at us, then nudged Andi's knee. "Don't be mad. It was just a precaution. Sit back and relax now. You done good."

What was that?

I cocked my head, zeroing in on the two of them across the fire. Twilight was darkening the sky around us, but I could still clearly see Andi's face—and the shame that now filled it.

The scum sitting next to her smiled around at the rest of us. "Andi here almost blew it, though, huh? Thought I was going to have to cut this bitch when shit went bad, but she pulled it together."

No.

"What is he talking about?" York spoke low and even, but there was a growl at the back of his throat.

"You're the 'she,'" I whispered.

"I wanted to—I thought that—"Andi stammered.

She moved to stand, but the dealer used his gun arm to force her back down. "Andi here's our little lookout. Kind of fucked it up, though, didn't she?"

He reared his gun up and moved as if to backhand Andi, but he stopped just short of her face and laughed. To Andi's credit, she didn't flinch.

"You work for them?" I said.

The dealer answered for her. "Oh yeah," he drawled. "Andi and I go way back. Caught her trying to lift a wallet out of some girl's purse while she was getting her ankle inked up at my friend Frankie's tattoo shop. Told her there was a much easier way to get cash. She's been running little errands for us ever since."

I heard every word he said, but I never took my eyes off Andi. Her face crumpled as he told the story, and I saw her deflate the same way she had in detention last year. She didn't need his cash. What she needed was an outlet for her rage—at Georgia, at her dad—and she'd gone looking for it in all the wrong places.

"I can explain," she said.

"Explain?" Boston said. "Explain?!" He leaped to his feet and stayed there, despite the thugs stepping closer and the gun now pointed at him. "You knew—you've known all along—"

"The paper," I interrupted. "With the time and place—"

"It fell out of my bag," Andi said miserably.

"You tried to pin that paper on us!" York cried.

The dealer reached into a cooler with his free hand and cracked open a beer. "Well, this is downright entertaining."

York spluttered at Andi. "You could have—you didn't—and then—"

"I tried to stop you!" Andi burst out. "I told you not to go to the docks! I said we should go back to the party!"

She did. She did try. But not hard enough.

"Didn't try to stop us from stealing their car, though, did you?" Boston raged.

York tried to pull him back down, but he wouldn't budge.

"Yeah, I'm a little pissed about that," the dealer said, sucking the foam off his beer can. "I think you owe me a new ride."

"I think you've already got everything you need," Andi said. She was trying to sound tough, but I heard a quiver in her voice.

"Just about," he agreed. He nodded over at Boston and York. "How 'bout you boys shove off those backpacks?"

They did as they were told, tossing the bags by the fire, where the thugs picked them up.

"You tried to get us to leave it all behind," I said to Andi.

She grasped at the lifeline. "I did! I did try! I knew the crooked-cop story wasn't going to fly with police, but I couldn't tell you why."

"You could have," I said, sympathy competing with deep disappointment. "You could have told us."

"You would have turned me in."

"Yeah, we would've!" Boston agreed.

Andi's eyes probed mine. "Sam, I swear. I thought if we just left them their stuff—and after they got it I was going to tell you, before we got back to—"

"The text messages," I said, realization dawning. *Call me or I will end you.* "You don't have a boyfriend, do you?"

Andi shook her head miserably.

"Andi here doesn't like boys." The dealer laughed. "Damn shame."

"She told us to leave the junk for you," I said to him. I should have been pissed at Andi, but all I felt was pity. I had seen Mama sucked into situations like this, seen how quickly they could spiral out of control—how the least guilty could take the hardest fall. "She kept trying to ditch the car, the drugs—she was just outnumbered."

The dealer was sipping his beer, listening.

"She didn't tell us anything, and she won't tell the cops. You can let her go."

He sneered at me. "You talk too much. And you—" He pointed at Andi. "All you had to do was keep your little party pals out of the way. Don't think you're still getting that hundred bucks."

"A hundred bucks?" York's hands clenched into fists on his knees, and his eyes drilled into Andi's. "You did all this for a *hundred fucking dollars?*"

No, I thought. *She did it for the thrill.* But her thrill ride had turned into a shit show for all of us.

"You don't even *need* money," Boston cried. "You have your own."

"No; I have *hers*." Andi took a sharp, sudden breath, almost like a hiccup, and looked away. "It's *all* I have of her."

I would have spent all the money in the world to buy back Mama's missing pieces, but for Andi, all the money in the world was the only piece she had left. *She steals because she refuses to spend.*

"I was just supposed to keep kids from the party away from the docks," Andi said. "It wasn't my fault. It was the police. They busted up the party, and they all ran." She waved an arm at us. "I couldn't stop them."

"You're garbage." York seethed.

A tear slipped down Andi's cheek, and she didn't bother to wipe it away. I wasn't sure she even knew it was there.

"The cabin," Boston said, his voice strained. "You told them where we were."

Andi shook her head, and the look she gave Boston was a warning, but he plowed on, catching up to what I'd already figured out.

"Those text messages! They were from him." He pointed at the dealer, who in turn cocked his head at Andi.

"So you *did* get my messages." He looked back at Boston. "If she had told me where you were, she'd be in a lot better favor right now. As it is, we used the GPS tracker in the wheel well. Took a while. Thanks for not finding it before we found you."

"They saw you," Andi said to the dealer, dragging his attention away from the boys and back to her. "They saw you by the docks, and the cops were right behind us. They could've identified you. When they took the car, I didn't know the stuff was still in it. I went with them to keep them from talking. I did it to protect you." As she said this last line, her eyes slipped, ever so slightly, over to me.

I gave her the tiniest nod in return. *I believe you.*

But apparently I was the only one.

The dealer waved the gun at his thugs. "Andi first," he said. "Then the rest."

I didn't have time to decipher what that might mean, because so much happened then at once. The twitchy meth-heads moved toward Andi just as Boston and York unleashed a flurry of curse words and accusations at her. Words like "traitor" and "scum" pierced the air in Boston's high-pitched scream, while York kept repeating "garbage" over and over again. The outburst startled the goons, and they paused halfway to Andi and turned to grab the boys instead.

York pushed one in the chest, then immediately held up his hands. "Okay, okay. Sorry. We're cool."

But Boston was not cool. He struggled against the guy trying to grip his arms and shrieked hysterically at Andi, "You did this! To all of us!" He flailed in the thug's arms. "Disgusting, lying piece of shit, nobody—"

A gunshot ripped through the air, and I curled instinctively into a ball on the ground, my hands over my ears. *Oh God, oh God, oh God.*

The dealer was on his feet, his gun aimed and freshly fired. I barely had time to register the thugs backing away, Boston still standing—shell-shocked and silent now, but unhurt—and York jumping blindly in front of his brother before the second bullet exploded from the gun.

The first shot had missed. This one found a target.

38

I'VE HEARD THAT the world moves in slow motion during traumatic moments like this—that pure terror can drag an instant out into an hour.

It wasn't like that for me.

It all happened very fast—blink-and-you-miss-it fast. For a second, all I knew was blood. Blood splattering over the campfire and onto my shoes; blood blooming on York's shirtsleeve; blood on Boston's hands as he gripped York's shoulder, trying to slow his brother's fall to the ground.

Then I was on my feet—*How did I get to my feet?*—and a bony shoulder was slamming into me, knocking me back to the ground. One of the thugs had run into me on his way out of the line of fire. He stumbled over my body and fell into the dirt, puking.

I guess blood and meth will make a guy a little queasy.

I rolled onto my back in time to see the dealer giving Andi a piggyback ride.

Wait, what? Did I hit my head when I fell?

But I wasn't hallucinating. Andi was on the guy's back, but it was no ride. Her black fingernails clawed at his face, and she wrapped her legs tight around his waist, one foot kicking repeatedly at his groin.

To my left, Boston pressed his hands against York's shoulder, crying, "What do I do? What do I do?"

My vision swam at the sight of the blood and the sound of the meth-head puking behind me. Only seconds had passed.

Andi screamed a guttural war cry, and I turned my head just in time to see her fingernails draw blood on the dealer's cheek. In the falling night, it looked like his face was bleeding black. Blood from every angle. There was nowhere to look that didn't make me sick.

From across the fire pit, the second thug leaped into the fight. He was trying to peel Andi's hands away from his boss's face, but the dealer was blind, and he lashed out at what he must have thought was a new enemy. He pressed the barrel of his gun into his own minion's chest and fired.

The thug fell still, then slumped forward, causing the totem pole of Andi and the dealer to collapse backward.

The gun thudded to the dirt in front of me, its open end gaping right at my eyeball. I didn't stop to think; I swallowed the bile that had crept into the back of my throat, took the gun in my hand, and stumbled to my feet.

Two shots into the air, and the chaos finally, mercifully, came to a standstill.

I was the last man left standing—literally. Bodies were sprawled all around my feet. York, flat on the ground and gasping, with

Boston kneeling at his side; Andi and the dealer in a tangle of arms and legs on the ground, both crawling out from under the dead body—*Holy shit, a dead body*—of one of the meth-heads; and the other druggie cowering behind me.

The coward druggie was the first to move. He skittered backward like a crab away from me.

I aimed the gun in his direction, shocked to find my arm steady, unwavering. I guess I was doing all of my shaking on the inside. He froze in midcrawl and began to cry. For a moment the near-dark played tricks on my eyes, and I imagined Mama trapped like a turtle on her back, Mama's eyes swirling wildly in their sockets, Mama's tears spilling down those cheeks.

"Go," I whispered fiercely.

He didn't need to be told twice. He scrambled to his feet and pulled a set of keys from his pocket, but to my surprise, he didn't turn to the truck. He spun around and ran straight for the speedboat. Pushing it with all his drug-induced adrenaline, he got it into the water and then hopped behind the wheel. Seconds later, the sound of the motor was fading down the Mississippi, and the only noise was the soft slap of water hitting the shore in the boat's wake.

I swung the gun back toward the campfire, careful to keep my gaze above the body on the ground. That could have been Mama, too. Dead, for running with the wrong people. Dead, for being too weak to fight a disease. Dead, just for trying to scratch an uncontrollable itch.

I pitied the dead.

But not the dealer.

I turned the gun on him, still on his ass in the dirt.

"Stand up."

At the command in my voice, they *all* stood up.

York leaned weakly on Boston. "You saved me," he said, but he wasn't talking to his brother. His unfocused gaze was aimed across the fire pit at Andi.

"I tried," she rasped through tears.

Once upon a time I would have envied those tears, the release they must have provided. But now I was thankful for my dry eyes. I didn't want a release. Everything that was pent up inside me was now keeping my gun arm taut.

Boston nodded once at Andi. "If you hadn't jumped on him . . ."

"Quiet!" I said. I didn't want to think about what would have happened to York if Andi hadn't altered the dealer's aim. Right now I needed to focus on the guy who wasn't talking.

He wasn't paying much attention, either. The dealer's eyes were combing the ground, probably looking for another weapon. He glanced at the gun a few times to confirm it was still pointed in his direction, but he ignored the girl holding it.

As if the gun were just floating in midair.

As if I were invisible.

"Look at me," I ordered him.

His eyes only searched the ground faster.

"LOOK AT ME!" I screamed.

And everyone did.

Everyone except York, whose eyes slipped closed as his knees gave out. Boston slumped under the weight of his brother's limp body, a sight that filled me with a quiet fury.

He won't be sitting on a golden toilet at the end of the world, because his world might end right here.

My eyes slid to the blood clotting at York's shoulder and the hands pressed tight against it. Boston had been more afraid than any of us to get his hands dirty, and look at them now. My anger stretched, running the length of my arm to the gun in my hand. I tightened my grip, and both Andi and the dealer, standing just feet apart, put their hands up.

It wasn't Andi holding her arms in the air as if I would shoot her that unnerved me so much as the look on her face that showed she believed she deserved it. Yes, I would probably be angry with her when the dust settled and my emotions caught up to me, but that anger wasn't part of this fury that filled me now. It burned in every cell of my body, leaving no room for fear or doubt or anything other than blind rage.

I now aimed that rage at the dealer. Blood dripped from his cheek to the corner of his mouth, and he tasted it with his tongue, licking his lips and smiling at me with teeth stained red.

"You gonna waste more of my ammo, or you gonna put the next bullet somewhere that counts?" he taunted.

I hated that he didn't feel the same fear my friends had at the end of his gun—hated the reckless disregard he'd shown for the life of the only boy to ever hold my hand. I hated that he'd lured my friend Andi into what seemed like a harmless crime for easy money; hated that he'd wasted his partner to save his own skin. But mostly I hated that smug smile on his bloody lips.

He wasn't just a dealer. And he sure as hell wasn't some cop who stole my mama away for a couple of nights in jail.

He was the devil who stole my entire childhood.

"Andi," I said, my voice cool. "Put your hands down."

She obeyed.

"Check his pockets for keys to the truck."

He twisted away as she came near him, but I held the gun straighter and stepped forward. He stood still then, the smile falling off his face.

Good.

Andi found the keys in his front pocket and held them up.

"Okay, let's get out of here," Boston said, struggling to support York's slumping form.

"Take the truck and go straight to the police," I said to Andi. My voice was ever steady, my rage focusing into something calm and absolute. "Tell them to send an ambulance here immediately. Tell them someone's been shot."

"No! We're going with her," Boston protested. "I'm taking my brother to the hospital!"

"Yes, you are," I said. I looked at Boston and Andi in turn, then at the pale, half-passed-out face of York. "That's not the gunshot victim I meant."

I took a deep breath and leveled the gun at the man—the devil—in front of me.

"Go," I told my friends. "Now."

AFTER

MAMA HAS FINALLY stopped crying, and I'm relieved, because I wouldn't want to mistake her tears as sympathy for that scum.

"Stop talking," she orders me. "Stop right there. They can monitor this conversation."

She twists around anxiously in her seat, checking to make sure the guard is still tucked away in the far corner of the visitation room.

I almost laugh. "Mama, I know how it works. I've been here before, remember?"

"Not on that side of the table," she says.

I clasp my hands together, the metal cuffs digging into my skin. "I already told all of this to the lawyer," I say.

For once I had told the whole truth and nothing but the truth. I plan to do the same on the stand, if it comes to that. And my attorney is pretty sure it *will* come to that. He's planning to claim temporary insanity—except he calls it the "duress defense," something about me being under extreme pressure and traumatized by fear. Whatever. Sounds like temporary insanity to me.

He says I'm lucky the guy isn't dead.

I'm not so sure.

I've seen firsthand how easy it is for attorneys to knock down drug charges to lesser offenses, and according to the news reports, they might let him off for the murder, since he shot his minion while under attack. He'll probably be in the hospital longer than he's in prison, and then he'll be back on the streets, selling his poison to someone else's mom.

A part of me wishes I had better aim.

And a stronger stomach. I'd passed out after the first shot and the sight of the blood—so much more than had poured from York's wound, and a lot messier. I'd woken up in the back of an ambulance, but I hadn't been able to see my friends at the hospital—not with the police officer stationed outside my room.

"Any word on the others?" I ask Mama.

She shakes her head. "You need to worry about you right now."

"Please."

Mama sighs. "The boy who was shot—"

"York."

"Right. He's out of the hospital. They said his wound was minor; the bullet just skimmed his shoulder."

Something tight in my gut releases all at once.

"Charges are pending," Mama says. "Leaving the scene of an accident."

Okay, that's not bad.

"He's lucky it's not aggravated assault on a police officer."

"Mama, it was truly an accident."

"Well, fortunately, the county attorney agrees. And the other one isn't going to be charged with anything. The little one."

"Boston." I smile. "He hates being called 'the little one.'"

"But that girl—Andi . . ." Mama points at my bench. "She's the one who should be sitting there."

It's hard to argue with Mama about Andi. I guess trouble knows trouble when it sees it.

"They're practically calling her a hero," Mama goes on. "She gave the police all kinds of information—rolling right over on her whole crew."

"They're not her crew. They're just some guys she got mixed up with."

We're her crew.

"I don't like her," Mama says. "I've been listening to your story, and she—"

"If you've been listening," I interrupt, "then you know things aren't always what they seem."

Mama falls quiet. She knows I'm handing her a free pass right now.

She already told me all about how the pills she took the night I went missing were nonaddictive and preapproved by her doctor for anxiety. And she made a big point of reminding me the reason for the anxiety was waking up at 1:00 a.m. to discover that I hadn't come home from work. But she failed to say how many of these preapproved, nonaddictive pills she'd taken or what she'd washed them down with.

She knows I don't believe her. I want to—desperately, I want to. She has four years of sobriety backing up her story, after all, but Mama's lies don't work on me. She slipped that night; I'm not sure how far, but I know it happened, and she knows I know. And so she blames herself for all of this.

But in this moment, I'm telling her I trust her. Mama holds my hand. She thinks I'm giving her a gift, but the gift is for me. I will always worry about Mama, but I can't be her keeper anymore. If she slips, it won't be *my fault, my fault, my fault.* It will be *her* fault. I squeeze her hand.

"I love you, Mama."

She sniffles.

"Oh, don't start that again," I warn, and we both laugh.

"I'm working on your bond," she says, serious again. "But if we can't post it, at the very least we can get you moved to juvie. You shouldn't be in here with the adults."

"They said the juvenile facility was overcrowded."

"They can make room for one more. I'll talk to someone—"

"Mama, I'm fine here." I give her a half smile. "Thanks to you, I already know most of the guards."

She flinches. "That's nothing to be proud of."

"Cherie?" A man's booming voice interrupts from the other side of the room, but he bellows it as "Cherry."

Mama and I give an identical eye roll and answer simultaneously, "Sherry."

"Sorry," the guard says as he approaches. His hand is outstretched, and in his fingers I see a tiny key. He reaches down to fit the key into a tiny hole on one of my cuffs.

"Switching to zip ties?" Mama asks.

I rub my emancipated wrists in relief.

"Nope—no ties, no cuffs," the guard says, and smiles at me. "You made bail."

I tilt my head back, startled. "I what?"

"But . . ." Mama shakes her head. "I didn't post it yet. We're short."

The guard shrugs. "Guess you've got a fairy godmother, then."

Mama promises to meet me out front, and I follow the guard in a daze to a small room, where I'm handed an unfamiliar set of clothes.

"These aren't mine," I say.

"Yours must be in evidence," he says, and shuts the door.

I hurry into a too-large pair of jeans and a too-small white T-shirt, and then I'm shuffled into a room marked "Discharge," where I blindly sign some papers and take a large envelope stuffed with my purse and the green knit hat.

Huh. Must not be any "evidence" on this.

I pull the hat over my curls and follow signs with arrows to the lobby. I'm walking around in a fog, trying to figure out who might have bailed me out. Not Aunt Ellen, or Mama would have known about it. But who else did I know with the money to . . .

A light, like a tiny ray of sunshine, pierces through the walls of this awful gray place as realization dawns. I *do* happen to know a girl with a lot of money.

And she still owes me two hundred bucks and one violin, I think with a grin.

My guess is confirmed when I push open the door to the lobby and see the grim look on Mama's face. She's staring through the glass walls toward the jail parking lot, her arms crossed.

"This really doesn't help your case," she says to me without taking her eyes off the lot.

When I step up next to her, I see what she sees.

And they see me, too.

All three of them, jumping up and down and waving like maniacs. I can tell they're cheering, even though I can't hear them through the thick glass.

Boston and York are holding signs and pumping them in the air like strikers on a picket line.

FREE SAM!

An intercom crackles to life in the lobby, and I hear a distorted voice say, "Disturbance in the east lot."

I move toward the door to warn them, but Mama grabs my arm, holding me back. I use my free hand to shoo them away, but either they can't see it or they don't care. Andi steps forward and tugs at her shirt, holding the front flat for me to see the words written there.

ALL OF US.

She turns around and stretches so I can read the words on the back.

OR NONE OF US.

I know things are bad right now. I know I've got some mistakes to pay for, some wrongs to right. And normally that would make me wish myself away to some far-off place—but seeing them all waiting for me outside, for once—*for once*—I don't want to be anywhere but right where I am.

Two officers cross through the lobby, brushing past me and Mama and heading straight for the door.

"Run!" I cry with glee as the sliding glass doors open.

The boys drop their signs and turn in the same direction, knocking heads. I'm laughing out loud now. I don't care what Mama thinks. Andi jumps in surprise at the sight of the officers coming their way. She gives me one last big wave, then takes off running after the boys, who are already halfway to the street.

The three of them zigzag across the lot as if dodging pursuers, but the officers outside are still by the doors, just shaking their heads at these crazy teenagers. Grandma would have called them fools. I call them friends. And as I watch my friends racing out of the lot like escaping inmates, I laugh.

I laugh until I cry.

ACKNOWLEDGEMENTS

WRITING CAN SOMETIMES be a solitary pursuit, but this book has been a collaborative effort from the start.

My first thanks goes to Jennifer Laughran. I am grateful every day for your honesty and advice. Every author should be lucky enough to have an agent they trust this much.

I have an incredible team at Bloomsbury. My editor, Mary Kate Castellani, helped me dig deeper to bring these four characters to life. Cindy Loh believed in this idea in its infancy. Beth Eller, Linette Kim, Erica Barmash, and Cristina Gilbert are the best book champions an author can ask for. And there would be no book to champion without the collective editorial skills and creative minds of Melissa Kavonic, Pat McHugh, Diane Aronson, Nicole Gastonguay, Colleen Andrews, and Donna Mark. Thank you all so much.

Extra special thanks to Kelly Thompson, who made the third act a million times better with one brilliant suggestion . . . to Gemma Cooper, who gave Sam her name and therefore her voice . . . and to Amy Dominy and Bill Konigsberg, who helped me believe in myself when my confidence failed at the eleventh hour. You are all brilliant.

To Mom and Dad and Kimmy K, who read that version of this book many years ago that no one else will ever see . . . thank you for loving these characters before they even had a story. To Matt, who dealt with more than the usual whining and moaning this go-around . . . thank you for your patience. To all my friends and family, who continue to support this crazy dream . . . thank you for your endless enthusiasm. I love you all to pieces.

And finally, to Derik, thank you for being the Will to my Grace. I think a girl only gets one of those in her lifetime, and you were mine. I miss you every day.